Contents

I have edited Clive Gilson's books for over a decade now – he's prolific and can turn his hand to many genres - poetry, short fiction, contemporary novels, folklore and science fiction – and the common theme is that none of them ever fails to take my breath away. There's something in each story that is either memorably poignant, hauntingly unnerving or sidesplittingly funny.

Lorna Howarth, *The Write Factor*

Tales From The World's Firesides is a grand project. I've collected thousands of traditional texts as part of other projects, and while many of the original texts are available through channels like Project Gutenberg, some of the narratives can be hard to read for modern audiences, and so the Fireside project was born. Put simply, I collect, collate and adapt traditional tales from around the world and publish them as a modern archive.

This is the third book in *Part 3 – Africa*, following on from the titles in *Parts 1* and *2* covering a host of nations and regions across Europe and North America.

I'm not laying any claim to insight or specialist knowledge, but these collections are born out of my love of story-telling and I hope that you'll share my affection for traditional tales, myths and legends.

Images by Open Clipart Vectors and Kalhh from Pixabay

Inkathaso Tales

-

Folklore, Fairy Tales and Legends from Southern Africa

Compiled & Edited by Clive Gilson

Tales from the World's Firesides

Book 3 in Part 3 of the series, Africa

Inkathaso Tales,

edited by Clive Gilson, Solitude, Bath, UK

www.clivegilson.com.com

First published as an eBook in 2021

2nd edition © 2021 Clive Gilson

3rd edition © 2023 Clive Gilson

Printed by IngramSpark

ISBN: 978-1-913500-47-4

ORIGINAL FICTION BY CLIVE GILSON

- Songs of Bliss
- Out of the Walled Garden
- The Mechanic's Curse
- The Insomniac Booth
- A Solitude of Stars

AS EDITOR – *FIRESIDE TALES – Part 1, Europe*

- Tales From the Land of Dragons
- Tales From the Land of The Brave
- Tales From the Land of Saints And Scholars
- Tales From the Land of Hope And Glory
- Tales From Lands of Snow and Ice
- Tales From the Viking Isles
- Tales From the Forest Lands
- Tales From the Old Norse
- More Tales About Saints and Scholars
- More Tales About Hope and Glory
- More Tales About Snow and Ice
- Tales From the Land of Rabbits
- Tales Told by Bulls and Wolves
- Tales of Fire and Bronze
- Tales From the Land of the Strigoi
- Tales Told by the Wind Mother
- Tales from Gallia
- Tales from Germania

EDITOR – *FIRESIDE TALES – Part 2, North America*

- Okaraxta - Tales from The Great Plains
- Tibik-Kìzis – Tales from The Great Lakes & Canada
- Jóhonaa'éí –Tales from America's Southwest
- Qugaaĝix̂ - First Nation Tales from Alaska & The Arctic
- Karahkwa - First Nation Tales from America's Eastern States
- Pot-Likker - Folklore, Fairy Tales, and Settler Stories from America

EDITOR – *FIRESIDE TALES – Part 3, Africa*

- Arokin Tales – Folklore & Fairy Tales from West Africa
- Hadithi Tales – Folklore & Fairy Tales from East Africa
- Inkathaso Tales – Folklore & Fairy Tales from Southern Africa
- Tarubadur Tales – Folklore & Fairy Tales from North Africa
- Elephant And Frog – Folklore from Central Africa

Preface

I've been collecting and telling stories for a couple of decades now, having had several of my own works published in recent years. My particular focus is on short story writing in the realms of magical realities and science fiction fantasies.

I've always drawn heavily on traditional folk and fairy tales, and in so doing have amassed a collection of many thousands of these tales from around the world. It has been one of my long-standing ambitions to gather these stories together and to create a library of tales that tell the stories of places and peoples from the four corners of our world.

One of the main motivations for me in undertaking the project is to collect and tell stories that otherwise might be lost or, at best forgotten. Given that a lot of my sources are from early collectors, particularly covering works produced in the late eighteenth century, throughout the nineteenth century, and in the early years of the twentieth century, I do make every effort to adapt stories for a modern reader. Early collectors had a different world view to many of us today, and often expressed views about race and gender, for example, that we find difficult to reconcile in the early years of the twenty-first century. I try, although with varying degrees of success, to update these stories with sensitivity while trying to stay as true to the original spirit of each story as I can.

I also want to assure readers that I try hard not to comment on or appropriate originating cultures. It is almost certainly true that the early collectors of these tales, with their then prevalent world views, have made assumptions about the originating cultures that have given us these tales. I hope that you'll accept my mission to preserve these tales, however and wherever I find them, as just that. I have, therefore, made sure that every story has a full attribution, covering both the original collector / writer and the collection title that this version has been adapted from, as well as having notes about publishers and other relevant and, I hope, interesting source data. Wherever possible I have added a cultural or indigenous attribution as well, although for some of the tiles, the country-based theme is obvious.

Inkathaso Tales includes a range of stories that originate in Southern Africa. South African Folklore is firmly rooted in an oral, historical tradition. It is tied to the region's landscape and fauna, with fantastic creatures playing an important role in these stories. Music and song is often used to tell the story and the tales' values are usually firmly African, with community and sharing being key.

Most of the sources that I have access to stem from the great tradition of the 19th century collectors, anthropologists and philologists, with much of the literature focused on the San people (Bushmen), nomadic hunter-gatherers who live in South Africa and in the neighbouring countries of Botswana, Namibia and Zimbabwe. Their focus is typically on animal stories and, in particular, stories about the jackal, a dangerous and comical trickster figure.

We also have some significant entries in this collection from the later tribal communities that formed in advance of European colonisation in the south.

There are also many stories about the lion and his family, along with tricky little rabbits, and other familiar animals such as doves, tortoises, and snakes, plus distinctively African animals like the ostrich and the eland. There are tales of tiny animals too, like the many different kinds of ants who live in fear of the dreaded anteater, or the little 'tink-tinkje" (finch) who has always wanted to be king of all the birds.

As in most folktales, there is a strong supernatural element where animals, reeds or trees take human form or assume human characteristics, gods take human women as brides, and thunder can deliver messages. Because the stories spring from an oral tradition, they often feature music, song and dance as an integral part of the plot, meaning that the refrains would have been known to the audience, who would have joined in with the storyteller.

The stories can, of course, be brutal and often contain death and disaster. In this, too, they reflect a certain African reality, although collectors and regular readers of folklore and fairy tales will recognise that brutality as a common theme in cautionary tales the world over.

As always, it is a delight to collect and adapt these stories, to discover new ways of thinking and to immerse yourself in the lore of such a fabulous land.

Clive,

Bath, 2023

The Mantis Assumes The Form Of A Hartebeest

This story has been edited and adapted from Specimens of Bushman Folklore, produced by Wilhelm Heinrich Immanuel Bleek and Lucy Lloyd, originally published in 1911 by George Allen and Company, London.

The Mantis is the one who cheated some children by resembling a dead-hartebeest. He feigned death and lay in front of the children when the children went to seek gambroo, which is a sort of cucumber, because he wanted the children to cut him up with their stone knives. These children did not possess metal knives.

The children saw him, when he stretched out, and while his horns were turned backwards. The children then said to each other, "It is a hartebeest that yonder lies. It is dead."

The children jumped for joy, saying, "Our hartebeest! We shall eat great meat."

Then they broke off stone knives by striking one stone against another. After that they skinned the Mantis, but the skin of the

Mantis snatched itself quickly out of the children's hands. One child said, "Hold that hartebeest skin firmly for me!"

The second child, "The hartebeest skin pulled at me."

Her elder sister said, "It does seem to me that the hartebeest has no wound from the people who shot it. It appears to me that the hartebeest seems to have died of itself. Although the hartebeest is fat and well fed and has no shooting wound."

The elder sister cut off a shoulder from the hartebeest, and put it down on a bush. The hartebeest's shoulder arose by itself, and it sat down nicely on the other side of the bush. She then cut off a thigh, and put it down on a bush, and again the thigh placed itself nicely beside the bush. She cut off another shoulder and put it upon another bush. It too arose, and sat upon a soft portion of the bush, as it felt that the bush upon which it lay was very prickly.

Another sister cut off the other thigh of the hartebeest, and as she did so she said, "This hartebeest's flesh does move, and that must be why it shrinks away from us."

The children continued to arrange their burdens, with one of them saying, "Cut and break off the hartebeest's neck, so that our younger sister may carry the hartebeest's head. Our other sister sitting over there shall carry the hartebeest's back, because she is big and strong. For, we must carry this great meat home even if its flesh moves and snatches itself out of our hand."

The children took up the flesh of the Mantis, saying to the youngest child, "Carry the hartebeest's head, so that father may put it to roast for you."

The youngest child slung the hartebeest's head onto her shoulder and called to her sisters "I've got it but help me up, for this hartebeest's head is not light."

Her sisters took hold of her and helped her up. Then they all started on their journey home. As they did so, the hartebeest's head slipped downwards, because the Mantis's head wished to stand on the ground. The youngest child lifted it up again, but the hartebeest's head, by turning a little, removed the carrying thong from its eye. The hartebeest's head was all the while whispering to the child, "O child! The thong is flapping in front of my eye. Take the thing away, please, for the thong is shutting my eye."

The child looked behind her, and the incognito Mantis winked at her child. The child whimpered. Her elder sister looked back at her, and called to her, "Come forward quickly, we must return home."

The child exclaimed, "This hartebeest's head is able to speak."

Her elder sister scolded her, "Stop lying. Come on, we have to go. We simply won't believe you about the hartebeest's talking head?"

The youngest child said to her elder sister, "The hartebeest has winked at me with the hartebeest's eye, and he asked me to take the thong away from his eye." Then she looked back again at the hartebeest's head, and the hartebeest opened and shut its eyes. The youngest child said to her elder sister, "The hartebeest's head must be alive, for it is opening and shutting its eyes."

The child, walking on, loosened the thong and let the hartebeest's head fall to the floor. The incognito Mantis scolded the child, and complained about his head, crying, "Oh! Oh! My poor head! Oh! You are a bad little person! You are hurting me in my head."

The young child and her sisters immediately dropped all of the flesh of the hartebeest. As soon as they did this the parts of the Mantis sprung together. The head quickly joined itself to the top of the neck. The neck quickly joined itself to the upper part of the Mantis's spine. The upper part of the spine joined itself to the Mantis's back. The thigh of the Mantis sprang forward and joined itself to the Mantis's back. His other thigh ran forward and joined itself to the other side of the Mantis's back. The chest then ran forward and joined itself to the front side of the upper part of the Mantis's spine. Eventually all of the parts of the creature were back together

Seeing this the children started to run, but the Mantis rose up from the ground and ran, chasing the children, turning himself into a man and running exactly like a man would on two legs and with pumping shoulders and arms. Luckily the children soon reached their home, and seeing this, the Mantis turned about and jogged down to the nearby river. He went along the riverbed, making a sliding, slurping noise as he stepped in the soft sand. When he felt that he had gone far enough he came out of the rive on the opposite side of the children's house and ran past their front door.

The children told their father what had happened. They said, "We have been and seen a hartebeest, which was dead. We cut up the hartebeest with stone knives, but its flesh quivered and quickly snatched itself out of our hands. It moved by itself around the bushes, and then the hartebeest's head started whispering. Our youngest sister, who sits there, carried it, and it fell to the floor and stood there, talking behind the child's back."

The youngest child then said to her father "O papa! Do you believe me when I say that hartebeest's head did talk to me? It is true that the hartebeest's head was looking at the nape of the neck, as I went along, and that was when the hartebeest's head told me that I should take away the thong away from his eye."

Her father said to the children, "Have you been and cut up the old man, the Mantis, while he lay pretending to be dead in front of you?"

The children said, "We thought that the hartebeest's horns were there, and the hartebeest had hair. The hartebeest had no arrow wounds. The hartebeest came and chased us when we dropped the flesh. Truly, the hartebeest's flesh jumped together and gathered itself, so that it might mend itself and chase us! Then the hartebeest ran forward, and his body was red, and he had no hair, and as he ran he swung his arm like a man.

"And when he saw that we reached the house, he whisked round, kicking up his heels and showing the white soles of his shoes. He ran before the wind, while the sun shone upon the soles of his feet, and he ran into the river with all his might, so that he might pass behind the back of the hill lying yonder."

Their parents said to the children, "You went and cut up the old man, sometimes known as 'Tinderbox Owner'."

The children said to their fathers, "He has gone round the house. He ran fast. It seems as if he is going to come over the little hill lying yonder whenever he sees that we are just reaching home. Our little sister, she was the one who the hartebeest's head spoke to as we went along. She told us, so we dropped the hartebeest's flesh, and we laid our karosses on our shoulders so that we could run very fast.

"While we ran, its flesh started mending itself, and when it finished mending itself, he rose up and ran forward and chased us very quickly and we got very tired.

"Then he descended into the small river, still moving very quickly. He picked up some wood, and then came out again while we sat and rested because we were so tired. He will always be out there deceiving children, and we were so tired and our hearts burnt on account of it. Oh papa! We shall not hunt for food. No! We shall stay at home together."

The Origin Of Death

This story has been edited and adapted from James A. Honey's South-African Folk Tales, originally published in 1910 by The Baker and Taylor Company.

The Moon, it is said, once sent an Insect to men, saying, "Go to men, and tell them, 'As I die, and dying live, so you shall also die, and dying live.'"

The Insect started with the message, but whilst on his way was overtaken by the Hare, who asked, "On what errand are you bound?"

The Insect answered, "I am sent by the Moon to men, to tell them that as she dies, and dying lives, they also shall die, and dying live."

The Hare said, "As you are an awkward runner, let me go and take the message."

With these words he ran off, and when he reached men, he said, "I am sent by the Moon to tell you, 'As I die, and dying perish, in the same manner you shall also die and come wholly to an end.'"

Then the Hare returned to the Moon, and told her what he had said to men. The Moon reproached him angrily, saying, "Did you dare tell the people a thing which I have not said?"

With these words she took up a piece of wood, and struck him on the nose. Since that day the Hare's nose is slit.

Story Of The Bird That Made Milk

This story has been edited and adapted from George McCall Theal's Kaffir (Xhosa) Folk-Lore, originally published in 1886 by S. Sonnenschein, Le Bas and Lowrey, London. This is a Xhosa story.

There was once upon a time a poor man living with his wife in a certain village. They had three children, two boys and a girl. They used to get milk from a tree by squeezing the trunk The milk was not as nice as that of a cow, and the people that drank it were always thin. For this reason, those people were never glossy like those who are fat.

One day the woman went to cultivate a garden. She began by cutting the grass with a pick, and then putting it in a big heap. That was the work of the first day, and when the sun was just about to set she went home. When she left, a bird came to that place, and sang this song:

"Weeds of this garden,

Weeds of this garden,

Spring up, spring up,

Work of this garden,

Work of this garden,

Disappear, disappear."

It was so.

The next morning, when she returned and saw that the garden was gone, she wondered greatly. She again put it in order, and this time she put some sticks in the ground to mark the place.

In the evening she went home and told her kinfolk that she had found the grass, which she had cut the day before, growing just as it had been.

Her husband said, "How can such a thing be? You were lazy and didn't work, and now you tell me this falsehood. Just get out of my sight, or I'll beat you."

On the third day she went to her work with a sorrowful heart, remembering the words spoken by her husband. She reached the place and found the grass growing as before. The sticks that she stuck in the ground were there still, but she saw nothing else of her labour. She wondered greatly.

She said in her heart, "I will not cut the grass again, I will just hoe the ground as it is." She commenced. Then the bird came and perched on one of the sticks.

It sang:

"Citi, citi, who is this cultivating the ground of my father?

Pick, come off,

Pick handle, break,

Sods, go back to your places!"

All these things happened.

The woman went home and told her husband what the bird had done. Then they made a plan. They dug a deep hole in the ground, and covered it with sticks and grass. The man hid himself in the hole, and put up one of his hands. The woman commenced to hoe the ground again. Then the bird came and perched on the hand of the man, and sang:

"This is the ground of my father.

Who are you, digging my father's ground?

Pick, break into small pieces

Sods, return to your places."

It was so.

Then the man tightened his fingers and caught the bird. He came up out of his place of concealment.

He said to the bird, "As for you, who spoil the work of this garden, you will not see the sun anymore. With this sharp stone I will cut off your head!"

Then the bird said to him, "I am not a bird that should be killed. I am a bird that can make milk."

The man said, "Make some, then."

The bird made some milk in his hand. The man tasted it. It was very nice milk.

The man said, "Make some more milk, my bird."

The bird did so. The man sent his wife for a milk basket. When she brought it, the bird filled it with milk.

The man was very much pleased. He said, "This pretty bird of mine is better than a cow."

He took it home and put it in a jar. After that he used to rise even in the night and tell the bird to make milk for him, but only he and his wife drank the bird's milk. The children continued to drink the milk of the tree. The names of the children were Gingci, the first-born son, Lonci, his brother, and Dumangashe, his sister. The father then got very fat indeed, so that his skin became shining.

The girl said to her brother Gingci, "Why does father get fat and we remain so thin?"

He replied, "I do not know. Perhaps he eats in the night."

They made a plan to watch. They saw him rise in the middle of the night. He went to the big jar and took an eating mat off it. He said, "Make milk, my bird." He drank much. Again he said, "Make milk, my bird," and again he drank till he was very full. Then he lay down and went to sleep.

The next day the woman went to work in her garden, and the man went to visit his friend. The children remained at home, but not in the house. Their father fastened the door of the house, and told them not to enter it on any account till his return.

Gingci said, "Today we will drink the milk that makes father fat and shining. We will not drink of the milk of the euphorbia tree today."

The girl said, "As for me, I also say let us drink father's milk today."

They entered the house. Gingci removed the eating mat from the jar, and said to the bird, "My father's bird, make milk for me."

The bird said, "If I am your father's bird, put me by the fireplace, and I will make milk."

The boy did so. The bird made just a little milk.

The boy drank, and said, "My father's bird, make more milk."

The bird said, "If I am your father's bird, put me by the door, then I will make milk."

The boy did this. Then the bird made just a little milk, which the boy drank.

The girl said My father's bird, make milk for me."

The bird said, "If I am your father's bird, just put me in the sunlight, and I will make milk."

The girl did so. Then the bird made a jar full of milk.

After that the bird sang:

"The father of Dumangashe came, he came,

He came unnoticed by me.

He found great fault with me.

The little fellows have met together.

Gingci the brother of Lonci.

The Umkomanzi cannot be crossed,

It is crossed by swallows

Whose wings are long."

When it finished its song it lifted up its wings and flew away. But the girl was still drinking milk.

The children called it, and said, "Return, bird of our father," but it did not come back. Then they said, "We shall be killed today."

They followed the bird. They came to a tree where there were many birds. The boy caught one, and said to it, "My father's bird, make milk."

It bled. They said. "This is not our father's bird."

This bird bled very much, and the blood ran like a river. Then the boy released it, and it flew away. The children were seized with fear. They said to themselves, "If our father finds us, he will kill us today."

In the evening the man came home. When he was yet far off, he saw that the door had been opened.

He said, "I did not shut the door that way."

He called his children, but only Lonci replied. He asked for the others.

Lonci said, "I went to the river to drink, when I returned they were gone."

He searched for them, and found the girl under the ashes and the boy behind a stone. He inquired at once about his bird. They were compelled to tell the truth concerning it.

Then the man took a strip of rawhide and hung those two children on a tree that projected over the river. He went away, leaving them there. Their mother pleaded with their father, saying that they should be released, but the man refused. After he was gone, the boy tried to escape. He climbed up the rawhide strip and held on to the tree, then he went up and loosened the strip that was tied to his sister. After that they climbed up the tree, and then went away from their home, They slept three times on the road.

They came to a big rock and the boy said, "We have no father and no mother, rock, be our house."

The rock opened, and they went inside. After that they lived there, and they obtained food by hunting animals.

When they had been in that place a long time, the girl grew to be quite tall. There were no people in that place. A bird came one day with a child, and left it there by their house.

The bird said, "I have done this for all of the people."

After that a crocodile came to that place. The boy was just going to kill it, but it said, "I am a crocodile, I am not to be killed, I am your friend."

Then the boy went with the crocodile to the house of the crocodile, in a deep hole under the water. The crocodile had many cattle and much millet. He gave the boy ten cows and ten baskets of millet.

The crocodile said to the boy You must send your sister to marry me."

The boy made a fold to keep his cattle in, while his sister made a garden and planted the millet. The crocodile sent more cattle. The boy made a very big fold, and it was full of cattle.

At this time another bird came. The bird said, "Your sister has performed the custom, and as for you, you should enter manhood."

The crocodile then gave one of his daughters to be the wife of the young man, while his sister went to the village of the crocodile to be his bride.

They said to her, "Whom do you choose to be your husband?"

The girl replied, "I choose Crocodile."

Her husband said to her, "Lick my face."

She did so. The crocodile cast off its skin, and turned into a man of great strength and fine appearance.

He said, "The enemies of my father's house did that, but you, my wife, are stronger than they are."

After this there was a great famine, and the mother of those two children came to their village. She did not recognise her children, but they knew her and gave her food. She went away, and then their father came. He did not recognise them either, but they knew him. They asked him what he wanted. He told them that his village was devoured by famine. They gave him food, and he went away.

He returned again.

The young man said, "You thought we would die when you hung us in the tree."

He was astonished, and said, "Are you indeed my child?"

Crocodile then gave the parents three baskets of corn, and told them to go and build on the mountains. The man did so and died there on the mountains.

!Gaunu-Tsaxau, The Baboons, And The Mantis

This story has been edited and adapted from Specimens of Bushman Folklore, produced by Wilhelm Heinrich Immanuel Bleek and Lucy Lloyd, originally published in 1911 by George Allen and Company, London.

!gaunu-tsaxau went to fetch sticks for his father, so that his father might take aim at the people who sit upon their heels. While collecting sticks he saw a troop of baboons, who were busy feeding. He went up to one of the older baboons and told him that he had to fetch many sticks for his father so that he could throw them at the lazy people.

The baboon exclaimed "Hie! Come to listen to this child." And one of the other, older baboons came over to listen to the child's story.

And so the baboons came, one by one, to hear !gaunu-tsaxau explain that he was collecting sticks for his father to throw at the lazy folk.

Eventually one of the oldest baboons, who recognised !gaunu-tsaxau as Mantis's son, exclaimed with a sneering kind of laugh,

"O-ho! It is us that this child's father wants to throw sticks at. We shall strike the child with our fists."

And so the baboons set about the task of striking !gaunu-tsaxau with their fists on account of his father's wish to throw sticks at them. They hit the boy with their fists, breaking his head. Another baboon struck with his fist, knocking out !gaunu-tsaxau's eye, and the child's eye rolled away.

This baboon exclaimed, "My ball! My ball!"

Then the baboons began to play a game of ball, while the child lay still and died.

One of the baboons started to sing:

And I want it, whose ball is it?

And I want it, whose ball is it?

And I want it."

While they were playing ball with the child's eye, the rest of the baboon troop sang:

My companion's ball it is, and I want it,

My companion's ball it is, and I want it,"

Meanwhile the Mantis was waiting for his child. He lay down at noon and started to dream about the child, and he dreamed that the baboons had killed the child, and that they had made a ball of the child's eye. Then he dreamed that he went to the baboons, who were still playing ball with the child's eye.

When he awoke he took up his bow and quiver, saying, "Rattling along, rattling along." As he got closer he could see the dust that the baboons were kicking up. Then the Mantis cried on account of it because the baboons really did appear to have killed his child. He quickly shut his mouth and dried the tears from his eyes, because he did not want the baboons to see tears in his eyes.

Then he came running up to the baboons, while the baboons stared at him, because they were startled by him. Then, while the baboons were still staring at him, he found a safe place to lay down the quiver. He took off his kaross, his skin cloak, putting it down quickly too. Then he took a feather brush from his bag, shaking it out fully, and he too started to play with the ball. He called out to the baboons, asking them why they were staring at him, and asking them to throw him their ball.

Then the baboons looked at one another, because they suspected that he really knew what they were doing. Mantis nearly caught hold of the ball as it was thrown from one baboon to another. At this, the child's eye recognised its father's scent, and it skittered this way and that way, leading the baboons a merry dance.

Eventually one baboon caught hold of the eye and threw it towards one of the other baboons. Then the Mantis sprang out and caught hold of the child's eye. The Mantis whirled around the child's eye, and he anointed it with the perspiration from his armpits. Then he threw the child's eye back towards the baboons, and the child's eye flew about in the sky. The baboons watched it as it flew about in the sky. Eventually the child's eye flew down and popped itself into a small bag tied to the side of Mantis's quiver.

Then the baboons and Mantis searched for the eye. As the baboons searched and searched they cried, "Give our companion the ball!"

The baboon who though he owned the ball said, "Give me the ball."

The Mantis said, "Look here! I have not got the ball."

The baboons all said, "Give my companion the ball."

The baboon whose ball it was, said, "Give me the ball."

Then the baboons said that the Mantis must shake the bag, for the ball seemed to be inside the bag. And the Mantis exclaimed, "Look here! Look here! The ball is not inside the bag."

He held the child's eye inside the bag while appearing to shake it and turn it inside out. "See? The ball cannot be inside the bag."

Then one of the baboons exclaimed, "Hit the old man with your fists."

Then another baboon exclaimed, "Give my companion the ball!", and he struck the Mantis about the head.

The Mantis cried, "I have not got the ball," while he struck back at the baboon's head.

In no time at all the baboons were all striking the Mantis with their fists, and the Mantis was striking back at them with his fist. The Mantis got the worst of it, so he cried out, "Ow! Hartebeest's Children! You must go! !Kau. !Yerriggu! You must go!"

The baboons stood and watched as Mantis flew up into the sky. He flew to the water, where he dived in while saying, "I |ke, tten !khwaiten!khwaiten, !kui ha i |ka!"

Then he walked out of the water and felt inside his bag. He took out the child's eye, walking on as he held it in his hand. He reached the grass at the top of the water's bank, where he sat down. He exclaimed, "Oh wwi ho!" as he put the child's eye back into the water.

"You must grow out, so that you might become again as you once were." Then he walked on, taking up his kaross and throwing it over his shoulder. He also took up the quiver, and then he returned to his home.

When he arrived at his home, the young Ichneumon exclaimed, "Who can have done this to my grandfather, the Mantis? He is covered with wounds?"

Then the Mantis replied, "The baboons killed !gaunu-tsaxau." The Mantis spoke very slowly and sadly. "I went as they were playing at ball with the child's eye. I went to play at ball with them. Then the child's eye vanished. The baboons said that I was the one who had taken it. So the baboons fought with me and I fought them, and then I flew home."

Then |kuammang-a said, "Why, grandfather, do you continue to go among strangers?"

The Mantis did not tell |kuammang-a and the others that he had put the child's eye into the water.

Then he stayed at home, and did not go anywhere near the water for many days. Then one day he did go to look at the place where he had put the child's eye. He approached gently, so as not to make a disturbance, but the child heard him, because he had made so much noise during the rest of his journey to the water. The child jumped up and splashed in the water. The Mantis laughed and his heart yearned for the child. After that he turned again and went home.

Down by the water the child grew and grew, and became exactly like he had always been. One day, as the Mantis came to see how the child fared, he saw the child sitting in the sun. The child heard him as he came rustling along, and the child sprang up and dived into the water.

The Mantis went home and this time he made a front kaross, an apron, and a ||koroko. When they were finished he put these things into a bag and returned gently to the water's edge. Again, he saw the child lying in the sun, so he approached as quietly as he could manage. The child heard him, of course. As the child jumped up to dive back into the water, the Mantis sprang forward and caught hold of the child. He anointed the child with his scent and asked, "Why are you afraid of me? I am your father, I am the Mantis, I am here, you are my son. You are !gaunu-tsaxau, and I am the Mantis."

The child sat down and he took the front kaross and the ||koroko from the bag The Mantis put the front kaross on to the child. He then put the ||koroko on to the child. Then he took the child with him, and they both travelled all the way home.

Then the young Ichneumon exclaimed, "Who is that coming here with the Mantis?"

And |kuammang-a replied, "Don't you remember that grandfather said he had gone to the baboons, while they were playing ball with the child's eye? Well, grandfather must have been playing a game with us, because, the child, his son, is coming home with him!"

Mantis and the child soon reached the house. Then the young Ichneumon spoke, and he said, "Why did you say that the baboons killed the child, when the child is here?"

Then the Mantis said, "Can you not see that he is not strong? I put his eye into the water, hoping that he would grow back to his former self. He has just come out of the water, and you can see that he is not yet strong. So, I will wait and take care of him, and I shall see whether he will become strong again."

The Story Of Five Heads

This story has been edited and adapted from George McCall Theal's Kaffir (Xhosa) Folk-Lore, originally published in 1886 by S. Sonnenschein, Le Bas and Lowrey, London. This is a Xhosa story.

There was once a man living in a certain place, who had two daughters big enough to be married. One day the man went over the river to another village, which was the residence of a great chief. The people asked him to tell them the news. He replied that there was no news in the place that he came from. Then the man inquired about the news of their place. They said the news of their place was that the chief wanted a wife.

The man went home and said to his two daughters, "Which of you wishes to be the wife of a chief?"

The eldest replied, "I wish to be the wife of a chief, my father." The name of that girl was Mpunzikazi.

The man said, "At that village which I visited, the chief wishes for a wife, and you, my daughter, shall go."

The man called all his friends, and assembled a large company to go with his daughter to the chief's village, but the girl would not consent that those people should go with her.

She said, "I will go alone to be the wife of the chief."

Her father replied, "How can you, my daughter, say such a thing? Is it not so that when a girl goes to present herself to her husband she should be accompanied by others? Be not foolish, my daughter."

The girl still said, "I will go alone to be the wife of the chief."

Then the man allowed his daughter to do as she chose. She went alone, no bridal party accompanying her, to present herself at the village of the chief who wanted a wife.

As Mpunzikazi was on the path, she met a mouse. The mouse said, "Shall I show you the way?"

The girl replied, "Just get away from before my eyes."

The mouse answered, " If you do like this, you will not succeed."

Then she met a frog. The frog said, "Shall I show you the way?"

Mpunzikazi replied, "You are not worthy to speak to me, as I am to be the wife of a chief."

The frog said, "Go on then, you will see afterwards what will happen."

When the girl got tired, she sat down under a tree to rest. A boy who was herding goats in that place came to her, he being very hungry.

The boy said, "Where are you going to, my eldest sister? "

Mpunzikazi replied in an angry voice, "Who are you that you should speak to me? Just get away from me."

The boy said, "I am very hungry. Will you not give me some of your food? "

She answered, "Get away quickly."

The boy said, "You will not return if you do this."

She went on her way again, and met with an old woman sitting by a big stone.

The old woman said, "I will give you advice. You will meet with trees that will laugh at you, but you must not laugh in return. You will see a bag of thick milk, but you must not eat it. You will meet a man whose head is under his arm, but you must not take water from him."

Mpunzikazi answered, "You ugly thing! Who are you that you should advise me?"

The old woman continued in saying those words.

The girl went on. Soon she came to a place where there were many trees. The trees laughed at her, and she laughed at them in return. She saw a bag of thick milk, and she ate some of it. She met a man carrying his head under his arm, and she took water to drink from him.

Then she came to the river by the chief's village. She saw a girl there dipping water from the river. The girl said, "Where are you going to, my sister? "

Mpunzikazi replied, "Who are you that you should call me sister? I am going to be the wife of a chief."

The girl drawing water was the sister of the chief. She said, "Wait, I will give you advice. Do not enter the village by this side."

Mpunzikazi did not stand to listen, but just went on.

She reached the village. The people asked her where she came from and what she wanted.

She answered, "I have come to be the wife of the chief."

They said, "Who ever saw a girl go without a retinue to be a bride?" They also said, "The chief is not at home. You must prepare food for him, so that when he comes home in the evening he may eat."

They gave her millet to grind. She ground it very coarse, and made bread that was not nice to eat.

In the evening she heard the sound of a great wind. That wind was the coming of the chief. He was a big snake with five heads and large eyes. Mpunzikazi was very much frightened when she saw him. He sat down before the door and told her to bring his food. She brought the bread which she had made. Makanda Mahlanu, or Five Heads as he was also known, was not satisfied with that bread. He said, "You shall not be my wife," and he struck her with his tail and killed her.

Afterwards the sister of Mpunzikazi said to her father, "I also wish to be the wife of a chief."

Her father replied, "It is well, my daughter, it is right that you should wish to be a bride."

The man called all his friends, and a great retinue prepared to accompany the bride. The name of the girl was Mpunzanyana.

On the way they met a mouse. The mouse said, "Shall I show you the road? "

Mpunzanyana replied, "If you will show me the way I shall be glad."

Then the mouse pointed out the way.

She came into a valley, where she saw an old woman standing by a tree. The old woman said to her, "You will come to a place where two paths branch off. You must take the little one, because if you take the big one you will not be fortunate."

Mpunzanyana replied, "I will take the little path, my mother." She went on.

Afterwards she met a cony. The cony said, "The village of the chief is close by. You will meet a girl by the river, you must speak nicely to her. They will give you millet to grind, and you must grind it well. When you see your husband, you must not be afraid."

She said, "I will do as you say, cony."

In the river she met the chief's sister carrying water. The chief's sister said, "Where are you going to?"

Mpunzanyana replied, "This is the end of my journey."

The chief's sister said, "What is the object of your coming to this place?"

Mpunzanyana replied, "I am with a bridal party. "

The chief's, sister said, "That is right, but will you not be afraid when you see your husband? "

Mpunzanyana answered, "I will not be afraid."

The chief's sister pointed out the hut in which she should stay. Food was given to the bridal party. The mother of the chief took millet and gave it to the bride, saying, "You must prepare food for your husband. He is not here now, but he will come in the evening."

In the evening Mpunzanyana heard a very strong wind, which made the hut shake. The poles fell, but she did not run out. Then she saw the chief Makanda Mahlanu coming. He asked for food. Mpunzanyana took the bread which she had made, and gave it to him. He was very much pleased with that food, and said, "You shall be my wife." He gave her very many ornaments.

Afterwards Makanda Mahlanu became a man, and Mpunzanyana continued to be the wife he loved best.

The Lost Message

This story has been edited and adapted from James A. Honey's South-African Folk Tales, originally published in 1910 by The Baker and Taylor Company.

The ant has had from time immemorial many enemies, and because he is small and destructive, there have been a great many slaughters among them. Not only were most of the birds their enemies, but Anteater lived almost wholly from them, and Centipede beset them every time and at all places when he had the chance.

So now there were a few among them who thought it would be well to hold council together and see if they could not come to some arrangement whereby they could retreat to some place of safety when attacked by robber birds and animals.

But at the gathering their opinions were most discordant, and they could come to no decision.

There was Red-ant, Rice-ant, Black-ant, Wagtail-ant, Gray-ant, Shining-ant, and many other varieties. The discussion was a true babel of diversity, which continued for a long time and came to nothing.

Some of the ants desired that they should all go into a small hole in the ground, and live there, while others wanted to have a large and strong dwelling built on the ground, where nobody could enter but an ant, while still others wanted to dwell in trees, so as to get rid of Anteater, forgetting entirely that there they would be the prey of birds, and yet another group seemed inclined to have wings and fly.

And, as has already been said, this deliberation amounted to nothing, and each party resolved to go to work in its own way, and on its own responsibility.

Greater unity than that which existed in each separate faction could be seen nowhere in the world. Every ant had its appointed task, each did his work regularly and well. And all worked together in the same way. From among them they chose a king - that is to say some of the groups did - and they divided the labour so that all went as smoothly as it possibly could.

But each group did it in its own way, and not one of them thought of protecting themselves against the onslaught of birds or Anteater.

The Red-ants built their house on the ground and lived under it, but Anteater levelled to the ground in a minute what had cost them many days of precious labour. The Rice-ants lived under the ground, and with them it went no better. For whenever they came out, Anteater visited them and took them out sack and pack. The Wagtail-ants fled to the trees, but there on many occasions sat Centipede waiting for them, or the birds gobbled them up. The Gray-ants had intended to save themselves from extermination by taking to flight, but this also availed them nothing, because the Lizard, the Hunting-spider, and the birds went a great deal faster than they.

When the Insect-king heard that they could come to no agreement he sent them the secret of unity, and the message of Work-together. But unfortunately he chose for his messenger the Beetle, and he has never yet arrived, so that the Ants are still today the embodiment of discord and consequently the prey of enemies.

Story Of The Girl Who Disregarded The Custom Of Ntonjane

This story has been edited and adapted from George McCall Theal's Kaffir (Xhosa) Folk-Lore, originally published in 1886 by S. Sonnenschein, Le Bas and Lowrey, London. This is a Xhosa story.

There was once a chief's daughter who had reached the age when it was necessary for her to observe the ntonjane. She was therefore placed in a hut, in which she was to remain during the period of the ceremony. One day her companions persuaded her to go and bathe in a stream near at hand, though this was against the custom of the ntonjane. When they came out of the water, they saw a snake with black blotches, called the Isinyobolokondwana, near their clothes. They were very much afraid, and did not know what to do at first. But by and-by one of them commenced to sing these words:

"Sinyobolokondwana,

Sinyobolokondwana,

Bring my mantle!"

The snake replied:

"Take it,

And pass on."

The companions of the chief's daughter, one after the other, asked the snake for their mantles in this manner, and obtained permission to take them. Last of all was the chief's daughter. But instead of speaking to the snake respectfully as the others had done, she said mockingly, "Ngcingcingci, ngcingcingci."

So the snake became very angry, and bit her, and she immediately turned the same hideous colour as it was. Her companions were so frightened that they left her and ran away home. They put another girl in the hut, and pretended that she was the chief's daughter. The girl, thus left alone, went to a forest close by, and climbed up a tree to hide herself.

About this time the chief was killing an ox on account of his daughter, and so he sent a young man to the forest to get pieces of wood with which to peg out the skin. The young man was cutting sticks, when he heard someone crying, "Man cutting sticks, tell my father and mother that the sinyobolokondwana bit me."

He heard this repeated twice, and, without looking to see what was crying, he ran home and told the chief. Two young men were then sent back with him to see what it was, one of these happening to be the girl's brother. These two were told to hide themselves and listen while the other cut the sticks. They did so, and heard the voice crying as before. Then the brother of the girl recognised his sister's voice, and they all went to the tree where she was, and took her home with them.

The chief was very much surprised to see his daughter in that state, and was so angry with her companions for taking her to the river, and then for substituting another girl so as to deceive him, that he caused them all to be killed.

Then he sent some of his men with forty cattle to take his daughter to a distant country, where she was to remain far away from him. They did as they were told, and built huts in that place to live in. After they had been there a long time, they found that the cows which the chief sent with them were giving more milk than they could consume, so they poured what was left in a hole in the ground. To their amazement, the milk rose, and rose, and rose, higher and still higher, till at last it stood up out of the ground like a great overhanging rock. They called the girl to see this wonderful thing that was happening. In her curiosity she went close to the precipice, when it fell down on her, and, as the milk ran over her, all her ugly blotched skin disappeared, and she was again beautiful as at first she had been.

Soon afterwards a young chief who was passing by saw the girl, and fell in love with her. He thought she was the daughter of one of the men who were there to protect her, but when he made inquiries they told him she was the daughter of their chief. Then he went to her father, and some of the men went also to tell how the milk had cured the girl. The young chief had very many cattle, which he offered to her father. So the old chief agreed to let him marry the girl, and she became his great wife, and was loved by him very dearly.

The Story Of The Leopard Tortoise

This story has been edited and adapted from Specimens of Bushman Folklore, produced by Wilhelm Heinrich Immanuel Bleek and Lucy Lloyd, originally published in 1911 by George Allen and Company, London.

The people had gone hunting. A woman lay ill in her hut when she perceived that a man had come up to her hut. She asked the man to rub her neck a little with fat, for, it ached. The man rubbed her neck with fat. And the man rubbed and rubbed the fat into the woman's aching neck until it was all gone. The man's hands were raw right down to the bone.

Again, she saw another man, who came hunting. And she also spoke to him, saying, "Rub me with fat a little."

And the man whose hands had decayed away while rubbing her neck, hid his hands, so that the other man should not see how they were rubbed down to the very bones.

And he said, "Yes, O my mate! Rub our elder sister a little with fat, for, the moon has been cut, while our elder sister lies ill. You shall also rub our elder sister with fat."

He was hiding his hands, so that the other one should not perceive them.

The woman, the Leopard Tortoise, said, "Put your hands into my neck."

And he, rubbing with fat, put his hands upon the Leopard Tortoise's neck, and the Leopard Tortoise drew in her head upon her neck, while his hands were altogether attached to her. He instantly dashed the Leopard Tortoise upon the ground, thinking he would break the shell and free his hands, but the Leopard Tortoise held him fast.

The first man had taken his hands from behind his back, and he exclaimed, "Feel what I also did feel!" and he showed the other man his hands, and all the while the second man's hands were altogether inside the Leopard Tortoise's neck.

Then the first man arose and he returned home, leaving the second man dashing the Leopard Tortoise upon the ground. Eventually after the moon had died and another moon had come, the second man freed his hands too and he joined the first man at home.

The people there exclaimed, "Where have you been?"

He answered, saying that he had got his hands stuck in the Leopard Tortoise, and that was why he had not returned home.

The people said, "Are you a fool? Did your parents not instruct you? The Leopard Tortoise always looks as if she is about to die, but she is always deceiving us."

The Monkey's Fiddle

This story has been edited and adapted from James A. Honey's South-African Folk Tales, originally published in 1910 by The Baker and Taylor Company.

Hunger and want forced Monkey one day to forsake his land and to seek elsewhere among strangers for much-needed work. Bulbs, earth beans, scorpions, insects, and such things were completely exhausted in his own land. But fortunately he received, for the time being, shelter with a great uncle of his, Orang Outang, who lived in another part of the country.

When he had worked for quite a while he wanted to return home, and as recompense his great uncle gave him a fiddle and a bow and arrow and told him that with the bow and arrow he could hit and kill anything he desired, and with the fiddle he could force anything to dance.

The first he met upon his return to his own land was Brer Wolf. This old fellow told him all the news and also that he had since early morning been attempting to stalk a deer, but all in vain.

Then Monkey laid before him all the wonders of the bow and arrow that he carried on his back and assured him that if he could but see the deer he would bring it down for him. When Wolf showed him the deer, Monkey was ready and down fell the deer.

They made a good meal together, but instead of Wolf being thankful, jealousy overmastered him and he begged for the bow and arrow. When Monkey refused to give it to him, he thereupon began to threaten him with his greater strength, and so, when Jackal passed by, Wolf told him that Monkey had stolen his bow and arrow. After Jackal had heard both of them, he declared himself unqualified to settle the case alone, and he proposed that they bring the matter to the court of Lion, Leopard, and the other animals. In the meantime he declared he would take possession of what had been the cause of their quarrel, so that it would be safe, as he said. But he immediately brought to earth all that was eatable, so there was a long time of slaughter before Monkey and Wolf agreed to have the affair in court.

Monkey's evidence was weak, and to make it worse, Jackal's testimony was against him. Jackal thought that in this way it would be easier to obtain the bow and arrow from Wolf for himself.

And so the sentence fell against Monkey. Theft was looked upon as a great wrong, and he must hang.

The fiddle was still at his side, and he received as a last favour from the court the right to play a tune on it. He was a master player of his time, and in addition to this he now added the wonderful power of his charmed fiddle. Thus, when he struck the first note of "Cockcrow" upon it, the court began at once to show an unusual and spontaneous liveliness, and before he came to the first waltzing turn of the old tune the whole court was dancing like a whirlwind.

Over and over, quicker and quicker, sounded the tune of "Cockcrow" on the charmed fiddle, until some of the dancers, exhausted, fell down, although still keeping their feet in motion. But Monkey, musician as he was, heard and saw nothing of what had happened around him. With his head placed lovingly against the instrument, and his eyes half closed, he played on, keeping time ever with his foot.

Wolf was the first to cry out in pleading tones breathlessly, "Please stop, Cousin Monkey! For love's sake, please stop!

But Monkey did not even hear him. Over and over sounded the resistless waltz of "Cockcrow."

After a while Lion showed signs of fatigue, and when he had gone the round once more with his young lion wife, he growled as he passed Monkey, "My whole kingdom is yours, ape, if you just stop playing."

"I do not want it," answered Monkey, "but withdraw the sentence and give me my bow and arrow, and you, Wolf, acknowledge that you stole it from me."

"I acknowledge, I acknowledge!" cried Wolf, while Lion cried, at the same instant, that he withdrew the sentence.

Monkey gave them just a few more turns of the "Cockcrow," gathered up his bow and arrow, and seated himself high up in the nearest camel thorn tree.

The court and other animals were so afraid that he might begin again that they hastily disbanded to new parts of the world.

The Children Are Sent To Throw The Sleeping Sun Into The Sky

This story has been edited and adapted from Specimens of Bushman Folklore, produced by Wilhelm Heinrich Immanuel Bleek and Lucy Lloyd, originally published in 1911 by George Allen and Company, London.

An old woman talked to another old woman, who then spoke to their children. She said that the children should gently approach the Sun to lift up the Sun-armpit so that the Bushman rice might become dry for them, for the sun travelled over the whole sky and made the world bright.

She said, "Oh, children! You must wait for the Sun to lie down to sleep, for, we are cold. You shall gently approach to lift him up, while he lies asleep. You shall take hold of him, all together, and lift him up, so that you may throw him up into the sky. You must sit down when ye have looked at him, yes, you must go sit down, while you wait for him."

Then the old woman said, "Oh, children going yonder! You must speak to him when you throw him up into the sky. You must tell him that he must altogether become the Sun, and he must be hot as he stands there in the sky so that the Bushman rice becomes dry.

So, the children went to sit down by the Sun, and they waited for him to lift up his elbow, so that his armpit shone upon the ground. When the children saw this happening, they threw him up into the sky. As they did this they said, "Oh, Sun! You must altogether stand fast in the sky, you must go along, you must stand fast while you are hot."

The old woman's husband then said, "The Suns' armpit is standing fast above yonder, for the children have thrown him up into the sky when he intended to sleep."

The children returned. Then, the children said, "Our companion here, he took hold of the Sun. We also took hold of him, and my younger brother took hold of him, and my other younger brother, we all took hold of the Sun. Then we all threw the old man up into the sky."

An older child then spoke, and he was a young man, saying, "Oh, my grandmother! We threw him up. We told him that he should altogether become the Sun, which is hot, for, we are cold. We said, 'Oh, my grandfather, Sun-armpit! Remain in the sky and become the Sun, which is hot, so that the Bushman rice may dry for us, and so that you may make the whole earth light and warm in the summer. You must shine, taking away the darkness, yes,, you must shine and make the darkness go away.' That is what we said."

And so, that is why the Sun comes and the darkness goes away. The Sun comes, the Sun sets, the darkness comes and the Moon comes at night. The day breaks, the Sun comes out, the darkness goes away, the Sun comes. The Moon comes out, the Moon brightens the darkness, the darkness departs, the Moon comes out, the Moon shines, taking away the darkness, it goes along, it has made bright the darkness, it sets. The Sun comes out, the Sun follows the darkness, the Sun takes away the Moon, the Moon stands, the Sun pierces it with the Sun's knife, and so the Moon decays away on account of it.

But the Moon says, "Oh, Sun! Leave my backbone for the children!"

Therefore, the Sun leaves the Moon's backbone for the children, and the Moon goes painfully away. The Moon returns in pain to his home, but he grows and he goes on to become another Moon, which is whole. He lives again, even though he seemed to die. He is a new Moon, and he feels that he has again put on a stomach, and he becomes large, and he is alive. He goes along at night, and he feels that he is a shoe that walks in the night.

When the Sun is here, all the earth is bright, and the people walk while the place is light, the earth is light, and the people perceive the bushes, they see the other people, they see the meat, which they are eating, they also see the springbok and the ostrich. The Sun shines upon the path. The people travel in summer, and they hunt the springbok and the gemsbok and the kudu in the summer.

The Story Of Demane And Demazana

This story has been edited and adapted from George McCall Theal's Kaffir (Xhosa) Folk-Lore, originally published in 1886 by S. Sonnenschein, Le Bas and Lowrey, London. This is a Xhosa story.

Once upon a time a brother and sister, who were twins and orphans, were obliged on account of ill-usage, to run away from their relatives. The boy's name was Demane, the girl's Demazana.

They went to live in a cave that had two holes to let in air and light, the entrance to which was protected by a very strong door, with a fastening inside. Demane went out hunting by day, and told his sister that she was not to roast any meat while he was absent, lest the cannibals should discover their retreat by the smell. The girl would have been quite safe if she had done as her brother commanded. But she was wayward, and one day she took some buffalo meat and put it on a fire to roast.

A cannibal smelt the flesh cooking, and went to the cave, but found the door fastened. So he tried to imitate Demane's voice, and asked to be admitted, singing this song:

"Demazana, Demazana,

Child of my mother,

Open this cave to me.

The swallows can enter it.

It has two apertures."

Demazana said, "No. You are not my brother, your voice is not like his."

The cannibal went away, but after a little time came back again, and spoke in another tone of voice, "Do let me in, my sister."

The girl answered, "Go away, you cannibal, your voice is hoarse, you are not my brother."

So he went away and consulted with another cannibal. He said, "What must I do to obtain what I desire?"

He was afraid to tell what his desire was, lest the other cannibal should want a share of the girl.

His friend said, "You must burn your throat with a hot iron."

He did so, and then no longer spoke hoarsely. Again he presented himself before the door of the cave, and sang:

"Demazana, Demazana,

Child of my mother,

Open this cave to me.

The swallows can enter it.

It has two apertures."

The girl was deceived. She believed him to be her brother come back from hunting, so she opened the door. The cannibal went in and seized her.

As she was being carried away, she dropped some ashes here and there along the path. Soon after this, Demane, who had taken nothing that day but a swarm of bees, returned and found his sister gone. He guessed what had happened, and followed the path by means of the ashes until he came to Zim's dwelling. The cannibal's family were out gathering firewood, but he was at home, and had just put Demazana in a big bag, where he intended to keep her till the fire was made.

Demane said, "Give me water to drink, father."

Zim replied, "I will, if you will promise not to touch my bag."

Demane promised. Then Zim went to get some water, and while he was away, Demane took his sister out of the bag, and put the bees in it, after which they both concealed themselves.

When Zim came with the water, his wife and son and daughter came also with firewood. He said to his daughter, "There is something nice in the bag, go bring, it."

She went, but the bees stung her hand, and she called out, "It is biting."

He sent his son, and afterwards his wife, but the result was the same. Then he became angry, and drove them outside, and having put a block of wood in the doorway, he opened the bag himself. The bees swarmed out and stung his head, particularly his eyes, so that he could not see.

There was a little hole in the thatch, and through this he forced his way. He jumped about, howling with pain. Then he ran and fell headlong into a pond, where his head stuck fast in the mud, and he became a block of wood like the stump of a tree. The bees made their home in the stump, but no one could get their honey, because, when anyone tried, his hand stuck fast.

Demane and Demazana then took all of Zim's possessions, which were very great, and they became wealthy people.

The Origin Of Death, Preceded By A Prayer Addressed To The Young Moon

This story has been edited and adapted from Specimens of Bushman Folklore, produced by Wilhelm Heinrich Immanuel Bleek and Lucy Lloyd, originally published in 1911 by George Allen and Company, London.

When someone shows us that the Moon has newly returned alive, we look towards the place where the Moon shines, and we see the Moon, and when we perceive it, we shut our eyes with our hands, and we exclaim, "!kabbi-a yonder! Take my face yonder! You shall give me your face yonder! You shall take my face yonder! You shall give me your face, which, when you have died, returns again to live. When we did not see you, you came to us again, lying down, and I may also resemble you. For, the joy yonder, that you always possess, is that you will return to us alive. The hare told you that you should do this, and you once said that we should also again return alive, after we died."

The hare was the one who wanted people to come back to life after they had died. At that time the hare was a person, but when is mother appeared to die, he would not be silent. He believed that his mother was altogether dead and would not return to him. Therefore, he would cry greatly for his mother.

The Moon said to the hare that he should leave off crying, for, his mother was not altogether dead, and that she would return again alive.

The hare replying, said that he was not willing to be silent, for, he knew that his mother would not return alive, for she was altogether dead.

And the Moon became angry with the hare for disagreeing with him. The Moon hit the hare with his fist, cleaving the hare's mouth, and as he hit the hare he exclaimed, "This person's mouth shall forever more be like this. The hare shall always bear a scar on his mouth. He shall spring away. He shall run backwards and forwards. The dogs shall chase him, and when they have caught him, they shall tear him to pieces, and he shall altogether die."

Then the Moon said, "And men shall altogether die and go away when they die and never return. And this is because the hare was not willing to agree with me, when I told him that he should not cry for his mother, for his mother would live again. Therefore, I say that he shall now altogether become a hare, a beast. And all of the people, they shall altogether die. They will not be like me, who returns to life after I die. He contradicted me, when I had told him about it."

That is what our mothers told us. Our mothers also told us that the hare has human flesh at his ||katten-ttu. When we have killed a hare, when we intend to eat the hare, we take out the 'biltong flesh', which is human flesh, and we leave it. We feel that this is not the true flesh of the hare, but is the flesh he had when he was formerly a man.

Our mothers told us that the Moon spoke again, saying, "You who are people, when you die you will vanish away. I, when I am dead, I return again living. I had intended that you who are men should be like me and do the things that I do. But I, the Moon, became angry with the hare, because the hare should not have spoken in this manner. He should have said, 'Yes, my mother lies sleeping, she will presently arise.' If the hare had agreed with me, the Moon, then you who are people would have been like me, the Moon.

The Moon also said that the hare should lie upon a bare place, and vermin should infest and bite him. He should not inhabit the bushes, for he must now lie upon a bare place. That is why the hare, when he springs up, goes along shaking his head, trying to make the vermin fall from his head.

The Leopard, The Ram, And The Jackal

This story has been edited and adapted from James A. Honey's South-African Folk Tales, originally published in 1910 by The Baker and Taylor Company.

Leopard was returning home from hunting on one occasion, when he lighted on the kraal of Ram. Now, Leopard had never seen Ram before, and accordingly, approaching submissively, he said, "Good day, friend! What may your name be?"

The other in his gruff voice, and striking his breast with his forefoot, said, "I am Ram. Who are you?"

"Leopard," answered the other, more dead than alive, and then, taking leave of Ram, he ran home as fast as he could.

Jackal lived at the same place as Leopard did, and the latter going to him, said, "Friend Jackal, I am quite out of breath, and am half dead with fright, for I have just seen a terrible looking fellow, with a large and thick head, and on my asking him what his name was, he answered, 'I am Ram.'"

"What a foolish fellow you are," cried Jackal, 'to let such a nice piece of flesh stand! Why did you do so? But we shall go tomorrow and eat it together."

Next day the two set off for the kraal of Ram, and as they appeared over a hill, Ram, who had turned out to look about him, and was calculating where he should that day crop a tender salad, saw them, and he immediately went to his wife and said, "I fear this is our last day, for Jackal and Leopard are both coming against us. What shall we do?"

"Don't be afraid," said the wife, "but take up the child in your arms, go out with it, and pinch it to make it cry as if it were hungry."

Ram did so as the confederates came on.

No sooner did Leopard cast his eyes on Ram than fear again took possession of him, and he wished to turn back. Jackal had provided against this, and made Leopard fast to himself with a leather thong, and said, "Come on."

Then Ram cried in a loud voice, pinching his child at the same time, "You have done well, Friend Jackal, to have brought us Leopard to eat, for you hear how my child is crying for food."

On these dreadful words Leopard, notwithstanding the entreaties of Jackal to let him go, to let him loose, set off in the greatest alarm. He dragged Jackal after him over hill and valley, through bushes and over rocks, and never stopped to look behind him until he carried himself and half-dead Jackal back to his place again. And so Ram escaped.

Motiratika

This story has been edited and adapted from Andrew Lang's Red Book of Heroes, originally published in 1909 by Longmans, Green and Company, London and New York. The original was adapted from the Ba-Ronga.

Once upon a time, in a very hot country, a man lived with his wife in a little hut, which was surrounded by grass and flowers. They were perfectly happy together till, by-and-by, the woman fell ill and refused to take any food. The husband tried to persuade her to eat all sorts of delicious fruits that he had found in the forest, but she would have none of them, and grew so thin he feared she would die. "Is there nothing you would like?" he said at last in despair.

"Yes, I think I could eat some wild honey," answered she. The husband was overjoyed, for he thought this sounded easy enough to get, and he went off at once in search of it.

He came back with a wooden pan quite full, and gave it to his wife.

"I can't eat that," she said, turning away in disgust. "Look! There are some dead bees in it! I want honey that is quite pure."

And the man threw the rejected honey on the grass, and started off to get some fresh. When he got back he offered it to his wife, who treated it as she had done the first bowlful. "That honey has got ants in it, throw it away," she said, and when he brought her some more, she declared it was full of earth. In his fourth journey he managed to find some that she would eat, and then she begged him to get her some water. This took him some time, but at length he came to a lake whose waters were sweetened with sugar. He filled a pannikin quite full, and carried it home to his wife, who drank it eagerly, and said that she now felt quite well. When she was up and had dressed herself, her husband lay down in her place, saying, "You have given me a great deal of trouble, and now it is my turn!"

"What is the matter with you?" asked the wife.

"I am thirsty and want some water," answered he, and she took a large pot and carried it to the nearest spring, which was a good way off.

"Here is the water," she said to her husband, lifting the heavy pot from her head, but he turned away in disgust.

"You have drawn it from the pool that is full of frogs and willows, you must get me some more."

So the woman set out again and walked still further to another lake.

"This water tastes of rushes," he exclaimed. "Go and get some fresh."

But when she brought back a third supply he declared that it seemed made up of water-lilies, and that he must have water that was pure, and not spoilt by willows, or frogs, or rushes. So for the fourth time she put her jug on her head, and passing all the lakes she had hitherto tried, she came to another, where the water was golden like honey. She stooped down to drink when a horrible head bobbed up on the surface.

"How dare you steal my water?" cried the head.

"It is my husband who has sent me," she replied, trembling all over. "But do not kill me! You shall have my baby if you will only let me go."

"How am I to know which is your baby?" asked the Ogre.

"Oh, that is easily managed. I will shave both sides of his head, and hang some white beads round his neck. And when you come to the hut you have only to call 'Motikatika!' and he will run to meet you, and you can eat him."

"Very well," said the ogre, "you can go home." And after filling the pot she returned, and told her husband of the dreadful danger she had been in.

Now, though his mother did not know it, the baby was a magician and he had heard all that his mother had promised the ogre, and he laughed to himself as he planned how to outwit her.

The next morning she shaved his head on both sides, and hung the white beads round his neck, and said to him, "I am going to the fields to work, but you must stay at home. Be sure you do not go outside, or some wild beast may eat you."

"Very well," answered he.

As soon as his mother was out of sight, the baby took out some magic bones, and placed them in a row before him. "You are my father," he told one bone, "and you are my mother. You are the biggest," he said to the third, 'so you shall be the ogre who wants to eat me, and you," to another, "are very little, therefore you shall be me. Now, then, tell me what I am to do."

"Collect all the babies in the village the same size as yourself," answered the bones, 'shave the sides of their heads, and hang white beads round their necks, and tell them that when anybody calls 'Motikatika,' they are to answer to it. And be quick for you have no time to lose."

Motikatika went out directly, and brought back quite a crowd of babies, and shaved their heads and hung white beads round their little necks, and just as he had finished, the ground began to shake, and the huge ogre came striding along, crying, "Motikatika! Motikatika!"

"Here we are! Here we are!" answered the babies, all running to meet him.

"It is Motikatika I want," said the ogre.

"We are all Motikatika," they replied. And the ogre sat down in bewilderment, for he dared not eat the children of people who had done him no wrong, or a heavy punishment would befall him. The children waited for a little, wondering, and then they went away.

The ogre remained where he was, till the evening, when the woman returned from the fields.

"I have not seen Motikatika," said he.

"But why did you not call him by his name, as I told you?" she asked.

"I did, but all the babies in the village seemed to be named Motikatika," answered the ogre, "you cannot think the number who came running to me."

The woman did not know what to make of it, so, to keep him in a good temper, she entered the hut and prepared a bowl of maize, which she brought him.

"I do not want maize, I want the baby," grumbled he "and I will have him."

"Have patience," answered she, "I will call him, and you can eat him at once." And she went into the hut and cried, "Motikatika!"

"I am coming, mother," replied he, but first he took out his bones, and, crouching down on the ground behind the hut, asked them how he should escape the ogre.

"Change yourself into a mouse," said the bones, and so he did, and the ogre grew tired of waiting, and told the woman she must invent some other plan.

"To-morrow I will send him into the field to pick some beans for me, and you will find him there, and can eat him."

"Very well," replied the ogre, "and this time I will take care to have him," and he went back to his lake.

Next morning Motikatika was sent out with a basket, and told to pick some beans for dinner. On the way to the field he took out his bones and asked them what he was to do to escape from the ogre. "Change yourself into a bird and snap off the beans," said the bones. And the ogre chased away the bird, not knowing that it was Motikatika.

The ogre went back to the hut and told the woman that she had deceived him again, and that he would not be put off any longer.

"Return here this evening," answered she, "and you will find him in bed under this white coverlet. Then you can carry him away, and eat him at once."

But the boy heard, and consulted his bones, which said, "Take the red coverlet from your father's bed, and put yours on his," and so he did. And when the ogre came, he seized Motikatika's father and carried him outside the hut and ate him. When his wife found out the mistake, she cried bitterly, but Motikatika said, "It is only just that he should be eaten, and not I, for it was he, and not I, who sent you to fetch the water."

The Moon Is Not To Be Looked At When Game Has Been Shot

This story has been edited and adapted from Specimens of Bushman Folklore, produced by Wilhelm Heinrich Immanuel Bleek and Lucy Lloyd, originally published in 1911 by George Allen and Company, London.

We may not look at the Moon, when we have shot game, because we are afraid of the Moon's shining. It is that which we fear. For, our mothers used to tell us that the Moon is not a good person, if we look at him. If we look at the Moon when we have shot game, then the beasts of prey will come and eat the game as it lies dying.

If the game does not die, it is because of the Moon's water. Our mothers used to tell us about it. The Moon's water, the water that we see on a bush, the water that resembles liquid honey, falls upon the game and the game rises. The water makes cool the poison with which we shot the game, and the game arises, and it goes on and shows no sign of poison at all. The Moon's water cures it.

That is why our mothers did not wish us to look at the things which are in the sky.

If we look at the Moon we will see how he goes, and he goes to a place far from here, and the day will break while he is still going along. If we look at the Moon then the game will also do the same. The day will break and the game will go along, and the game will try to take us away to a place where there is no water. We will die of thirst if the game leads us astray, and takes us to a place where there is no water.

The World's Reward

This story has been edited and adapted from James A. Honey's South-African Folk Tales, originally published in 1910 by The Baker and Taylor Company.

Once there was a man that had an old dog, so old that the man desired to put him aside. The dog had served him very faithfully when he was still young, but ingratitude is the world's reward, and the man now wanted to dispose of him. The old dumb creature, however, ferreted out the plan of his master, and so at once resolved to go away of his own accord.

After he had walked quite a way he met an old bull in the veldt

"Don't you want to go with me?" asked the dog.

"Where?" was the reply.

"To the land of the aged," said the dog, "where troubles don't disturb you and thanklessness does not deface the deeds of man."

"Good," said the bull, "I am your companion."

The two now walked on and found a ram.

The dog laid the plan before him, and all moved off together, until they afterwards came successively upon a donkey, a cat, a cock, and a goose.

These joined their company, and the seven set out on their journey.

Late one night they came to a house and through the open door they saw a table spread with all kinds of nice food, and some robbers were having their fill of it. It would not help much if they asked for admittance, and seeing that they were hungry, they must think of something else.

Therefore the donkey climbed up on the bull, the ram on the donkey, the dog on the ram, the cat on the dog, the goose on the cat, and the cock on the goose, and with one accord they all let out terrible, threatening noises.

The bull began to bellow, the donkey to bray, the dog to bark, the ram to bleat, the cat to mew, the goose to giggle gaggle, and the cock to crow, all without cessation.

The people in the house were frightened perfectly limp. They glanced out through the front door, and there they stared at the strange sight. Some of them took to the ropes over the back lower door, some disappeared through the window, and in a few moments the house was empty.

Then the seven old animals climbed down from one another, stepped into the house, and satisfied themselves with the delicious food.

But when they had finished, there still remained a great deal of food, too much to take with them on their remaining journey, and so together they contrived a plan to hold their position until the next day after breakfast

The dog said, "See here, I am accustomed to watch at the front door of my master's house," and thereupon flopped himself down to sleep.

The bull said, "I go behind the door," and there he took his position.

The ram said, "I will go up on to the loft".

The donkey said, "I at the middle door".

The cat replied, "I in the fireplace".

The goose said, "I in the back door".

Finally the cock said, "I am going to sleep on the bed."

The captain of the robbers after a while sent one of his men back to see if these creatures had yet left the house.

The man came very cautiously into the neighbourhood. He listened and listened, but he heard nothing. He peeped through the window, and saw in the grate just two coals still glimmering, and thereupon started to walk through the front door.

There the old dog seized him by the leg. He jumped into the house, but the bull was ready, swept him up with his horns, and tossed him on to the loft. Here the ram received him and pushed him off the loft again. Reaching ground, he made for the middle door, but the donkey set up a terrible braying and at the same time gave him a kick that landed him in the fireplace, where the cat flew at him and scratched him nearly to pieces. He then jumped out through the back door, and here the goose got him by the trousers. When he was some distance away the cock crowed. He thereupon ran so that you could hear the stones rattle in the dark.

Purple and crimson and out of breath, he came back to his companions. "Frightful, frightful!" was all that they could get from him at first, but after a while he told them.

"When I looked through the window I saw in the fireplace two bright coals shining, and when I wanted to go through the front door to go and look, I stepped into an iron trap. I jumped into the house, and there someone seized me with a fork and pitched me up on to the loft, there again someone was ready, and threw me down on all fours. I wanted to fly through the middle door, but there some one blew on a trumpet, and smote me with a sledgehammer so that I did not know where I landed, but coming to very quickly, I found I was in the fireplace, and there another flew at me and scratched the eyes almost out of my head. I thereupon fled out of the back door, and lastly I was attacked on the leg by the sixth with a pair of fire tongs, and when I was still running away, someone shouted out of the house, 'Stop him, stop h - i - m!'"

The Runaway Children, Or, The Wonderful Feather

This story has been edited and adapted from George McCall Theal's Kaffir (Xhosa) Folk-Lore, originally published in 1886 by S. Sonnenschein, Le Bas and Lowrey, London. This is a Xhosa story.

Once in a time of famine a woman left her home and went to live in a distant village, where she became a cannibal. She had one son, whose name was Magoda. She ate all the people in that village, until only herself and Magoda remained. Then she was compelled to hunt animals, but she caught people still when she could. In hunting she learned to be very swift of foot, and could run so fast that nothing she pursued could escape from her.

Her brother, who remained at home when she left, had two daughters, whom he did not treat very kindly. One day he sent them to the river for water, which they were to carry in two pots. These pots were made of clay, and were the nicest and most valuable in the village. One of the girls fell down on a rock and broke the pot she was carrying. Then she did not know what to do, because she was afraid to go back to her father. She sat down and cried, but that did not help, for the pot would not be whole again. Then she said to her sister, "Let us go away to another place, where our father will not be able to find us."

She was the younger and the cleverer of the two, and so she persuaded her sister. They walked away in the opposite direction from their home, and for two days had nothing but gum to eat. Then they saw a fire at a distance, and went to it, where they saw a house. It was the house of their aunt, but they did not know it. They were afraid to go in, but Magoda came out and talked to them. When he heard who they were, he was sorry for them, and told them that their aunt was a cannibal, giving them advice not to stay there. But just then they heard her corning, so they went into Magoda's house and hid themselves, for he lived in one house and his mother in another.

The woman came and said, "I smell something nice, what is it, my son?"

Magoda said there was nothing.

She replied, "Surely I smell fat children."

But as she did not go in, they remained concealed that night.

The next morning, Nomagoda (so called because she was the mother of Magoda) went out to hunt, but she did not go far, so the children could not get away. They went into her house, where they saw a person with only one arm, one side, and one leg.

The person said to them, "See, the cannibal has eaten the rest of me, take care of yourselves."

When it was nearly dark, Nomagoda came home again, bringing some animals which she had killed. She smelt that children had been in the house, so she went to her son's house and looked in.

She said to Magoda, "Why do you not give me some? Do I not catch animals for you?"

Then she saw the children, and was very glad. She took them to her house, and told them to sleep. They lay down, but were too frightened to close their eyes. They heard their aunt say, "Axe, be sharp, axe, be sharp," and to let her know that they were awake, they spoke of vermin biting them.

After a while the cannibal went to sleep, when they crept out, first putting two blocks of wood in their places, and ran away as fast as they could. When Nomagoda awoke, she took the axe and went to kill them, but the axe fell on the blocks of wood.

As soon as it was day, the cannibal pursued the children. They looked behind, and saw clouds of dust which she made as she ran. There was a tall tree just in front of them, so they hastened to climb up it, and sat down among the branches. Nomagoda came to the tree and commenced to cut it down, but when a chip fell out, a Ntengu, the bird, sang:

"Ntengu, ntengu,

Chips, return to your places,

Chips, return to your places,

Chips, be fast."

The chip then went back to its place and was fast again. This happened three times, but Nomagoda, who was very angry, caught the bird and swallowed it. When she put it in her mouth, one of the feathers dropped to the ground. Then she began to chop at the tree again, but as soon as a chip was loose the feather sang:

"Ntengu, ntengu,

Chips, return to your places,

Chips, return to your places,

Chips, be fast."

The chip then stuck fast again. The cannibal chopped till she was tired, but the feather continued to keep the tree from receiving harm. Then she tried to catch the feather, but it flew about too quickly for her, until she sank down exhausted on the ground at the foot of the tree.

The children, up in the branches, could see a long way off, and as they strained their eyes, they observed three dogs as big as calves, and they knew these dogs belonged to their father, who was searching for them. So they called them by name, and the dogs came running to the tree and ate up the cannibal, who was too tired to make her escape.

Thus the children were delivered, and their father was so glad to get them back again that he forgave them for breaking the pot and running away.

The Story Of A Dam

This story has been edited and adapted from James A. Honey's South-African Folk Tales, originally published in 1910 by The Baker and Taylor Company.

There was a great drought in the land, and Lion called together a number of animals so that they might devise a plan for retaining water when the rains fell.

The animals which attended at Lion's summons were Baboon, Leopard, Hyena, Jackal, Hare, and Mountain Tortoise.

It was agreed that they should scratch a large hole in some suitable place to hold water, and the next day they all began to work, with the exception of Jackal, who continually hovered about in that locality, and was overheard to mutter that he was not going to scratch his nails off in making water holes.

When the dam was finished the rains fell, and it was soon filled with water, to the great delight of those who had worked so hard at it. The first one, however, to come and drink there, was Jackal, who not only drank, but filled his clay pot with water, and then proceeded to swim in the rest of the water, making it as muddy and dirty as he could.

This was brought to the attention of Lion, who was very angry and ordered Baboon to guard the water the next day, armed with a huge knobkerrie. Baboon was concealed in a bush close to the water, but Jackal soon became aware of his presence there, and guessed what he was doing there. Knowing the fondness of baboons for honey, Jackal at once hit upon a plan, and marching to and fro, every now and then dipped his fingers into his clay pot, and licked them with an expression of intense relish, saying, in a low voice to himself, "I don't want any of their dirty water when I have a pot full of delicious honey." This was too much for poor Baboon, whose mouth began to water. He soon began to beg Jackal to give him a little honey, as he had been watching for several hours, and was very hungry and tired.

After taking no notice of Baboon at first, Jackal looked round, and said, in a patronizing manner, that he pitied such an unfortunate creature, and would give him some honey on certain conditions. He asked Baboon to give him the knobkerrie and then allow himself to be bound by Jackal. He foolishly agreed, and was soon tied in such a manner that he could not move hand or foot.

Jackal now proceeded to drink of the water, to fill his pot, and to swim in plain sight of Baboon, from time to time telling him what a foolish fellow he had been to be so easily duped, and that he, Jackal, had no honey or anything else to give him, excepting a good blow on the head every now and then with his own knobkerrie.

The other animals soon appeared and found poor Baboon in this sorry plight, looking the picture of misery. Lion was so exasperated that he caused Baboon to be severely punished, and to be denounced as a fool.

Tortoise hereupon stepped forward, and offered his services for the capture of Jackal. It was at first thought that he was merely joking, but when he explained how he proposed to catch him, his plan was considered so feasible that his offer was accepted. He proposed that a thick coating of "bijenwerk" (a kind of sticky black substance found on beehives) should be spread all over him, and that he should then go and stand at the entrance to the dam, on the water level, so that Jackal might tread upon him and stick fast. This was accordingly done and Tortoise took position there.

The next day, when Jackal came, he approached the water very cautiously, and wondered to find no one there. He then ventured to the entrance of the water, and remarked how kind they had been in placing there a large black stepping-stone for him. As soon, however, as he trod upon the supposed stone, he stuck fast, and saw that he had been tricked, for Tortoise now put his head out and began to move. Jackal's hind feet being still free he threatened to smash Tortoise with them if he did not let him go.

Tortoise merely answered, "Do as you like."

Jackal thereupon made a violent jump, and found, with horror, that his hind feet were now also stuck fast. "Tortoise," said he, "I have still my mouth and teeth left, and will eat you alive if you do not let me go."

"Do as you like," Tortoise again replied.

Jackal, in his endeavours to free himself, at last made a desperate bite at Tortoise, and found himself fixed, both head and feet. Tortoise, feeling proud of his successful capture, now marched quietly up to the top of the bank with Jackal on his back, so that he could easily be seen by the animals as they came to the water.

They were indeed astonished to find how cleverly the crafty Jackal had been caught, and Tortoise was much praised, while the unhappy Baboon was again reminded of his misconduct when set to guard the water.

Jackal was at once condemned to death by Lion, and Hyena was to execute the sentence. Jackal pleaded hard for mercy, but finding this useless, he made a last request to Lion that he should not have to suffer a lingering death. As he said, Lion was always so fair and just in his dealings.

Lion inquired of him in what manner he wished to die, and he asked that his tail might be shaved and rubbed with a little fat, and that Hyena might then swing him round twice and dash his brains out upon a stone. This, being considered sufficiently fair by Lion, was ordered by him to be carried out in his presence.

When Jackal's tail had been shaved and greased, Hyena caught hold of him with great force, and before he had fairly lifted him from the ground, the cunning Jackal had slipped away from Hyena's grasp, and was running for his life, pursued by all the animals.

Lion was the foremost pursuer, and after a great chase Jackal got under an overhanging precipice, and, standing on his hind legs with his shoulders pressed against the rock, called loudly to Lion to help him, as the rock was falling, and would crush them both. Lion put his shoulders to the rock, and exerted himself to the utmost. After some little time Jackal proposed that he should creep slowly out, and fetch a large pole to prop up the rock, so that Lion could get out and save his life. Jackal did creep out, and left Lion there to starve and die.

The Girl Of The Early Race, Who Made Stars

This story has been edited and adapted from Specimens of Bushman Folklore, produced by Wilhelm Heinrich Immanuel Bleek and Lucy Lloyd, originally published in 1911 by George Allen and Company, London.

My mother told me that a girl arose, and she put her hands into the wood ashes, and she threw the wood ashes up into the sky. She said to the wood ashes, "The wood ashes which are here, they must altogether become the Milky Way. They must lie white in the sky, and the Stars may stand outside of the Milky Way."

The Milky Way must go round with the stars. The Milky Way lies flat in the sky while the Stars sail along. Eventually the Milky Way and the Stars and the Sun turn back to fetch the daybreak, and all will stand nicely in the sky. The Stars and the Milky Way become white when the Sun comes out. When the Sun sets, they stand white and red in the dark sky. It glows and the people can travel across the dark land.

It is said that this girls was one of the people of the early race, the !Xwe-|na-ssho-!ke. She was the 'first' girl, and she acted badly. She was finally shot by her husband. These !Xwe-|na-ssho-!ke are said to have been stupid people, and not to have understood things well.

The girl also thought that she would throw up into the air the roots of the !huing, in order that the !huing roots should also become Stars, and so some Stars are red.

The girl was angry with her mother, because her mother had not given her many !huing roots. She did not yet go out to seek food herself for she was too young, so she lay in the hut and was hungry. She did not yet eat the young men's hunted game. She only ate the game caught by her father, who was an old man. While she thought that the hands of the young men would become cool. Then, the arrow would become cool. The arrowhead, which is at the top, it would be cold, while the arrowhead felt that the bow was cold, while the bow felt that the young man's hands were cold. She feared the young men's game. Her father was the one from whom she alone ate game.

Crocodile's Treason

This story has been edited and adapted from James A. Honey's South-African Folk Tales, originally published in 1910 by The Baker and Taylor Company.

Crocodile was, in the days when animals still could talk, the acknowledged foreman of all water creatures and if one should judge from appearances one would say that he still is. But in those days it was his especial duty to have a general care of all water animals, and when one year it was exceedingly dry, and the water of the river where they had lived dried up and became scarce, he was forced to make a plan to trek over to another river a short distance from there.

He first sent Otter out to spy out the land. He stayed away two days and brought back a report that there was still good water in the other river, real sea-cow holes, that not even a drought of several years could dry up.

After he had ascertained this, Crocodile called to his side Tortoise and Alligator. "Look here," said he, "I need you two tonight to carry a report to Lion. So then get ready, the veldt is dry, and you will probably have to travel for a few days without any water. We must make peace with Lion and his subjects, otherwise we utterly perish this year. And he must help us to trek over to the other river, especially past the farm that lies in between, and to travel unmolested by any of the animals of the veldt, so long as the trek lasts. A fish on land is sometimes a very helpless thing, as you all know."

The two had it mighty hard in the burning sun, and on the dry veldt, but eventually they reached Lion and handed him the treaty.

"What is going on now?" thought Lion to himself when he had read it. "I must consult Jackal first," said he. But to the commissioners he gave back an answer that the following evening he would with his advisers be at the appointed place, at the big vaarland willow tree, at the farther end of the water hole where Crocodile had his headquarters.

When Tortoise and Alligator came back, Crocodile was exceedingly pleased with himself at the turn the case had taken.

He allowed Otter and a few others to be present and ordered them on that evening to have ready plenty of fish and other eatables for their guests under the vaarland willow.

That evening as it grew dark Lion appeared with Wolf, Jackal, Baboon, and a few other important animals, at the appointed place, and they were received in the most open-hearted manner by Crocodile and the other water creatures.

Crocodile was so glad at the meeting of the animals that he now and then let fall a great tear of joy that disappeared into the sand. After the other animals had done well by the fish, Crocodile laid bare to them the condition of affairs and opened up his plan. He wanted only peace among all animals, for they not only destroyed one another, but men, too, would in time destroy them all.

The local Boer farmer had already stationed at the source of the river no less than three steam pumps to irrigate his land, and the water was becoming scarcer every day. More than this, he took advantage of their unfortunate position by making them sit in the shallow water and then, one after the other, bringing about their death. As Lion was, on this account, inclined to make peace, it was to his glory to take this opportunity and give his hand to these peace-making water creatures, and carry out their part of the contract, namely, to escort them from the dried-up water, past the Boer's farm and to the long sea-cow pools.

"And what benefit shall we receive from it?" asked Jackal.

"Well," answered Crocodile, 'the peace made is of great benefit to both sides. We will not exterminate each other. If you desire to come and drink water, you can do so with an easy mind, and not be the least bit nervous that I, or any one of us will seize you by the nose, and so also with all the other animals. And from your side we are to be freed from Elephant, who has the habit, whenever he gets the opportunity, of tossing us with his trunk up into some open and narrow fork of a tree and there allowing us to become biltong."

Lion and Jackal stepped aside to consult with one another, and then Lion wanted to know what form of security he would have that Crocodile would keep to his part of the contract.

"I give you my word of honour," was the prompt answer from Crocodile, and he let drop a few more long tears of honesty into the sand.

Baboon then said it was all square and honest as far as he could see into the case. He thought it was nonsense to attempt to dig pitfalls for one another, because he personally was well aware that his race would benefit somewhat from this contract of peace and friendship. And more than this, they must consider that use must be made of the fast disappearing water, for even in the best of times it was an unpleasant thing to be always carrying your life about in your hands. He would, however, like to suggest to the King that it would be well to have everything put down in writing, so that there would be nothing to regret in case it was needed.

Jackal did not want to listen to the agreement. He could not see that it would benefit the animals of the veldt. But Wolf, who had fully satisfied himself with the fish, was in an exceptionally peace-loving mood, and he advised Lion again to close the agreement.

After Lion had listened to all his advisers, and also the pleading tones of Crocodile's followers, he held forth in a speech in which he said that he was inclined to enter into the agreement, seeing that it was clear that Crocodile and his subjects were in a very tight place.

There and then a document was drawn up, and it was resolved, before midnight, to begin the trek. Crocodile's messengers swam in all directions to summon together the water animals for the trek.

Frogs croaked and crickets chirped in the long water grass. It was not long before all the animals had assembled at the vaarland willow. In the meantime Lion had sent out a few despatch riders to his subjects to raise a commando for an escort, and long before midnight these also were at the vaarland willow in the moonlight.

The trek then was regulated by Lion and Jackal. Jackal was to take the lead to act as spy, and when he was able to draw Lion to one side, he said to him, "See here, I do not trust this affair one bit, and I want to tell you straight out, I am going to make tracks! I will spy for you until you reach the sea-cow pool, but I am not going to be the one to await your arrival there."

Elephant had to act as advance guard because he could walk so softly and could hear and smell so well. Then came Lion with one division of the animals, then Crocodile's trek with a flank protection of both sides, and Wolf received orders to bring up the rear.

Meanwhile, while all this was being arranged, Crocodile was smoothly preparing his treason. He called Yellow Snake to one side and said to him, "It is to our advantage to have these animals, who go among us every day, and who will continue to do so, fall into the hands of the Boer. Listen, now! You remain behind unnoticed, and when you hear me shout you will know that we have arrived safely at the sea-cow pool. Then you must harass the Boer's dogs as much as you can, and the rest will look out for themselves."

Thereupon the trek moved on. It was necessary to go very slowly as many of the water animals were not accustomed to the journey on land, but they trekked past the Boer's farm in safety, and toward break of day they were all safely at the sea-cow pool. There most of the water animals disappeared suddenly into the deep water, and Crocodile also began to make preparations to follow their example. With tearful eyes he said to Lion that he was, oh, so thankful for the help, that, from pure relief and joy, he must first give vent to his feelings by a few screams. Thereupon he suited his words to actions so that even the mountains echoed, and then he thanked Lion on behalf of his subjects, and purposely continued with a long speech, dwelling on all the benefits both sides would derive from the agreement of peace.

Lion was just about to say good day and take his departure, when the first shot fell, and with it Elephant and a few other animals.

"I told you all so!" shouted Jackal from the other side of the sea-cow pool. "Why did you allow yourselves to be misled by a few Crocodile tears?"

Crocodile had disappeared long ago into the water. All one saw was just a lot of bubbles, and on the banks there was an actual war against the animals. It simply crackled the way the Boers shot them. But most of them, fortunately, came out of it alive.

Shortly after, they say, Crocodile received his well-earned reward, when he met a driver with a load of dynamite. And even now when the Elephant gets the chance he pitches them up into the highest forks of the trees.

Story Of The Cannibal's Wonderful Bird

This story has been edited and adapted from George McCall Theal's Kaffir (Xhosa) Folk-Lore, originally published in 1886 by S. Sonnenschein, Le Bas and Lowrey, London. This is a Xhosa story.

A number of girls once went away from their homes early in the morning for the purpose of getting imbola, which is a red dye used to colour their bodies and clothes. Among them was the daughter of a chief, a very pretty girl. After they had collected the imbola, they were about to return home, when one of them proposed that they should bathe in a large pool of water that was there. To this they all agreed, and so they went into the water and played about in it for a long time.

At last they dressed themselves again, and set out for home, but when they had gone some distance, the chief's daughter noticed that she had forgotten one of her ornaments, which she had taken off when they went to bathe. So she asked her cousin to return with her to get it. The cousin refused. Then she asked another girl, and another, but one and all refused to go back. She was thus obliged to return to the water alone, while the other girls went home.

On arriving at the pool, a big ugly cannibal with only one leg came up to her, caught her, and put her in his bag. She was so frightened that she lay quite still. The cannibal then took her round to the different villages and made her sing for him. He called her his bird.

When he came to a village he asked for meat, and when it was given to him he said "Sing, my bird." But he would never open the bag so that anyone could see what sort of a bird he had.

When the girls reached home, they told the chief that his daughter had reached the age of ntonjane, and they selected one of themselves and shut her up in a hut. The chief believed that story, and so he killed a large ox and said the people must eat. That day they ate fat beef, and were very merry. The boys took meat, and went away from the village to eat it.

The cannibal, who did not know that the girl's father was chief at this place, came there just at this time. He said to the boys if they would give him meat he would make his bird sing for them. So they gave him meat, and he said, "Sing, my bird."

The girl's brother was among those boys, and he thought the bird sang like his sister, but he was afraid to ask the cannibal to let him see. He advised the cannibal to go to the village where the men were, and told him there was plenty of meat that day.

The cannibal then went to the village and made his bird sing. The chief wanted very much to see the bird, but the cannibal would not open the bag. The chief offered him an ox for the bird, but the cannibal declined the offer. Then the chief made a plan. He asked the cannibal to go for some water, and said he would give him plenty of beef when he returned. The cannibal said he would go if they would promise not to open his bag while he was away. They all promised not to touch the bag. They gave the cannibal a leaky pot to carry the water in, so that he was gone a long time. As soon as he was out of sight the chief opened the bag and took his daughter out. At first he could not believe it was his daughter, for he thought she was observing ntonjane. But when he knew how those other girls had deceived him he said they must all die, and so they were killed. Then he put snakes and toads in the bag, and tied it up again.

When the cannibal came back he complained about the leaky pot, but they gave him plenty of meat to satisfy him, so he picked up his bag and went away. He did not know what had happened while he was absent. When he came near his own house he called to his wife, "Make ready to cook." He sent and called all the other cannibals to come to a feast, and they came expecting to get something nice. He let them wait a little to get very hungry. Then he opened his bag and thought to take the girl out, but found only snakes and toads in it. The other cannibals were so angry when they saw this, that they killed him and made their feast of him.

The Great Star, !Gaunu, Which, Singing, Named The Stars

This story has been edited and adapted from Specimens of Bushman Folklore, produced by Wilhelm Heinrich Immanuel Bleek and Lucy Lloyd, originally published in 1911 by George Allen and Company, London.

!gaunu was once a great Star, and it is said that it was he who named the other Stars. He sang while he uttered the Stars' names. He said "‖Xwahai" to Stars which are very small.

And so the porcupine, when he sees these stars fade in fade in the sky, will not remain on the hunting ground, for, he knows that it is dawn. When ‖Xwahai has faded he returns home, for, he is used to looking at these Stars, and he knows that they are the dawn's Stars.

What The Stars Say, And A Prayer To A Star

This story has been edited and adapted from Specimens of Bushman Folklore, produced by Wilhelm Heinrich Immanuel Bleek and Lucy Lloyd, originally published in 1911 by George Allen and Company, London.

The Bushmen understand things. They understand that the Star shall take their heart when they hunger, and the Star shall give them the Star's heart, for the Star is not small and the Star seems as if it has food. Therefore, they say, that the Star shall give them the Star's heart that they may not hunger.

The Stars are wont to call, "Tsau! Tsau!"

The Bushmen say that the Stars curse for them the springboks' eyes.

The Stars say, "Tsau!" They say, "Tsau! Tsau!"

My grandfather told me, when we sat in the coolness outside, that the Stars spoke thus. The Stars said, "Tsau!", while they cursed the springboks' eyes for the people. I too have heard the Stars saying, "Tsau! Tsau!" Summer is when the Stars speak.

My grandfather used to speak to Canopus when Canopus had newly come out. He said, "You shall give me your heart, with which you do sit in plenty. You shall take my heart with which I am desperately hungry. That I might also be full, like you. For, I hunger. For, you seem to be satisfied with food, and that is why you are not small. I am hungry. You shall give me your stomach. You shall take my stomach, that you may also hunger. Give you me also your arm, you shall take my arm, with which I do not kill. For, I miss my aim. You shall give me your arm. For, my arm which is here, I miss my aim with it."

My grandfather wished that the arrow might hit the springbok for him, hence, he wished the Star to give him the Star's arm, while the Star took his arm, with which he missed his aim.

The Story Of Mbulukazi

This story has been edited and adapted from George McCall Theal's Kaffir (Xhosa) Folk-Lore, originally published in 1886 by S. Sonnenschein, Le Bas and Lowrey, London. This is a Xhosa story.

There was once a man who had two wives, one of whom had no children, and for that reason she was not loved by her husband. Her name was Numbakatali. The other wife had one daughter who was very plain, and several children besides, but they were all crows. The one who had no offspring was very downcast on that account, and used to go about weeping all day.

Once when she was working in her garden, and crying as usual, two doves came and perched near her. One of them said to the other, "Dove, ask the woman why she is crying." So the dove questioned her.

She replied, "It is because I have no children, and my husband does not love me. His other wife's children are crows, which come and eat my corn, and she laughs at me."

The dove said, "Go home and get two earthen jars, and bring them here,"

Numbakatali went and got them. Then the doves scratched her knees till the blood flowed, and put the blood in the jars. The woman gave the doves some corn to eat, after which she took the jars home to her hut, and set them carefully down in a corner. Every day the two doves came to be fed, and always told the woman to look at what was in the jars.

At last, when she looked one day, she saw two children, one a boy, the other a girl, and both very handsome. She was very much delighted at the sight, but she did not tell anyone.

When the children grew a little she made a snug place for them in the hut, where they were to sit all day, because she did not wish them to be seen. Always before she went to her work she charged them not to go out, and as her husband never came to see her, no one knew of the existence of these children except herself and a servant girl.

But one day, when they were big, she went out, and after she was away some time, the boy said to his sister, " Come, let us help our mother by bringing water from the river."

So they went for water, but they had not reached the river when they met a company of young men with a chief's son, who was looking for a pretty girl to be his wife. The young chief was called Broad Breast, because his chest was very wide, and it was also made of a glittering metal that shone in the sun. These men asked for water to drink. The boy gave them all some water, but the young chief would only take it from the girl. He was very much smitten with her beauty, and watched her when she left, so as to find out where she lived.

As soon as the young chief saw the hut that the girl went to, he returned home with his party and asked his father for cattle with which to marry her. The chief, who was very rich, gave his son many fine cattle, with which the young man went to the girl's mother's husband, and said, "I want to marry your daughter."

So the girl who was very plain was told to come, but the young chief said, "She is not the one I want, the one I saw was much prettier."

The father replied I have no other children but crows."

But Broad Breast persisted, so the man called his wives, both of whom denied that there was such a girl. However, the servant girl went to the father and privately told him the truth. In the evening he went to his wife's hut, and to his great joy saw the boy and his sister. He was so delighted that he remained there that night, and after talking it over with his wife, he agreed to let Broad Breast marry the girl.

In the morning a mat was spread in the yard, and the young chief was asked to sit down. The two children and the servant girl who told their father about them were also called, and they all sat down on the mat.

The young chief, as soon as he saw her, said, "This is the girl I meant."

He stayed part of the day, and then with his attendants went to his father for more cattle, which he brought back for the father of the girl.

The mother of the very plain girl and the crows was very jealous when she saw such a fine young chief coming with so many cattle. She wanted her daughter to be the one that was to be married, so she dressed her as finely as she could, but she did not have clothes as pretty as the other girl had. Her name was Mahlunguluza, for she was called after the crows, who were her siblings. The pretty girl's name was Mbulukazi, which name was given to her because her handsome dress was made of the skin of a mbulu.

The mother of Mahlunguluza spoke to the young chief about her daughter, and so he married both the girls. Their father gave to each an ox, with which they went to their new home. Mbulukazi's ox was a pretty young one, and Mahlunguluza's ox was an old and poor one. When they arrived, Broad Breast gave to Mbulukazi a very nice new house to live in, but to Mahlunguluza he gave an old one quite in ruins.

Then the very plain one saw she was not loved, and she became jealous, so she made a plan to kill her sister. One day she told her she heard their father was sick, and proposed that they should go to see him. Mbulukazi consented, and as soon as they obtained leave from their husband they left. Their road led them along the edge of a cliff, below which was a deep pool of water.

Mahlunguluza lay down on the rock, and said, "Come, see what is here in the water."

Her sister lay down with her head over the edge of the rock, when Mahlunguluza jumped up quickly and pushed her over. Mbulukazi sank in the water and was drowned. Then the very plain girl returned home, and when her husband asked where Mbulukazi was, she said that she was still with their father.

The next day the ox of the drowned one came running to the village and walked about lowing for a while, after which it tore down the old, ruined house of Mahlunguluza with its horns. Its actions attracted the notice of the men, and they said, "Surely this ox means something, why is it doing this?"

Then it went to the deep pool of water, and the men followed it. The ox smelt all over the rock, and then jumped into the water and brought out the body of Mbulukazi. The ox licked her till her life came back, and as soon as she was strong once more, she told what had happened.

They all went home rejoicing greatly, and informed Broad Breast. When the young chief heard the story he was angry with Mahlunguluza, and said to her, "Go home to your father, I never wanted you at all, it was your mother who brought you to me."

So she had to go away in sorrow, and Mbulukazi remained the great wife of the chief.

The Son Of The Wind

This story has been edited and adapted from Specimens of Bushman Folklore, produced by Wilhelm Heinrich Immanuel Bleek and Lucy Lloyd, originally published in 1911 by George Allen and Company, London.

The son of the Wind was once very still. One day he rolled a ball to !na-ka-ti saying, "O !na-ka-ti! There it goes!"

And !na-ka-ti exclaimed, "O my friend! There it goes!" because !nq-ka-ti did not know the other one's name.

So, !na-ka-ti went to question his mother about the other one's name. He said, "Oh, our mother! Tell me the name of the friend who is yonder. He knows my name, but I do not know his name. I would like to speak his name when I roll the ball to him."

His mother said, "I will not utter to you your friend's comrade's name. You must wait for father to provide us with the shelter of a hut. Then I will tell you the name of your friend. And you must scamper home to the hut as soon as I have said the name of your friend, or else the Wind will blow you away."

!na-ka-ti's mother said, "He is called |erriten-!kuang-!kuang", and he is !gau-!gaubu-ti." Then she said, "You must not, at first, utter your friend's name. You must be silent, until he says your name. when you do say his name must run home before the wind blows you away."

So, !na-ka-ti went to roll the ball, and while there he did not utter the other one's name. He waited until he saw his father sitting down on the mat, and so he knew that the hut was finished and ready. As soon as he saw that the hut was ready he said, "There it goes! Oh |erriten-!kuang-!kuang! There it goes !gau-!gaubu-ti! There it goes!"

Immediately he had said these names he scampered away home, while |erriten-!kuang-!kuang! began to lean over and fall down. He lay kicking violently upon the vlei, and the winds blew, and the people's huts vanished away. The wind blew, breaking their sheltering bushes, together with the huts, and the people could not see for the dust.

Then the wind's mother came out of her own hut. She grasped him to raise him up and set him on his feet. But |erriten-!kuang-!kuang! was unwilling to stand, for he wanted to lie still. His mother took hold of him and set him on his feet. Therefore, the blowing wind became still.

Therefore, we who are Bushmen, we are wont to say, "The wind seems to be lying down, for, it does not gently blow. For, when it stands upright, then it is still.

The Lioness And The Ostrich

This story has been edited and adapted from James A. Honey's South-African Folk Tales, originally published in 1910 by The Baker and Taylor Company.

It is said, once a lioness roared, and the ostrich also roared. The lioness went toward the place where the ostrich was. They met.

The lioness said to the ostrich, "Please roar."

The ostrich roared. Then the lioness roared. The voices were equal.

The lioness said to the ostrich, "You are my match."

Then the lioness said to the ostrich, "Let us hunt game together."

They saw eland and made toward it. The lioness caught only one, the ostrich killed a great many by striking them with the claw, which was on his leg, but the lioness killed only one. When they had met after the hunting they went over to their game, and the lioness saw that the ostrich had killed a great deal.

Now, the lioness also had young cubs. They went to the shade to rest themselves. The lioness said to the ostrich, "Get up and rip the beasts open, let us eat."

Said the ostrich, "Go and rip open the beasts, I shall eat the blood."

The lioness stood up and ripped open their game, and ate with the cubs. And when she had eaten, the ostrich got up and ate the blood. Then they all went to sleep.

The cubs played about. While they were playing, they went to the ostrich, who was asleep. When he went to sleep he also opened his mouth. The young lions saw that the ostrich had no teeth. They went to their mother and said, "This fellow, who says he is your equal, has no teeth, he is insulting you."

Then the lioness went to wake the ostrich, and said, "Get up, let us fight", and they fought.

And the ostrich said, "Go to that side of the ant-hill, and I will go to this side of it."

The ostrich struck the ant-hill, and sent it toward the lioness. Then, the second time he struck the lioness in a vulnerable spot, near the liver, and killed her.

Story Of The Wonderful Horns

This story has been edited and adapted from George McCall Theal's Kaffir (Xhosa) Folk-Lore, originally published in 1886 by S. Sonnenschein, Le Bas and Lowrey, London. This is a Xhosa story.

There was once a boy whose mother that bore him was dead, and he was ill-treated by his other mothers. On this account he determined to go away from his father's place. One morning he went, riding on an ox which was given to him by his father. As he was travelling, he came to a herd of cattle with a bull.

His ox said, "I will fight and overcome that bull."

The boy got off his ox's back. The fight took place, and the bull was defeated. The boy then mounted his ox again.

About midday, feeling hungry, he struck the right horn of his ox, and food came out. After satisfying his hunger, he struck the left horn, and the rest of the food went in again.

The boy saw another herd of dun-coloured cattle. His ox said, "I will fight and die there. You must break off my horns and take them with you. When you are hungry, speak to them, and they will supply you with food."

In the fight the ox was killed, as he had said. The boy took his horns, and went on walking till he came to a village where he found the people cooking a weed called tyutu, having no other food to eat.

He entered one of the houses. He spoke to his horn, and food came out, enough to satisfy the owner of the house and himself. After they had eaten, they both fell asleep. The owner of the house got up and took away the horns. He concealed them, and put two others in their place.

The boy started next morning with the horns, thinking they were the right ones. When he felt hungry, he spoke to the horns, but nothing came out. He therefore went back to the place where he had slept the night before. As he drew near, he heard the owner of the place speaking to the horns, but without getting anything out of them.

The boy took his horns from the thief, and went on his way. He came to a house, and asked to be entertained. The owner refused, and sent him away, because his clothes were in tatters, and his body soiled with travel.

After that he came to a river and sat down on the bank. He spoke to his horns, and a new mantle and handsome ornaments came out. He dressed himself, and went on. He came to a house where there was a very beautiful girl. He was received by the girl's father, and stayed there. His horns provided food and clothing food for them all.

After a time he married the girl. He then returned home with his wife, and was welcomed by his father. He spoke to his horns, and a fine house came out, in which he lived with his wife.

The Little Hare

This story has been edited and adapted from Andrew Lang's All Sorts of Stories Book, originally published in 1911 by Longmans, Green and Company, London and New York. The original was adapted from the Basuto.

A long, long way off, in a land where water is very scarce, there lived a man and his wife and several children. One day the wife said to her husband, "I am pining to have the liver of a nyamatsane, a type of bok, for my dinner. If you love me as much as you say you do, you will go out and hunt for a nyamatsane, and will kill it and get its liver. If not, I shall know that your love is not worth having."

"Bake some bread," was all her husband answered, 'then take the crust and put it in this little bag."

The wife did as she was told, and when she had finished she said to her husband, "The bag is ready and quite full."

"Very well," said he, "and now good-bye, I am going after the nyamatsane."

But the nyamatsane was not so easy to find as the woman had hoped. The husband walked on and on and on without ever seeing one, and every now and then he felt so hungry that he was obliged to eat one of the crusts of bread out of his bag. At last, when he was ready to drop from fatigue, he found himself on the edge of a great marsh, which bordered on one side the country of the nyamatsanes. But there were no more nyamatsanes here than anywhere else. They had all gone on a hunting expedition, as their larder was empty, and the only person left at home was their grandmother, who was so feeble she never went out of the house.

Our friend looked on this as a great piece of luck, and made haste to kill her before the others returned, and to take out her liver, after which he dressed himself in her skin as well as he could. He had scarcely done this when he heard the noise of the nyamatsanes coming back to their grandmother, for they were very fond of her, and never stayed away from her longer than they could help.

They rushed clattering into the hut, exclaiming, "We smell human flesh! Some man is here," and began to look about for him, but they only saw their old grandmother, who answered, in a trembling voice, "No, my children, no! What should any man be doing here?" The nyamatsanes paid no attention to her, and began to open all the cupboards, and peep under all the beds, crying out all the while, "A man is here! a man is here!" but they could find nobody, and at length, tired out with their long day's hunting, they curled themselves up and fell asleep.

Next morning they woke up quite refreshed, and made ready to start on another expedition, but as they did not feel happy about their grandmother they said to her, "Grandmother, won't you come today and feed with us?" And they led their grandmother outside, and all of them began hungrily to eat pebbles. Our friend pretended to do the same, but in reality he slipped the stones into his pouch, and swallowed the crusts of bread instead. However, as the nyamatsanes did not see this they had no idea that he was not really their grandmother.

When they had eaten a great many pebbles they thought they had done enough for that day, and all went home together and curled themselves up to sleep. Next morning when they woke they said, "Let us go and amuse ourselves by jumping over the ditch," and every time they cleared it with a bound. Then they begged their grandmother to jump over it too, and with a tremendous effort she managed to spring right over to the other side. After this they had no doubt at all of this being their true grandmother, and went off to their hunting, leaving our friend at home in the hut.

As soon as they had gone out of sight our hero made haste to take the liver from the place where he had hidden it, threw off the skin of the old nyamatsane, and ran away as hard as he could, only stopping to pick up a very brilliant and polished little stone, which he put in his bag by the side of the liver.

Towards evening the nyamatsanes came back to the hut full of anxiety to know how their grandmother had got on during their absence. The first thing they saw on entering the door was her skin lying on the floor, and then they knew that they had been deceived, and they said to each other, "So we were right, after all, and it was human flesh we smelt." Then they stooped down to find traces of the man's footsteps, and when they had got them they set out instantly in hot pursuit.

Meanwhile our friend had journeyed many miles, and was beginning to feel quite safe and comfortable, when, happening to look round, he saw in the distance a thick cloud of dust moving rapidly. His heart stood still within him, and he said to himself, "I am lost. It is the nyamatsanes, and they will tear me in pieces," and indeed the cloud of dust was drawing near with amazing quickness, and the nyamatsanes almost felt as if they were already devouring him. Then as a last hope the man took the little stone that he had picked up out of his bag and flung it on the ground. The moment it touched the soil it became a huge rock, whose steep sides were smooth as glass, and on the top of it our hero hastily seated himself. It was in vain that the nyamatsanes tried to climb up and reach him, they slid down again much faster than they had gone up, and by sunset they were quite worn out, and fell asleep at the foot of the rock.

No sooner had the nyamatsanes tumbled off to sleep than the man stole softly down and fled away as fast as his legs would carry him, and by the time his enemies were awake he was a very long way off. They sprang quickly to their feet and began to sniff the soil round the rock, in order to discover traces of his footsteps, and they galloped after him with terrific speed. The chase continued for several days and nights, and several times the nyamatsanes almost reached him, and each time he was saved by his little pebble.

Between his fright and his hurry he was almost dead of exhaustion when he reached his own village, where the nyamatsanes could not follow him, because of their enemies the dogs, which swarmed over all the roads. So they returned home.

Then our friend staggered into his own hut and called to his wife, "Ichou! How tired I am! Quick, give me something to drink. Then go and get fuel and light a fire."

So she did what she was bid, and then her husband took the nyamatsane's liver from his pouch and said to her, "There, I have brought you what you wanted, and now you know that I love you truly."

And the wife answered, "It is well. Now go and take out the children, so that I may remain alone in the hut," and as she spoke she lifted down an old stone pot and put on the liver to cook.

Her husband watched her for a moment, and then said, "Be sure you eat it all yourself. Do not give a scrap to any of the children, but eat every morsel up." So the woman took the liver and ate it all herself.

Directly the last mouthful had disappeared she was seized with such violent thirst that she caught up a great pot full of water and drank it at a single draught. Then, having no more in the house, she ran in next door and said, "Neighbour, give me, I pray you, something to drink." The neighbour gave her a large vessel quite full, and the woman drank it off at a single draught, and held it out for more.

But the neighbour pushed her away, saying, "No, I shall have none left for my children."

So the woman went into another house, and drank all the water she could find, but the more she drank the thirstier she became. She wandered in this manner through the whole village till she had drunk every water-pot dry. Then she rushed off to the nearest spring, and swallowed that, and when she had finished all the springs and wells about she drank up first the river and then a lake. But by this time she had drunk so much that she could not rise from the ground.

In the evening, when it was time for the animals to have their drink before going to bed, they found the lake quite dry, and they had to make up their minds to be thirsty till the water flowed again and the streams were full. Even then, for some time, the lake was very dirty, and the lion, as king of the beasts, commanded that no one should drink till it was quite clear again.

But the little hare, who was fond of having his own way, and was very thirsty besides, stole quietly off when all the rest were asleep in their dens, and crept down to the margin of the lake and drank his fill. Then he smeared the dirty water all over the rabbit's face and paws, so that it might look as if it were he who had been disobeying Big Lion's orders.

The next day, as soon as it was light, Big Lion marched straight for the lake, and all the other beasts followed him. He saw at once that the water had been troubled again, and was very angry.

"Who has been drinking my water?" said he, and the little hare gave a jump, and, pointing to the rabbit, he answered, "Look there! It must be he! Why, there is mud all over his face and paws!"

The rabbit, frightened out of his wits, tried to deny the fact, exclaiming, "Oh, no, indeed I never did."

But Big Lion would not listen, and commanded them to cane him with a birch rod.

Now the little hare was very much pleased with his cleverness in causing the rabbit to be beaten instead of himself, and went about boasting of it. At last one of the other animals overheard him, and called out, "Little hare, little hare! What is that you are saying?"

But the little hare hastily replied, "I only asked you to pass me my stick."

An hour or two later, thinking that no one was near him, he said to himself again, "It was really I who drank up the water, but I made them think it was the rabbit."

But one of the beasts whose ears were longer than the rest caught the words, and went to tell Big Lion about it. "Do you hear what the little hare is saying?"

So Big Lion sent for the little hare, and asked him what he meant by talking like that.

The little hare saw that there was no use trying to hide it, so he answered pertly, "It was I who drank the water, but I made them think it was the rabbit." Then he turned and ran as fast as he could, with all the other beasts pursuing him.

They were almost up to him when he dashed into a very narrow cleft in the rock, much too small for them to follow, but in his hurry he had left one of his long ears sticking out, which they just managed to seize. But pull as hard as they might they could not drag him out of the hole, and at last they gave it up and left him, with his ear very much torn and scratched.

When the last tail was out of sight the little hare crept cautiously out, and the first person he met was the rabbit. He had plenty of impudence, so he put a bold face on the matter, and said, "Well, my good rabbit, you see I have had a beating as well as you."

But the rabbit was still sore and sulky, and he did not care to talk, so he answered, coldly, "You have treated me very badly. It was really you who drank that water, and you accused me of having done it."

"Oh, my good rabbit, never mind that! I've got such a wonderful secret to tell you! Do you know what to do so as to escape death?"

"No, I don't."

"Well, we must begin by digging a hole."

So they dug a hole, and then the little hare said, "The next thing is to make a fire in the hole," and they set to work to collect wood, and lit quite a large fire.

When it was burning brightly the little hare said to the rabbit, "Rabbit, my friend, throw me into the fire, and when you hear my fur crackling, and I call "Itchi, Itchi," then be quick and pull me out."

The rabbit did as he was told, and threw the little hare into the fire, but no sooner did the little hare begin to feel the heat of the flames than he took some green bay leaves he had plucked for the purpose and held them in the middle of the fire, where they crackled and made a great noise. Then he called loudly "Itchi, Itchi! Rabbit, my friend, be quick, be quick! Don't you hear how my skin is crackling?"

And the rabbit came in a great hurry and pulled him out.

Then the little hare said, "Now it is your turn!" and he threw the rabbit in the fire. The moment the rabbit felt the flames he cried out "Itchi, Itchi, I am burning, pull me out quick, my friend!"

But the little hare only laughed, and said, "No, you may stay there! It is your own fault. Why were you such a fool as to let yourself be thrown in? Didn't you know that fire burns?" And in a very few minutes nothing was left of the rabbit but a few bones.

When the fire was quite out the little hare went and picked up one of these bones, and made a flute out of it, and sang this song:

"Pii, pii, O flute that I love,

Pii, pii, rabbits are but little boys.

Pii, pii, he would have burned me if he could,

Pii, pii, but I burned him, and he crackled finely.”

When he got tired of going through the world singing this the little hare went back to his friends and entered the service of Big Lion. One day he said to his master, "Grandfather, shall I show you a splendid way to kill game?"

"What is it?" asked Big Lion.

"We must dig a ditch, and then you must lie in it and pretend to be dead."

Big Lion did as he was told, and when he had lain down the little hare got up on a wall blew a trumpet and shouted:

“Pii, pii, all you animals come and see,

Big Lion is dead, and now peace will be.”

Directly they heard this they all came running. The little hare received them and said, "Pass on, this way to the lion."

So they all entered into the Animal Kingdom. Last of all came the monkey with her baby on her back. She approached the ditch, and took a blade of grass and tickled Big Lion's nose, and his nostrils moved in spite of his efforts to keep them still. Then the monkey cried, "Come, my baby, climb on my back and let us go. What sort of a dead body is it that can still feel when it is tickled?" And she and her baby went away in a fright.

Then the little hare said to the other beasts, "Now, shut the gate of the Animal Kingdom."

And it was shut, and great stones were rolled against it. When everything was tight closed the little hare turned to Big Lion and said "Now!" and Big Lion bounded out of the ditch and tore the other animals in pieces.

But Big Lion kept all the choice bits for himself, and only gave away the little scraps that he did not care about eating, and the little hare grew very angry, and determined to have his revenge. He had long ago found out that Big Lion was very easily taken in, so he laid his plans accordingly. He said to him, as if the idea had just come into his head, "Grandfather, let us build a hut," and Big Lion consented.

And when they had driven the stakes into the ground, and had made the walls of the hut, the little hare told Big Lion to climb upon the top while he stayed inside. When he was ready he called out, "Now, grandfather, begin," and Big Lion passed his rod through the reeds with which the roofs are always covered in that country.

The little hare took it and cried, "Now it is my turn to pierce them," and as he spoke he passed the rod back through the reeds and gave Big Lion's tail a sharp poke.

"What is pricking me so?" asked Big Lion.

"Oh, just a little branch sticking out. I am going to break it," answered the little hare, but of course he had done it on purpose, as he wanted to fix Big Lion's tail so firmly to the hut that he would not be able to move. In a little while he gave another prick, and Big Lion called again, "What is pricking me so?"

This time the little hare said to himself, "He will find out what I am at. I must try some other plan." So he called out, "Grandfather, you had better put your tongue here, so that the branches shall not touch you."

Big Lion did as he was bid, and the little hare tied it tightly to the stakes of the wall. Then he went outside and shouted, "Grandfather, you can come down now," and Big Lion tried, but he could not move an inch.

Then the little hare began quietly to eat Big Lion's dinner right before his eyes, paying no attention at all to his growls of rage. When he had quite done he climbed up on the hut, and, blowing his flute, he chanted:

"Pii, pii, fall rain and hail."

Directly the sky was full of clouds, the thunder roared, and huge hailstones whitened the roof of the hut. The little hare, who had taken refuge within, called out again, "Big Lion, be quick and come down and dine with me." But there was no answer, not even a growl, for the hailstones had killed Big Lion.

The little hare enjoyed himself vastly for some time, living comfortably in the hut, with plenty of food to eat and no trouble at all in getting it. But one day a great wind arose, and flung down the Big Lion's half-dried skin from the roof of the hut. The little hare bounded with terror at the noise, for he thought Big Lion must have come to life again, but on discovering what had happened he set about cleaning the skin, and propped the mouth open with sticks so that he could get through. So, dressed in Big Lion's skin, the little hare started on his travels.

The first visit he paid was to the hyaenas, who trembled at the sight of him, and whispered to each other, "How shall we escape from this terrible beast?"

Meanwhile the little hare did not trouble himself about them, but just asked where the king of the hyaenas lived, and made himself quite at home there. Every morning each hyaena thought to himself, "Today he is certain to eat me," but several days went by, and they were all still alive.

At length, one evening, the little hare, looking round for something to amuse him, noticed a great pot full of boiling water, so he strolled up to one of the hyaenas and said, "Go and get in." The hyaena dared not disobey, and in a few minutes was scalded to death. Then the little hare went the round of the village, saying to every hyaena he met, "Go and get into the boiling water," so that in a little while there was hardly a male left in the village.

One day all the hyaenas that remained alive went out very early into the fields, leaving only one little daughter at home. The little hare, thinking he was all alone, came into the enclosure, and, wishing to feel what it was like to be a hare again, threw off Big Lion's skin, and began to jump and dance, singing:

I am just the little hare,

the little hare, the little hare,

I am just the little hare

who killed the great hyaenas.

The little hyaena gazed at him in surprise, saying to herself, "What! was it really this tiny beast who put to death all our best people?" when suddenly a gust of wind rustled the reeds that surrounded the enclosure, and the little hare, in a fright, hastily sprang back into Big Lion's skin.

When the hyaenas returned to their homes the little hyaena said to her father, "Father, our tribe has very nearly been swept away, and all this has been the work of a tiny creature dressed in the lion's skin."

But her father answered, "Oh, my dear child, you don't know what you are talking about."

She replied, "Yes, father, it is quite true. I saw it with my own eyes."

The father did not know what to think, and told one of his friends, who said, "Tomorrow we had better keep watch ourselves."

And the next day they hid themselves and waited till the little hare came out of the royal hut. He walked gaily towards the enclosure, threw off Big Lion's skin, and sang and danced as before:

I am just the little hare,

the little hare, the little hare,

I am just the little hare

who killed the great hyaenas.

That night the two hyaenas told all the rest, saying, "Do you know that we have allowed ourselves to be trampled on by a wretched creature with nothing of the lion about him but his skin?"

When supper was being cooked that evening, before they all went to bed, the little hare, looking fierce and terrible in Big Lion's skin, said as usual to one of the hyaenas "Go and get into the boiling water." But the hyaena never stirred.

There was silence for a moment, then a hyaena took a stone, and flung it with all his force against the lion's skin. The little hare jumped out through the mouth with a single spring, and fled away like lightning, with all the hyaenas in full pursuit uttering great cries. As he turned a corner the little hare cut off both his ears, so that they should not know him, and pretended to be working at a grindstone which lay there.

The hyaenas soon came up to him and said, "Tell me, friend, have you seen the little hare go by?"

"No, I have seen no one."

"Where can he be?" said the hyaenas one to another. "Of course, this creature is quite different, and not at all like the little hare."

Then they went on their way, but, finding no traces of the little hare, they returned sadly to their village, saying, "To think we should have allowed ourselves to be swept away by a wretched creature like that!"

#Kaga'ra And !Haunu, Who Fought Each Other With Lightning

This story has been edited and adapted from Specimens of Bushman Folklore, produced by Wilhelm Heinrich Immanuel Bleek and Lucy Lloyd, originally published in 1911 by George Allen and Company, London.

#kagara once went to fetch his younger sister from the home of !haunu, and he took her back to her parents.

!haunu, the Sorcerer of the Rains, gave chase to his brother-in-law. As he passed along behind the hill the clouds came, clouds which were unequalled in beauty before they vanished away.

#kagara said, "You must walk on." His younger sister walked, carrying a heavy burden of her husband's things. #kagara said, "You must walk on, for, home is not near at hand."

As they approached their house #kagara said, "Walk on! Walk on!" He waited for his younger sister to come up to his side. He exclaimed, "What are all of these things that you are carrying?"

Then !haunu sneezed, and blood poured out of his nostrils, and he fired stealthy lightning at his brother-in-law. #kagara fended him off quickly, but !haunu sent more. #kagara said, "You must come and walk close beside me so that I can protect you."

#kagara and !haunu went along, still angry with each other. #kagara continued to fend off his younger sister's husband, !haunu. Then !haunu stealthily fired black lightning at his younger sister's husband, and whisked him up and carried him a little distance away.

Black lightning is the lightning that kills us. We do not see it. It resembles a gun. We are merely startled by the clouds' thundering, while the other man lies there all shrivelled up. #kagara lay injured, with his head aching. He bound up his head with a net, then he continued on his way while !haunu continued thundering.

Eventually #kagara went to lie down in his hut, while !haunu lay all about thundering. He rubbed himself and his sister with buchu, and he lay down.

When the clouds were thick, and the clouds resembled a mountain, and there was thunder and lightning, my grandmothers used to say, "#kagara and his companion are those who fight in the East, he and !haunu."

The Hyena's Revenge

This story has been edited and adapted from Specimens of Bushman Folklore, produced by Wilhelm Heinrich Immanuel Bleek and Lucy Lloyd, originally published in 1911 by George Allen and Company, London.

The Hyena went to Lion's house. Although they feasted, Hyena felt that Lion had acted grudgingly towards him about the quagga's flesh, so Hyena decided to deceive Lion. Later, when Lion came to Hyena's house, Hyena was boiling ostrich flesh in his pot.

Hyena gave soup to Lion, but Lion took hold of the pot, while the pot was hot. Hyena also grasped the pot with his, hands, and Hyena said, "Oh Lion! Allow me to pour soup into the inside of your mouth."

Hyena poured soup into Lion's mouth. Then he put the mouth of the pot over Lion's head, while the pot was hot, and the soup burned Lion's eyes. The soup also burned the inside of his mouth. Then, he swallowed hot soup with his throat, he swallowed, causing himself to die, with his head all the while inside the pot.

Hyena took up his stick, and he beat Lion with the stick, while his head was inside the pot. Hyena struck, cleaving the pot asunder, and so Hyena deceived Lion.

Tink-Tinkje

This story has been edited and adapted from James A. Honey's South-African Folk Tales, originally published in 1910 by The Baker and Taylor Company.

The birds wanted a king. Men have a king, so have animals, and why shouldn't they? All had assembled.

"The Ostrich, because he is the largest," one called out.

"No, he can't fly."

"Eagle, on account of his strength."

"Not he, he is too ugly."

"Vulture, because he can fly the highest."

"No, Vulture is too dirty, his odour is terrible."

"Peacock, he is so beautiful."

"His feet are too ugly, and also his voice."

"Owl, because he can see well."

"Not Owl, he is ashamed of the light."

And so they got no further. Then one shouted aloud, "He who can fly the highest will be king."

"Yes, yes," they all screamed, and at a given signal they all ascended straight up into the sky.

Vulture flew for three whole days without stopping, straight toward the sun. Then he cried aloud, "I am the highest, I am king."

"T-sie, t-sie, t-sie," he heard above him, for there Tink-tinkje was flying. He had held fast to one of the great wing feathers of Vulture, and had never been felt, he was so light. "T-sie, t-sie, t-sie, I am the highest, I am king," piped Tink-tinkje.

Vulture flew for another day still ascending. "I am highest, I am king."

"T-sie, t-sie, t-sie, I am the highest, I am king," Tink-tinkje mocked. There he was again, having crept out from under the wing of Vulture.

Vulture flew on the fifth day straight up in the air. "I am the highest, I am king," he called.

"T-sie, t-sie, t-sie," piped the little fellow above him. "I am the highest, I am king."

Vulture was tired and now flew direct to earth. The other birds were mad through and through. Tink-tinkje must die because he had taken advantage of Vulture's feathers and hidden himself there. All of the birds flew after him and he had to take refuge in a mouse hole. But how were they to get him out? Someone must stand guard to seize him the moment he put out his head.

"Owl must keep guard, he has the largest eyes, he can see well," they exclaimed.

Owl went and took up his position before the hole. The sun was warm and soon Owl became sleepy and presently he was fast asleep.

Tink-tinkje peeped out, saw that Owl was asleep, and zip, away he went. Shortly afterwards the other birds came to see if Tink-tinkje were still in the hole. "T-sie, t-sie," they heard in a tree, and there the little vagabond was sitting.

White-crow, perfectly disgusted, turned around and exclaimed, "Now I won't say a single word more."

And from that day to this White-crow has never spoken. Even though you strike him, he makes no sound, he utters no cry.

The Lion Jealous Of The Voice Of The Ostrich

This story has been edited and adapted from Specimens of Bushman Folklore, produced by Wilhelm Heinrich Immanuel Bleek and Lucy Lloyd, originally published in 1911 by George Allen and Company, London.

The Lions conspired together that they might deceive the Ostrich, for, the women folk praised the Ostrich for calling finely, but the women did not praise the Lions.

One Lion asked, "In what manner shall we deceive them?"

Another Lion answered, "We must tell the women to make a game of #gebbi-ggu, so that we may see whether the women will continue to admire the Ostrich. Then we shall see what the Ostrich will do."

And another Lion spoke, "Why does the Ostrich calls so well?"

The other Lion answered, "The Ostrich calls with his lungs, deep in his chest. You call with your mouth, so, you do not call nicely."

The first Lion replied, "You must make a game of #gebbi-ggu, so that you can kill the Ostrich and take out the Ostrich's lungs, so that you may eat them. Then you will sound like the Ostrich."

The women then made a game of #gebbi-ggu. The Ostrich was still yonder at his house. When the Lion called, the women did not applaud the Lion, because they felt that the Lion did not call well. Then the Ostrich came and the Ostrich called, sounding afar. And the women exclaimed, "I do wish that the Lion called in this manner. Sadly he sounds as if he had put his tail into his mouth, while the Ostrich calls in such a resounding manner."

And the Lion, answering, said, "Do you see how the women are? It is only the Ostrich whom they cherish, because he possesses this sweet call."

The other Lions became angry because it was the Ostrich whom the women cherished. The Ostrich looked as though he was about to leave, so the Lion scratched the Ostrich's ||hatten-ttu, scratched, tearing it. And he called out, "is it a thing which calls sweetly?" while he kicked the Ostrich's ||hatten-ttu. And the Ostrich also turned back and kicked, tearing the Lion's |uan-ttu.

Then the Ostrich spoke, saying, "This person is angry with me, because he sounds like he holds his tail in his mouth when he calls, and this is why the women do not praise him, while the women feel that he does not call nicely for the women. If he sounded like me then the women would have praised him, and that is why they will not make a #gebbi-ggu for him."

My grandfather told me about it, and about how the Lions then killed the Ostrich. He said that we should also do as the Lion once did. We too should eat the Ostrich's lungs. My grandfather gave us the Ostrich's lungs to eat, that we might also resemble the Ostrich.

We asked our grandfather whether we should bake the Ostrich's lungs, and our grandfather said that we should not cook the Ostrich's lungs. We should eat them raw, for that is the only way to sound like the Ostrich. He said that we should swallow them down whole. If we should chew the Ostrich's lungs we would likewise not sound like the Ostrich.

Grandfather said, "You must come and stand by me, so that I may cut pieces from the Ostrich's lungs and give them to you to eat.

We answered, "Oh my grandfather! We do not wish to eat the Ostrich's lungs when they are raw."

Grandfather said, " You must eat them if you want to be like the Lions. If your friends eat the lungs raw and then you hear them and you have not eaten the lungs raw, then you will become angry and you will fight them because the women will not applaud you."

And this is why to this day the Lion will not leave the Ostrich after it has killed and eaten it.

The Story Of The Glutton

This story has been edited and adapted from George McCall Theal's Kaffir (Xhosa) Folk-Lore, originally published in 1886 by S. Sonnenschein, Le Bas and Lowrey, London. This is a Xhosa story.

There was once a man who quarrelled with his wife, so that she left him, and went home to her father's place. When she got home she found nobody, for all the people had been swallowed by a monster. She went into the house that used to be her father's, and noticed that there were footprints of animals and spots of blood all over the floor. She then got into the top of the hut and hid herself.

She heard the monster coming, saying:

"O man, O man,

I have eaten,

And I am still living."

She kept awake. Shortly the house was filled with all kinds of animals, who made a fire, cooked their food, ate it up, and slept. Next morning they awoke, and all went out to search for something else to eat.

The woman had two children born while the animals were away. She came down from her hiding-place, and took up a stone used for raising pots above the fire, and went again into her hiding-place.

The animals returned in the evening, and while their pots were on the fire, she threw down the stone into one of them. The animals all rushed out of the house. Outside they held a consultation, and their chief decided that those living in holes should go to the holes, that those living in forests should go to the forests, and that those living in rivers should go to the rivers.

After this, the woman set a trap, and succeeded in catching a buffalo, but she could not skin it. She saw a glutton coming, also known as an igongqongqo, a fabulous monster, like a man, but capable of devouring enormous quantities of food, and she asked him to help her. He consented.

He pulled out his knife and skinned the buffalo. She gathered some wood, and kindled a fire for the purpose of roasting the liver. The glutton roasted it. She went away and picked up an empty calabash, and when she returned she found the glutton roasting the legs, having already eaten the liver. She then said, "I am going for water."

She got behind a bush, and blew the empty calabash. The glutton wondered what this was, and called her. She continued blowing until the glutton was so frightened that he took his bag and put the remainder of the meat into it, and ran away.

She followed him, still blowing, until he threw away the bag containing the meat. She still followed, blowing. The glutton stumbled, and fell into a thorny bush, where he was held fast. The woman then ceased blowing, and heard him blubbering out:

"Let me alone, lu bo bo,

Let me alone, lu bo bo."

She blew again, and he struggled and got free. He ran away with all his might. She then took the bag home with her, made a fire, and cooked the meat. When it was ready, she took it to her hiding-place, and lived on it till her children were able to run about outside.

One day, these twins asked their mother to make bows and arrows for them. Their mother advised them not to wander away from the house, saying to them, "The glutton will swallow you."

But at a certain time they left home, and went in the direction where the monster lived. They found it asleep, and shot it with their arrows in both eyes. The boys returned home and told their mother. Next day they went to the place, and found the glutton dead.

The boys heard people talking inside the glutton. Having told their mother, she took a knife and cut it open, when people came out, and cattle, and dogs. The people asked, "Who killed the glutton?"

The mother of the twins told them, and they rewarded the boys with a large number of cattle.

The Magic Mirror

This story has been edited and adapted from Andrew Lang's All Sorts of Stories Book, originally published in 1911 by Longmans, Green and Company, London and New York. The original was adapted from a native Zimbabwean tale told by the Sena.

A long, long while ago there lived a man called Gopani-Kufa.

One day, as he was out hunting, he came upon a strange sight. An enormous python had caught an antelope and coiled itself around it. The antelope, striking out in despair with its horns, had pinned the python's neck to a tree, and so deeply had its horns sunk in the soft wood that neither creature could get away.

"Help!" cried the antelope, " I was doing no harm, yet I have been caught, and would have been eaten, had I not defended myself."

"Help me," said the python, "for I am Insato, King of all the Reptiles, and will reward you well!"

Gopani-Kufa considered for a moment, then stabbing the antelope with his assegai, he set the python free.

"I thank you," said the python, "come back here with the new moon, when I shall have eaten the antelope, and I will reward you as I promised."

"Yes," said the dying antelope, "he will reward you, and your reward shall be your own undoing!"

Gopani-Kufa went back to his kraal, and with the new moon he returned again to the spot where he had saved the python.

Insato was lying upon the ground, still sleepy from the effects of his huge meal, and when he saw the man he thanked him again, and said, "Come with me now to Pita, which is my own country, and I will give you what you will of all my possessions."

Gopani-Kufa at first was afraid, thinking of what the antelope had said, but finally he consented and followed Insato into the forest.

For several days they travelled, and at last they came to a hole leading deep into the earth. It was not very wide, but large enough to admit a man. "Hold on to my tail," said Insato, "and I will go down first, drawing you after me." The man did so, and Insato entered.

Down, down, down they went for days, all the while getting deeper and deeper into the earth, until the darkness ended and they dropped into a beautiful country. Around them grew short green grass, on which browsed herds of cattle and sheep and goats. In the distance Gopani-Kufa saw a great collection of houses, all square, built of stone and very tall, and their roofs were shining with gold and burnished iron.

Gopani-Kufa turned to Insato, but found, in the place of the python, a man, strong and handsome, with the great snake's skin wrapped round him for covering, and on his arms and neck were rings of pure gold.

The man smiled. "I am Insato," said he, "but in my own country I take man's shape - even as you see me - for this is Pita, the land over which I am king." He then took Gopani-Kufa by the hand and led him towards the town.

On the way they passed rivers in which men and women were bathing and fishing and boating, and farther on they came to gardens covered with heavy crops of rice and maize, and many other grains which Gopani-Kufa did not even know the name of. And as they passed, the people who were singing at their work in the fields, abandoned their labours and saluted Insato with delight, bringing also palm wine and green cocoanuts for refreshment, as to one returned from a long journey.

"These are my children!" said Insato, waving his hand towards the people. Gopani-Kufa was much astonished at all that he saw, but he said nothing. Presently they came to the town, and everything here, too, was beautiful, and everything that a man might desire he could obtain. Even the grains of dust in the streets were of gold and silver.

Insato conducted Gopani-Kufa to the palace, and showing him his rooms, and the maidens who would wait upon him, told him that they would have a great feast that night, and on the morrow he might name his choice of the riches of Pita and it should be given him. Then he was away.

Now Gopani-Kufa had a wasp called Zengi-mizi. Zengi-mizi was not an ordinary wasp, for the spirit of the father of Gopani-Kufa had entered it, so that it was exceedingly wise. In times of doubt Gopani-Kufa always consulted the wasp as to what had better be done, so on this occasion he took it out of the little rush basket in which he carried it, saying, "Zengi-mizi, what gift shall I ask of Insato tomorrow when he would know the reward he shall bestow on me for saving his life?"

"Biz-z-z," hummed Zengi-mizi, "ask him for Sipao the Mirror." And it flew back into its basket.

Gopani-Kufa was astonished at this answer, but knowing that the words of Zengi-mizi were true words, he determined to make the request. So that night they feasted, and on the morrow Insato came to Gopani-Kufa and, giving him greeting joyfully, he said, "Now, O my friend, name your choice amongst my possessions and you shall have it!"

"O king!" answered Gopani-Kufa, "Out of all your possessions I will have the Mirror, Sipao."

The king started. "O friend, Gopani-Kufa," he said, "ask anything but that! I did not think that you would request that which is most precious to me."

"Let me think over it again then, O king," said Gopani-Kufa, "and tomorrow I will let you know if I change my mind."

But the king was still much troubled, fearing the loss of Sipao, for the mirror had magic powers, so that he who owned it had but to ask and his wish would be fulfilled, and to it Insato owed all that he possessed.

As soon as the king left him, Gopani-Kufa again took Zengi-mizi, out of his basket. "Zengi-mizi," he said, "the king seems loth to grant my request for the Mirror. Is there not some other thing of equal value for which I might ask?"

And the wasp answered, "There is nothing in the world, O Gopani-Kufa, which is of such value as this Mirror, for it is a Wishing Mirror, and accomplishes the desires of him who owns it. If the king hesitates, go to him the next day, and the day after, and in the end he will bestow the Mirror upon you, for you saved his life."

And it was even so. For three days Gopani-Kufa returned the same answer to the king, and, at last, with tears in his eyes, Insato gave him the Mirror, which was of polished iron, saying, "Take Sipao, then, O Gopani-Kufa, and may your wishes come true. Go back now to your own country, Sipao will show you the way."

Gopani-Kufa was greatly rejoiced, and, taking farewell of the king, said to the Mirror, "Sipao, Sipao, I wish to be back upon the Earth again!"

Instantly he found himself standing upon the upper earth, but, not knowing the spot, he said again to the Mirror, "Sipao, Sipao, I want the path to my own kraal!"

And behold! Right before him lay the path!

When he arrived home he found his wife and daughter mourning for him, for they thought that he had been eaten by lions, but he comforted them, saying that while following a wounded antelope he had missed his way and had wandered for a long time before he had found the path again.

That night he asked Zengi-mizi, in whom sat the spirit of his father, what he had better ask Sipao for next?

"Biz-z-z," said the wasp, "would you not like to be as great a chief as Insato?"

And Gopani-Kufa smiled, and took the Mirror and said to it, "Sipao, Sipao, I want a town as great as that of Insato, the King of Pita, and I wish to be chief over it!"

Then all along the banks of the Zambesi river, which flowed nearby, sprang up streets of stone buildings, and their roofs shone with gold and burnished iron like those in Pita, and in the streets men and women were walking, and young boys were driving out the sheep and cattle to pasture, and from the river came shouts and laughter from the young men and maidens who had launched their canoes and were fishing. And when the people of the new town beheld Gopani-Kufa they rejoiced greatly and hailed him as chief.

Gopani-Kufa was now as powerful as Insato the King of the Reptiles had been, and he and his family moved into the palace that stood high above the other buildings right in the middle of the town. His wife was too astonished at all these wonders to ask any questions, but his daughter Shasasa kept begging him to tell her how he had suddenly become so great, so at last he revealed the whole secret, and even entrusted Sipao the Mirror to her care, saying, "It will be safer with you, my daughter, for you dwell apart, whereas men come to consult me on affairs of state, and the Mirror might be stolen."

Then Shasasa took the Magic Mirror and hid it beneath her pillow, and after that for many years Gopani-Kufa ruled his people both well and wisely, so that all men loved him, and never once did he need to ask Sipao to grant him a wish.

Now it happened that, after many years, when the hair of Gopani-Kufa was turning grey with age, there came white men to that country. Up the Zambesi they came, and they fought long and fiercely with Gopani-Kufa, but, because of the power of the Magic

Mirror, he beat them, and they fled to the sea-coast. Chief among them was one Rei, a man of much cunning, who sought to discover from where sprang Gopani-Kufa's power. So one day he called to him a trusty servant named Butou, and said, "Go to the town and find out for me what is the secret of its greatness."

And Butou, dressing himself in rags, set out, and when he came to Gopani-Kufa's town he asked for the chief, and the people took him into the presence of Gopani-Kufa. When the white man saw him he humbled himself, and said, "O Chief! Take pity on me, for I have no home! When Rei marched against you I alone stood apart, for I knew that all the strength of the Zambesi lay in your hands, and because I would not fight against you he turned me forth into the forest to starve!"

And Gopani-Kufa believed the white man's story, and he took him in and feasted him, and gave him a house.

In this way the end came. For the heart of Shasasa, the daughter of Gopani-Kufa, went forth to Butou the traitor, and from her he learnt the secret of the Magic Mirror. One night, when all the town slept, he felt beneath her pillow and, finding the Mirror, he stole it and fled back with it to Rei, the chief of the white men.

So it befell that, one day, as Gopani-Kufa was gazing up at the river from a window of the palace he again saw the war-canoes of the white men, and at the sight his spirit misgave him.

"Shasasa! My daughter!" he cried wildly, "Go fetch me the mirror, for the white men are at hand."

"Woe is me, my father!" she sobbed. "The Mirror is gone! For I loved Butou the traitor, and he has stolen Sipao from me!"

Then Gopani-Kufa calmed himself, and drew out Zengi-mizi from its rush basket. "O spirit of my father!" he said, "What now shall I do?"

"O Gopani-Kufa!" hummed the wasp, "There is nothing now that can be done, for the words of the antelope which you slew are being fulfilled."

"Alas! I am an old man, and I had forgotten!" cried the chief. "The words of the antelope were true words. My reward shall be my undoing. They are being fulfilled!"

Then the white men fell upon the people of Gopani-Kufa and slew them together with the chief and his daughter Shasasa, and since then all the power of the Earth has rested in the hands of the white men, for they have in their possession Sipao, the Magic Mirror.

The Resurrection Of The Ostrich

This story has been edited and adapted from Specimens of Bushman Folklore, produced by Wilhelm Heinrich Immanuel Bleek and Lucy Lloyd, originally published in 1911 by George Allen and Company, London.

A Bushman killed an Ostrich that was looking after a nest full of eggs, and he carried the dead Ostrich to his house. The Bushman's wife plucked the Ostrich's short feathers because they were bloody. She placed them on the bushes outside of the hut. The Bushman and his wife ate the Ostrich meat.

Then a little whirlwind blew, scattering the Ostrich feathers. One of the smaller Ostrich feathers, covered in blood, blew up into the sky. A short while later the little feather floated down out of the sky and fell into a small lake. The feather became wet in the water, and that made the feather conscious. As it lay in the water it started to turn into Ostrich flesh. Then the flesh started to grow feathers. Soon after that the creature grew wings and legs.

Eventually a fully formed Ostrich walked out of the water and basked in the sun upon the water's edge. It was a young Ostrich. Its feathers were young feathers, and they were black, for the creature was a little male Ostrich. He dried his feathers lying upon the water's bank, and he slowly stretched his legs and strengthened his feet. He started to walk, strengthening his feet and hardening his breast so that his breastbone may become strong again.

As he walked away, he ate young, bushes. He swallowed many young plants. He walked towards the old nest, where once died, so that he could scratch in the old nest house and fetch his wives. He decided then to marry another she Ostrich. Now that his breastbone was strong, he roared as he walked, hardening his ribs.

When he found his nest house he scratched out a new nest and roared, summoning the Ostrich wives. When he saw them coming back to him he went to meet them and he ran round the females so that he could look at his wives' feathers, and his wives' feathers appeared most fine.

When his flesh was full and strong again, and he felt heavy, and his legs were grown and big, and his knees were large, he grew great feathers. He was now fully grown again. He thought that the nest was ready for the females to lay new eggs. He scratched out the nest while the females stood eating. He scratched to dry out the nest house because it was damp.

One of the she Ostriches lay down to try the nest. At first she slept opposite the house while it dried out properly. Then, when the nest was dry, she made the ground inside the house soft so that another female might come and lay an egg. One by one the females laid their eggs and flapped their wings. Two small eggs stood there.

The male Ostrich went away to eat. Two of his wives lay in the nest house, while the third wife went with him. The following day the male and female returned early. They sent the two wives off th feed and the wife who had been with him overnight, laid another egg. Then she joined the other two wives while he lay down to sleep at the nest house. He stays there to drive away the jackal, when he thinks that the jackal is coming to steal and eat the eggs. He takes care of the eggs because they are his children. If the jackal comes he will kick the jackal with his feet.

The White Man And Snake

This story has been edited and adapted from James A. Honey's South-African Folk Tales, originally published in 1910 by The Baker and Taylor Company.

A white man, it is said, met Snake upon whom a large stone had fallen and covered her so that she could not rise. The White Man lifted the stone off Snake, but when he had done so, she wanted to bite him. The White Man said, "Stop! Let us both go first to some wise people."

They went to Hyena, and the White Man asked him, "Is it right that Snake should want to bite me, when I helped her as she lay under a stone and could not rise?"

Hyena, who thought he would get his share of the White Man's body, said, "If you were bitten what would it matter?"

Then Snake wanted to bite him, but the White Man said again, "Wait a little, and let us go to other wise people, that I may hear whether this is right."

They went and met Jackal. The White Man said to Jackal, "Is it right for Snake to want to bite me, when I lifted up the stone which lay upon her?"

Jackal replied, "I do not believe that Snake could be covered by a stone so she could not rise. Unless I saw it with my two eyes, I would not believe it. Therefore, come let us go and see the place where you say it happened to decide if it can be true."

They went, and arrived at the place where it had happened. Jackal said, "Snake, lie down, and let yourself be covered."

Snake did so, and the White Man covered her with the stone, but although she exerted herself very much, she could not rise. Then the White Man wanted again to release Snake, but Jackal interfered, and said, "Do not lift the stone. She wanted to bite you, therefore she may rise by herself."

Then they both went away and left Snake under the stone.

The Vultures, Their Elder Sister, And Her Husband

This story has been edited and adapted from Specimens of Bushman Folklore, produced by Wilhelm Heinrich Immanuel Bleek and Lucy Lloyd, originally published in 1911 by George Allen and Company, London.

The Vultures once upon a time turned their elder sister into a person, and they lived with her. When their elder sister's husband brought home a springbok, they ate up the entire springbok, and their elder sister's husband cursed and scolded them.

Then their elder sister took up the skin of the springbok. She singed it and she boiled the skin of the springbok. They took hold of the pieces of skin and swallowed them down. Once again their elder sister's husband scolded them because they had just eaten the body of the springbok, and now they had eaten the springbok's skin.

The Vultures were afraid of their elder sister's husband, so they went away, flying in all directions. They did, though, keep a furtive eye on their elder sister's husband.

One day their elder sister's husband went hunting. Once again he killed a springbok, and he brought the springbok home, slung upon his back. The Vultures came back again, and they ate up the springbok. Once again their elder sister's husband scolded them, and they flew a little way off and sat down. Their elder sister singed the springbok's skin and then she boiled the springbok's skin. As before, the Vulture's elder sister gave them pieces of the skin, which they swallowed down.

The next morning their elder sister's husband said that his wife must go with him, and that she should altogether eat on the hunting ground with him instead of eating the springbok with her brothers.

The Vultures left the house when their sister went out, and they sat down opposite the house. They decided to lay their plans. One of the Vultures said, "You shall fly high so that you can tell us what the place seems to be like."

Another Vulture said, "Little sister shall be the one to try, and then, she must tell us."

And then, their little sister Vulture flew high in the sky.

They said, "Let's see what little sister will do."

She flew so high that they could no longer see her.

The Vultures sat and waited for her to return. Eventually she flew back down and sat in the midst of them.

And they exclaimed Ah! What is the place like?"

And their younger sister said, "Our sister here shall ascend and take a look, for we will need her opinion on what we can see."

Then, her elder sister ascended, into the sky. After a short while she too descended from above, and sat in the midst of the other people.

And the other people said, "What is the place like?"

And she said, "There is nothing the matter with the place, for, the place is clear. The place is very beautiful, for, I do behold the whole place, the stems of the trees. I do behold them, and the place looks just right for a springbok to be lying under a tree, for the place is very beautiful."

Then they all flew into the sky, and hurried to join their elder sister so that they could eat before their elder sister's husband scolded them. When they espied their elder sister's husband coming, they ate in great haste. They said, "We must eat! We must eat! We must eat in great haste! That accursed man comes yonder, and he cannot endure us."

They finished the springbok and flew heavily away, while their elder sister's husband came to pick up the bones.

Later, when spied another springbok, they descended, and their elder sister saw them too. She followed them. The Vultures then said, as they were eating, "We must eat, but we should look around, and we shall leave some meat for our elder sister. We will leave the poorest undercut for her."

When the Vultures saw that their elder sister was really coming they exclaimed, "Elder sister really seems to be coming yonder. We must leave the meat which is in the springbok's skin." And, they left the meat just as they said.

Their elder sister said, "Fie! how can you act in this manner towards me? As if I had been the one who scolded you!" Then their elder sister took the springbok and returned home, while the Vultures flew about looking for yet another springbok, which they intended again to eat.

Dai-Xerreten, The Lioness, And The Children

This story has been edited and adapted from Specimens of Bushman Folklore, produced by Wilhelm Heinrich Immanuel Bleek and Lucy Lloyd, originally published in 1911 by George Allen and Company, London.

Dai-Xerreten was a man of the early race, and his head was made of stone. Dai-Xerreten believed that the Lioness had gathered together the people's children, because she was an invalid on account of her chest. She gathered together the people's children so that the children might live with her and work for her, for, she was an invalid, and she could not do hard work.

Dai-Xerreten went to her house when she was away dipping up water. Dai-Xerreten went to the children and sat down. He said, "O children sitting here! Your people's hearth fire is at the top of the ravine which comes down from the top of the hill."

Two children arose and went away to their own people.

Dai-Xerreten again said, "O children sitting here! Your people's hearth fire is at the top of the ravine which comes down from the top of the hill."

Three more children went away to their own people.

And he again said, "O children sitting here! Your people's hearth fire is at the top of the ravine which comes down from the top of the hill."

Another child arose and went away to its own people.

He again said, "O children sitting here! The fire of your people is that which is below the top

Once again he said, "O children sitting here! Your people's hearth fire is at the top of the ravine which comes down from the top of the hill."

Two more children arose and went away to their own people.

He said again, "O children sitting here! Your people's hearth fire is at the top of the ravine which comes down from the top of the hill."

Another two children arose and went away.

And he again said, "O children sitting here! Your people's hearth fire is at the top of the ravine which comes down from the top of the hill."

The rest of the children got up and went away to their own people.

Dai-Xerreten sat waiting for the Lioness.

When the Lioness came home from the water she could not see any of the children. She stammered with rage and exclaimed, "Why do the chil…chil…chil…children not play here, as they usually do? It must have something to do with this man who sits at the house. His head resembles Dai-Xerreten." And she became very angry.

She roared, "Dai-Xerreten indeed sits here!"

She walked up to the house. She exclaimed, "Where are my children?"

Dai-Xerreten said, "They are not our children."

The Lioness roared, "Out! Leave off! You must give me the children!"

Dai-Xerreten said, "They were not our children."

The Lioness caught hold of his head. She cried, "Xabbabbu" and growled and bit his head. Then she exclaimed, "Oh! Oh dear! Oh dear! Oh dear! Oh dear! My teeth! This must be why this cursed man's big head came to sit in front of my house!"

Dai-Xerreten said, "I told you that they were not our children."

The Lioness exclaimed, "Destruction! You came and sat here with your big stone head."

Dai-Xerreten arose and returned home, while the Lioness sat in anger at her house, because he had come and taken away from her the children. She was very angry. The Lioness believed that the children had all been living peacefully with her, for she felt that she had treated them well, and she had come to love them.

Cloud-Eating

This story has been edited and adapted from James A. Honey's South-African Folk Tales, originally published in 1910 by The Baker and Taylor Company.

Jackal and Hyena were together, it is said, when a white cloud rose. Jackal descended upon it, and ate some of the cloud as if it were fat.

When he wanted to come down, he said to Hyena, "My sister, as I am going to share this cloud with you, catch me well." So she caught him, and broke his fall. Then she also went up and ate there, high up on the top of the cloud.

When she was satisfied, she said, "My greyish brother, now catch me well too."

The greyish rogue said to his friend, "My sister, I shall catch you well. Come down."

He held up his hands, and she came down from the cloud, and when she was near, Jackal cried out, painfully jumping to one side, "My sister, do not take it ill. Oh me! Oh me! A thorn has pricked me and sticks in me."

Thus she fell down from above, and was sadly hurt.

Since that day, it is said that Hyena's hind feet have been shorter and smaller than the front ones.

The Mason Wasp And His Wife

This story has been edited and adapted from Specimens of Bushman Folklore, produced by Wilhelm Heinrich Immanuel Bleek and Lucy Lloyd, originally published in 1911 by George Allen and Company, London.

The Mason Wasp was once walking along, while his wife walked behind him. His wife said, "O my husband! Shoot that hare for me!"

And the Mason Wasp laid down his quiver and said, "Where is the hare?"

And his wife said, "The hare lies there."

The Mason Wasp took out an arrow, and stooped low to creep up on the hare. His wife said, "Put down your kaross! Why won't you put down your kaross?"

The Mason Wasp loosened the strings of his kaross as he walked along. His wife then said, "Do you really look like this?? That must have been why you were not willing to lay down the kaross."

The Mason Wasp stepped to one side and took aim at his wife. He shot, hitting his wife's breastbone with the arrowhead. His wife fell down dead.

Then the Mason Wasp exclaimed, "Yi ii hihi! O my wife hi!"

Then he cried, lamenting the fact that he had been the one to have done this terrible thing. He had shot his wife and she died.

Story Of The Great Chief Of The Animals

This story has been edited and adapted from George McCall Theal's Kaffir (Xhosa) Folk-Lore, originally published in 1886 by S. Sonnenschein, Le Bas and Lowrey, London. This is a Xhosa story.

THERE was once a woman who had occasion to leave her home for a short time, and who left her children in charge of a hare. The place where they lived was close to a path, along which droves of wild animals were accustomed to pass.

Soon after the woman left, the animals appeared, and the hare at sight of them became frightened. So she ran a short distance away and stood there to watch. Among the animals was one terrible monster, which called to the hare, and demanded to know who those children were. The hare told the monster their names, upon which the animal swallowed them entire.

When the woman returned, the hare told her what had happened. Then the woman gathered some dry wood, and sharpened two pieces of iron, which she took with her and went along the path.

Now this monster was the chief of the animals. When the woman came up a hill and began to call out that she was looking for her children., the animal replied, "Come nearer, I cannot hear you."

When she went nearer, he swallowed her also. Once inside the monster, the woman found her children alive, and also many other people, and oxen, and dogs. The children were hungry, so the woman cut some pieces of flesh from the monster's ribs with her pieces of iron. She then made a fire and cooked the meat, and the children ate.

The other people said, "We also are hungry, give us something to eat."

Then she cut and cooked for them also.

The monster felt uncomfortable under this treatment, and called his councillors together for advice, but they could suggest no remedy. He lay down and rolled in the mud, but that did not help him, and at last he went and put his head in the kraal fence, and there he died.

His councillors were standing a little distance away, afraid to approach him, so they sent a monkey to see how he was. The monkey returned and said, "Those whose home is on the mountains must hasten to the mountains, those whose home is on the plains must hasten to the plains, as for me, I go to the rocks."

Then the animals all dispersed.

By this time the woman had succeeded in cutting a hole through the chief's side, and out she climbed, followed by her children.

Then an ox came out, and said "Bo! Bo! Who helped me?"

Then a dog came out and said, "Ho! Ho! Who helped me?

Then a man came out and said, "Zo! Zo! Who helped me?"

Afterwards all the people and cattle came out. They agreed that the woman who helped them should be their chief.

When her children became men, they were out hunting one day, and saw a monstrous cannibal, who was sticking fast in a mud hole. They killed him, and then returned to tell the men of their tribe what they had done. The men went and skinned the cannibal, and once again a great number of people came out of him too. These people joined their deliverers, and so the people became a great nation.

Elephant And Tortoise

This story has been edited and adapted from James A. Honey's South-African Folk Tales, originally published in 1910 by The Baker and Taylor Company.

Two powers, Elephant and Rain, had a dispute. Elephant said, "If you say that you nourish me, in what way is it that you say so?"

Rain answered, "If you say that I do not nourish you, when I go away, will you not die?" And Rain then departed.

Elephant said, "Vulture! Cast lots to make rain for me."

Vulture said, "I will not cast lots."

Then Elephant said to Crow, "Cast lots!"

Crow answered, "Give me the things with which I may cast lots." Crow then cast lots and rain fell. It rained at the lagoons, but they dried up, and only one lagoon remained.

Elephant went a-hunting. On the way he met Tortoise, to whom Elephant said, "Tortoise, remain at the water!" Thus Tortoise was left behind when Elephant went a-hunting.

Then Giraffe came along , and said to Tortoise, "Give me water!"

Tortoise answered, "The water belongs to Elephant."

Then Zebra came along, who said to Tortoise, "Give me water!"

Tortoise answered, "The water belongs to Elephant."

Then Gemsbok came along, and said to Tortoise, "Give me water!"

Tortoise answered, "The water belongs to Elephant.

Then Wildebeest arrived and said, "Give me water!"

Tortoise said, "The water belongs to Elephant."

Then Roodebok came along and said to Tortoise, "Give me water!"

Tortoise answered, "The water belongs to Elephant."

Springbok came along too, and said to Tortoise, "Give me water!"

Tortoise said, "The water belongs to Elephant."

Then Jackal fetched up and said to Tortoise, "Give me water!"

Tortoise said, "The water belongs to Elephant."

Finally Lion came up and said, "Little Tortoise, give me water!"

When little Tortoise was about to say something, Lion got hold of him and beat him. Then Lion drank some water, and ever since then all animals drink water.

When Elephant came back from the hunting, he said, "Little Tortoise, is there water?"

Tortoise answered, "The animals have drunk the water."

Elephant asked, "Little Tortoise, shall I chew you or swallow you down?"

Little Tortoise said, "Swallow me, if you please!" and Elephant swallowed him whole.

After Elephant had swallowed Little Tortoise, Little Tortoise tore off his liver, heart, and kidneys.

Elephant said, "Little Tortoise, you kill me."

So Elephant died, but little Tortoise came out of his dead body, and went wherever he liked.

Tortoises Hunting Ostriches

This story has been edited and adapted from James A. Honey's South-African Folk Tales, originally published in 1910 by The Baker and Taylor Company.

One day, it is said, the Tortoises held a council to decide how they might hunt Ostriches, and they said, "Let us, on both sides, stand in rows near each other, and let one go to hunt the Ostriches, so that they must flee along through the midst of us."

They did so, and as they were many, the Ostriches were obliged to run along through the midst of them. During this the tortoises did not move, but, remaining always in the same places, called each to the other, "Are you there?" and each one answered, "I am here."

The Ostriches hearing this, ran so tremendously that they quite exhausted their strength, and fell down. Then the Tortoises assembled by-and-by at the place where the Ostriches had fallen, and devoured them.

The Sacred Milk Of Koumongoe

This story has been edited and adapted from Andrew Lang's Strange Story Book, originally published in 1913 by Longmans, Green and Company, London and New York. The original was adapted from a Basuto tale.

Far away, in a very hot country, there once lived a man and woman who had two children, a son named Koane and a daughter called Thakane.

Early in the morning and late in the evenings the parents worked hard in the fields, resting, when the sun was high, under the shade of some tree. While they were absent the little girl kept house alone, for her brother always got up before the dawn, when the air was fresh and cool, and drove the cattle out to the sweetest patches of grass he could find.

One day, when Koane had slept later than usual, his father and mother went to their work before him, and there was only Thakane to be seen busy making the bread for supper.

"Thakane," he said, "I am thirsty. Give me a drink from the tree Koumongoe, which has the best milk in the world."

"Oh, Koane," cried his sister, "you know that we are forbidden to touch that tree. What would father say when he came home? For he would be sure to know."

"Nonsense," replied Koane, "there is so much milk in Koumongoe that he will never miss a little. If you won't give it to me, I shan't take the cattle out. They will just have to stay all day in the hut, and you know that they will starve." And he turned from her in a rage, and sat down in the corner.

After a while Thakane said to him, "It is getting hot, had you better drive out the cattle now?"

But Koane only answered sulkily, "I told you I am not going to drive them out at all. If I have to do without milk, they shall do without grass."

Thakane did not know what to do. She was afraid to disobey her parents, who would most likely beat her, yet the beasts would be sure to suffer if they were kept in, and she would perhaps be beaten for that too. So at last she took an axe and a tiny earthen bowl. She cut a very small hole in the side of Koumongoe, and out gushed enough milk to fill the bowl.

"Here is the milk you wanted," said she, going up to Koane, who was still sulking in his corner.

"What is the use of that?" grumbled Koane, "why, there is not enough to drown a fly. Go and get me three times as much!"

Trembling with fright, Thakane returned to the tree, and struck it a sharp blow with the axe. In an instant there poured forth such a stream of milk that it ran like a river into the hut.

"Koane! Koane!" cried she, "Come and help me to plug up the hole. There will be no milk left for our father and mother." But

Koane could not stop it any more than Thakane, and soon the milk was flowing through the hut downhill towards their parents in the fields below.

The man saw a white stream a long way off, and guessed what had happened. "Wife, wife," he called loudly to the woman, who was working at a little distance, "Do you see Koumongoe running fast down the hill? That is some mischief of the children's, I am sure. I must go home and find out what is the matter." And they both threw down their hoes and hurried to the side of Koumongoe.

Kneeling on the grass, the man and his wife made a cup of their hands and drank the milk from it. And no sooner had they done this, than Koumongoe flowed back again up the hill, and entered the hut.

"Thakane," said the parents, severely, when they reached home panting from the heat of the sun, "what have you been doing? Why did Koumongoe come to us in the fields instead of staying in the garden?"

"It was Koane's fault," answered Thakane. "He would not take the cattle to feed until he drank some of the milk from Koumongoe. So, as I did not know what else to do, I gave it to him."

The father listened to Thakane's words, but made no answer. Instead, he went outside and brought in two sheepskins, which he stained red and sent for a blacksmith to forge some iron rings. The rings were then passed over Thakane's arms and legs and neck, and the skins fastened on her before and behind. When all was ready, the man sent for his servants and said, "I am going to get rid of Thakane."

"Get rid of your only daughter?" they answered, in surprise. "But why?"

"Because she has eaten what she ought not to have eaten. She has touched the sacred tree which belongs to her mother and me alone." And, turning his back, he called to Thakane to follow him, and they went down the road which led to the dwelling of an ogre.

They were passing along some fields where the corn was ripening, when a rabbit suddenly sprang out at their feet, and standing on its hind legs, it sang:

"Why do you give to the ogre

Your child, so fair, so fair?"

"You had better ask her," replied the man. "She is old enough to give you an answer."

Then, in her turn, Thakane sang:

"I gave Koumongoe to Koane,

Koumongoe to the keeper of beasts,

For without Koumongoe

they could not go to the meadows,

Without Koumongoe they would starve in the hut,

That was why I gave him the Koumongoe of my father."

And when the rabbit heard that, he cried, "Wretched man! It is you whom the ogre should eat, and not your beautiful daughter."

But the father paid no heed to what the rabbit said, and only walked on the faster, bidding Thakane to keep close behind him. By-and-by they met with a troop of great deer, called elands, and they stopped when they saw Thakane and sang:

"Why do you give to the ogre

Your child, so fair, so fair?"

"You had better ask her, replied the man. "She is old enough to give you an answer."

Then, in her turn, Thakane sang:

"I gave Koumongoe to Koane,

Koumongoe to the keeper of beasts,

For without Koumongoe

they could not go to the meadows,

Without Koumongoe they would starve in the hut,

That was why I gave him the Koumongoe of my father."

And the elands all cried, "Wretched man! It is you whom the ogre should eat, and not your beautiful daughter."

By this time it was nearly dark, and the father said they could travel no further that night, and must go to sleep where they were. Thakane was thankful indeed when she heard this, for she was very tired, and found the two skins fastened round her almost too heavy to carry. So, in spite of her dread of the ogre, she slept till dawn, when her father woke her, and told her roughly that he was ready to continue their journey.

Crossing the plain, the girl and her father passed a herd of gazelles feeding. They lifted their heads, wondering who was out so early, and when they caught sight of Thakane, they sang:

"Why do you give to the ogre

Your child, so fair, so fair?"

"You had better ask her, replied the man. "She is old enough to answer for herself."

Then, in her turn, Thakane sang:

"I gave Koumongoe to Koane,

Koumongoe to the keeper of beasts,

For without Koumongoe

they could not go to the meadows,

Without Koumongoe they would starve in the hut,

That was why I gave him the Koumongoe of my father."

And the gazelles all cried, "Wretched man! It is you whom the ogre should eat, and not your beautiful daughter."

At last they arrived at the village where the ogre lived, and they went straight to his hut. He was nowhere to be seen, but in his place was his son Masilo, who was not an ogre at all, but a very polite young man. He ordered his servants to bring a pile of skins for Thakane to sit on, but told her father he must sit on the ground. Then, catching sight of the girl's face, which she had kept down, he was struck by its beauty, and put the same question that the rabbit, and the elands, and the gazelles had done.

Thakane answered him as before, and he instantly commanded that she should be taken to the hut of his mother, and placed under her care, while the man should be led to his father. Directly the ogre saw him he bade the servant throw him into the great pot which always stood ready on the fire, and in five minutes he was done to a turn. After that the servant returned to Masilo and related all that had happened.

Now Masilo had fallen in love with Thakane the moment he saw her. At first he did not know what to make of this strange feeling, for all his life he had hated women, and had refused several brides whom his parents had chosen for him. However, they were so anxious that he should marry, that they willingly accepted Thakane as their daughter-in-law, though she did not bring any marriage portion with her.

After some time a baby was born to her, and Thakane thought it was the most beautiful baby that ever was seen. But when her mother-in-law saw it was a girl, she wrung her hands and wept, saying, "O miserable mother! Miserable child! Alas for you! Why were you not a boy!"

Thakane, in great surprise, asked the meaning of her distress, and the old woman told her that it was the custom in that country that all the girls who were born should be given to the ogre to eat.

Then Thakane clasped the baby tightly in her arms, and cried, "But it is not the customer in my country! There, when children die, they are buried in the earth. No one shall take my baby from me."

That night, when everyone in the hut was asleep, Thakane rose, and carrying her baby on her back, went down to a place where the river spread itself out into a large lake, with tall willows all around the bank. Here, hidden from everyone, she sat down on a stone and began to think what she should do to save her child.

Suddenly she heard a rustling among the willows, and an old woman appeared before her. "What are you crying for, my dear?" said she.

And Thakane answered, "I was crying for my baby. I cannot hide her for ever, and if the ogre sees her, he will eat her, and I would rather she was drowned than that."

"What you say is true," replied the old woman. "Give me your child, and let me take care of it. And if you will fix a day to meet me here I will bring the baby."

Then Thakane dried her eyes, and gladly accepted the old woman's offer. When she got home she told her husband she had thrown it in the river, and as he had watched her go in that direction he never thought of doubting what she said.

On the appointed day, Thakane slipped out when everybody was busy, and ran down the path that led to the lake. As soon as she got there, she crouched down among the willows, and sang softly:

"Bring to me Dilah,

Dilah the rejected one,

Dilah, whom her father Masilo cast out!"

And in a moment the old woman appeared holding the baby in her arms. Dilah had become so big and strong, that Thakane's heart was filled with joy and gratitude, and she stayed as long as she dared, playing with her baby. At last she felt she must return to the village, lest she should be missed, and the child was handed back to the old woman, who vanished with her into the lake.

Children grow up very quickly when they live under water, and in less time than anyone could suppose, Dilah had changed from a baby to a woman. Her mother came to visit her whenever she was able, and one day, when they were sitting talking together, they were spied out by a man who had come to cut willows to weave into baskets. He was so surprised to see how similar the face of the girl was to Masilo, that he left his work and returned to the village.

"Masilo," he said, as he entered the hut, "I have just beheld your wife near the river with a girl who must be your daughter, she is so like you. We have been deceived, for we all thought she was dead."

When he heard this, Masilo tried to look shocked because his wife had broken the law, but in his heart he was very glad. "But what shall we do now?" asked he.

"Make sure for yourself that I am speaking the truth by hiding among the bushes the first time Thakane says she is going to bathe in the river, and wait till the girl appears."

For some days Thakane stayed quietly at home, and her husband began to think that the man had been mistaken, but at last she said to her husband, "I am going to bathe in the river."

"Well, you can go," answered he. But he ran down quickly by another path, and got there first, and hid himself in the bushes. An instant later, Thakane arrived, and standing on the bank, she sang:

"Bring to me Dilah,

Dilah the rejected one,

Dilah, whom her father Masilo cast out!"

Then the old woman came out of the water, holding the girl, now tall and slender, by the hand. And as Masilo looked, he saw that she was indeed his daughter, and he wept for joy that she was not lying dead in the bottom of the lake.

The old woman, however, seemed uneasy, and said to Thakane, "I feel as if someone was watching us. I will not leave the girl today, but will take her back with me", and sinking beneath the surface, she drew the girl after her. After they had gone, Thakane returned to the village, which Masilo had managed to reach before her.

All the rest of the day he sat in a corner weeping, and his mother who came in asked, "Why are you weeping so bitterly, my son?"

"My head aches," he answered, "it aches very badly." And his mother passed on, and left him alone.

In the evening he said to his wife, "I have seen my daughter, in the place where you told me you had drowned her. Instead, she lives at the bottom of the lake, and has now grown into a young woman."

"I don't know what you are talking about," replied Thakane. "I buried my child under the sand on the beach."

Then Masilo implored her to give the child back to him, but she would not listen, and only answered, "If I were to give her back you would only obey the laws of your country and take her to your father, the ogre, and she would be eaten."

But Masilo promised that he would never let his father see her, and that now she was a woman no one would try to hurt her, so Thakane's heart melted, and she went down to the lake to consult the old woman.

"What am I to do?" she asked, when, after clapping her hands, the old woman appeared before her. "Yesterday Masilo beheld Dilah, and ever since he has entreated me to give him back his daughter."

"If I let her go he must pay me a thousand head of cattle in exchange," replied the old woman. And Thakane carried her answer back to Masilo.

"Why, I would gladly give her two thousand!" cried he, "for she has saved my daughter."

And he bade messengers hasten to all the neighbouring villages, and tell his people to send him at once all the cattle he possessed. When they were all assembled he chose a thousand of the finest bulls and cows, and drove them down to the river, followed by a great crowd wondering what would happen.

Then Thakane stepped forward in front of the cattle and sang:

"Bring to me Dilah,

Dilah the rejected one,

Dilah, whom her father Masilo cast out!"

And Dilah came from the waters holding out her hands to Masilo and Thakane, and in her place the cattle sank into the lake, and were driven by the old woman to the great city filled with people, which lies at the bottom.

The Zebra Stallion

This story has been edited and adapted from James A. Honey's South-African Folk Tales, originally published in 1910 by The Baker and Taylor Company.

The Baboons, it is said, used to disturb the Zebra Mares in drinking. But one of the Mares became the mother of a foal. The others then helped her to suckle the young stallion, so that he might soon grow up.

When he was grown up and they were in want of water, he brought them to the water. The Baboons, seeing this, came, as they formerly were used to do, to stand in their way and keep them from the water

While the Mares stood there, the Stallion stepped forward, and spoke to one of the Baboons, "You gum-eater's child!"

The Baboon said to the Stallion, "Please open your mouth, that I may see what you live on." The Stallion opened his mouth, and it was milky.

Then the Stallion said to the Baboon, "Please open your mouth also, that I may see."

The Baboon did so, and there was some gum in it. But the Baboon quickly licked some milk off the Stallion's tongue. The Stallion became angry, took the Baboon by his shoulders, and pressed him upon a hot, flat rock. Since that day the Baboon has a bald place on his back.

The Baboon said, lamenting, "I, my mother's child, I, the gum-eater, am outdone by this milk-eater!"

The Young Man Of The Ancient Race, Who Was Carried Off By A Lion, When Asleep In The Field

This story has been edited and adapted from Specimens of Bushman Folklore, produced by Wilhelm Heinrich Immanuel Bleek and Lucy Lloyd, originally published in 1911 by George Allen and Company, London.

A young man was out hunting one day when he ascended a hill. He was feeling very sleepy, even while he sat looking around for game. So, he thought that he would first lie down, and he wondered what could have happened to him today because he had not previously felt like this?

As he slept a lion came up and went to the water. It was now noonday and the heat was making the lion thirsty. The Lion saw the sleeping man and carried the man off.

The man awoke startled, and he saw that it was a lion which had taken him up. And he thought that he would not stir, for the lion would bite him and kill him if he stirred. He decided to first see what the lion intended to do, for the lion appeared to think that he was dead.

The lion carried him to a zwart-storm tree, where the lion laid him safely halfway up. Then the lion thought that it would still be thirsty, even if it ate the man, so it would first go to the water, that it might go to drink. The lion would come back afterwards to eat the man up.

So the Lion pressed the man firmly by the head into a fork in the tree's branches, and went back to the water. Then the man turned his head a little. The lion saw this slight movement and wondered why had the man's head had moved? The Lion thought that it had not pressed the man's head firmly enough into the tree, so it returned and trod the man's head more firmly into the tree's branches.

Then the Lion licked the man's tears as the man wept. The man cried because he was in the lion's power and because he could feel a stick piercing the hollow at the back of his head. The man turned his head a little, and this time he looked steadfastly at the lion. Once again the lion pressed the man's head even more firmly into the tree.

This time the man lay still and quiet, pretending to be dead, although the stick was piercing him. And the lion saw that the man was now safely stored in the tree, so the lion went a few steps away, and it looked back towards the man. The man watched the lion through his eyelashes, and he watched as the lion went away, ascending the hill. The lion then descended the hill on the other side, while the man gently turned his head because he wanted to see whether the lion had really gone away. And he saw that the lion appeared to have descended the hill on the other side, and then he saw that the lion was sneaking a quick look back from the top of far hill just in case the man was actually still alive.

The lion, it seemed thought that the man might still be feigning death and intended to rise up and run away. When the lion saw that the man was still lying down, it thought that it would quickly run to the water to have a drink and then hurry back so that it might eat. The lion was hungry.

The man lay still and watched. Only when he thought that it had altogether gone did he dare to stir. Even then he lay still for a long while to see whether the lion would sneak a quick look, for a lion is a thing which is cunning, and the man was sure that the lion would try to deceive him.

After a long time had passed since the lion last came back to peep at him, he arose slowly at first and then he sprang up and ran to a different part of the land where he believed that the lion would never look for him. He even ran in a zigzag line to be sure that the lion could not smell out his footsteps. That way, he thought, he could outwit the lion and return to his house in a round and about way.

When he came out at the top of the hill, he called out to the people at home about the fact that he had just been 'lifted up' by a lion while the sun stood high. The people looked out many hartebeest-skins, and they rolled the man up in them, for, he had just been 'lifted up' by a lion while the sun was high. The lion was sure to come back and the hartebeest-skins would cover up the man's scent, and the people, in their hearts, did not want the lion to eat this young man..

Later the people went out to seek for an edible root called !kui-sse, and they dug out !kui-sse, and they brought some home at noon, and they baked !kui-sse. An old Bushman, as he went along getting wood for his wife, in order that his wife might make a fire above the !kui-sse, saw the lion as the lion came over the top of the hill from the same direction that the young man had come from. He told the house folk about it, and he spoke, saying, "Look at the top of the hill where the young man came from. What can you see?"

And the young man's mother spoke. She said, "You must not allow the lion to come into the huts. You must shoot it dead, before it comes to the huts."

And the people slung on their quivers, and they went to meet the lion, and they shot at the lion many times, but the lion would not die.

And another old woman spoke. She said, "You must give a child to the lion so that the lion may go away from us."

The lion answered. It said that it did not want a child. It wanted the person whose tears it had licked. He was the one whom it wanted.

And the people asked, "How were you shooting at the lion? Why could you not manage to kill the lion?"

And another old man spoke, saying, "Can you not see that the lion must really be a sorcerer? It will not die when we are shooting at it, for, it insists upon having the man whom it carried off."

The people threw children to the lion, but the lion did not want the children which the people threw to it. The lion left the children alone.

The people were shooting at it, while it sought for the man. The people said, "You must bring us assegais, and then we must kill the lion."

Some people continued to shoot at the lion, while many others stabbed at it with their assegais, but the lion continued to search for the young man. The lion said that it wanted the young man whose tears it had licked. He was the one whom it wanted.

The lion scratched and tore apart the people's huts. The people cried, "Can you not see that the lion will not eat the children whom we have given to it?"

And the people said, "Can you not see that this lion must be a sorcerer?"

And other people said, "'You must give a girl to the lion. Maybe we will see whether the lion will eat her and go away."

The lion did not want the girl, for, the lion only wanted the man whom it had carried off. He was the one whom it wanted.

And the people cried out. They did not know how to act towards the lion. They had started shooting at the lion in the morning, but it would not die and now it was late in the day.

And so the people said, "Let's talk to the young man's mother about it. Although she loves the young man, she must give the young man to the lion, even if he be the child of her heart. The sun is about to set, and the lion is threatening us. The lion will not go away and leave us in peace, for it insists upon having the young man."

And the young man's mother spoke. She said, "You may give my child to the lion, but you must not let the lion walk away after it has eaten my child. You will kill the lion by laying it upon my child, and there it must die, like my child must die. "

When the young man's mother had spoken, the people took the young man out from the hartebeest-skins and they gave the young man to the lion. And the lion bit the young man to death. As it did so the people shot at it and stabbed at it.

Finally the lion spoke, and it said to the people that this was the right time for it to die, for it had got hold of the man for whom it had been searching. And it died. The man also lay dead, and the lion lay on top of him, also dead.

Why Has Jackal A Long Black Stripe On His Back?

This story has been edited and adapted from James A. Honey's South-African Folk Tales, originally published in 1910 by The Baker and Taylor Company.

The Sun, it is said, was one day on earth, and the men who were travelling saw him sitting by the wayside, but they passed him without appearing to notice that he was there.

Jackal, however, who came after them, and saw him also sitting, went to him and said, "Such a fine little child is left behind by the men." He then took Sun up, and put it into his awa-skin on his back.

When it burnt him, he said, "Get down," and shook himself, but Sun stuck fast to his back, and burnt Jackal's back black from that day.

Horse Cursed By Sun

This story has been edited and adapted from James A. Honey's South-African Folk Tales, originally published in 1910 by The Baker and Taylor Company.

It is said that once Sun was on earth, and caught Horse to ride it. But Horse was unable to bear his weight, and therefore Ox took the place of Horse, and carried Sun on its back. Since that time Horse is cursed in these words because it could not carry Sun's weight:

"From today you shall have a time of dying.

This is your curse, that you have a time of dying.

And day and night shall you eat,

But the desire of your heart shall not be at rest,

Though you graze till morning and again until sunset.

Behold, this is the judgment which I pass upon you," said Sun.

Since that day Horse has been mortal and always has a certain time of dying.

Ubuqili Buka Bongoza

This story has been edited and adapted from Levine Henrietta Samuelson's book, Some Zulu Customs and Folk-lore, originally published in 1905 by The Church Printing Company, London.

In the early days when the Boers invaded Zululand the Zulus twice set traps for them, which were very successful. They were completely caught in both.

Dingane, who was at that time King of the Zulus, prepared the first one himself. He gave a great beer drink in his cattle kraal, and invited all the Boers, with their leader, Piet Retief. These readily accepted the invitation, came, and were highly entertained in various ways. A good many Zulus were asked by Dingane to come and help to entertain by singing and dancing while the tyuala, their beer, was being passed round. The Boers enjoyed the beer immensely, as well as the singing and dancing, little guessing what was in store for them that day.

When Dingane thought he had spent enough time with them, he gave a sign to his people, which had been agreed upon beforehand. He just passed the palm of his hand over his mouth, and that meant, "Sweep them all off the face of the earth." After having given this sign, he himself went out of the kraal unnoticed.

Hundreds of Zulus who had been waiting outside the kraal ready armed set to at once, and those who had been singing and dancing joined in as soon as the sign was given them. There was a confusion of beer pots and assegais. The assegais came like a hailstorm upon the unfortunate Boers. Their leader was the only one who escaped by leaping over the cattle kraal fence and disappearing in a most mysterious way.

A few years after Piet Retief came forward again with another big commando, in hopes of settling old scores, when he was led into another trap beyond the White Umfolozi, at a place called Opate. He had been troubling the Zulus a great deal all round about Mahlabatini. Dingane was quite at a loss what to do with them, for he wished to put an end to it all. Amongst his numerous chiefs he had one very smart general called Nobongoza, who thought of a plan to catch the Dutchmen. He had a private interview with the king, and made his plans known to him. They were thought to be very good indeed, for Dingane left the management of everything to him after that.

Opate is a nice open plain, surrounded with bushes and hills. To get to it one had to go through a narrow pass. Nobongoza ordered a good number of his men to drive the king's cattle to this plain for safety, but he really had quite another object in view in doing this. All the natives were to go armed, in readiness to defend the cattle in case the Boers should find their hiding place and try to take them.

A day after the cattle had been taken to Opate, Nobongoza sent a big army to hide in the bush all around the place, then he turned traitor and went over to the Boers, saying he was tired of fighting against them, therefore he was now willing to lead them to a place where the king had hidden his cattle, and they could just help themselves and go away. Piet Retief believed what Nobongoza said, and was quite pleased. He allowed this chief to go as their leader, and even promised to pay him for his trouble. So he led them through this narrow pass, and when they had got through a fine sight came in view - a sight that would make any Dutchman's heart leap for joy. The plain was alive with fine cattle. They at once made a dash for them, when Nobongoza suddenly disappeared in the forest close by, where thousands of armed Zulus were waiting for their prey. They rushed out from the bush all round, closed in upon the Boers, and killed every one of them. The cattle were then driven back triumphantly to the King's kraal, and Nobongoza was looked upon as a hero ever after.

A Woman Of The Early Race And The Rain Bull

This story has been edited and adapted from Specimens of Bushman Folklore, produced by Wilhelm Heinrich Immanuel Bleek and Lucy Lloyd, originally published in 1911 by George Allen and Company, London.

Once upon a time the Rain courted a young woman, although the young woman was staying in her hut because she felt ill. The Rain loved the young woman's scent, and on account of it he visited the young woman, bringing with him weather that was misty. The young woman held her child by her on the kaross. As she lay there she too smelled the Rain's scent, and her hut was fragrant, and full of the mist that came with the Rain's breath.

And the young woman became aware of him, as he came up and while he lowered his tail, for the Rain, in those days, took the form of a bull. And the young woman exclaimed, "Who can this man be who comes to me?"

The young woman took up some buchu in her hand and threw that buchu upon the Rain's forehead. Then she arose, and she pressed the buchu down upon his forehead with her hand. She pushed him away, took up her kaross and tied it securely. With that the young woman took up the child and laid the child down upon the kaross and wrapped the child up safe and sound. She wanted to keep the child safe for her husband while she went away, for she feared that she might never come back.

The young woman then mounted the Rain, and the Rain took her away. As she went along she looked at the trees, and then she spoke, saying, "You must go to the tree standing yonder, the one that is big. You shall go and set me down at it. I ache, so you shall first go to set me down there."

Therefore, the Rain trotted on, taking her straight to the |kuerriten|kuerriten. And the young woman said, "You must go underneath, close to the stem of the tree."

The Rain went underneath, close to the stem of the tree. The young woman looked at him, and took out buchu, which she rubbed him with. This made the Rain fall fast asleep.

When she saw that the Rain slept, she climbed up the |kuerriten|kuerriten and she stole softly away. The young woman made it all the way home, but the Rain soon awoke and felt that the place was becoming strangely cool. The Rain rose up and walked to the middle of the spring that was his own home, all the while believing that the young woman was still sitting upon his back.

Meanwhile the young woman went to burn buchu, because she still smelt strongly of the Rain's scent or ||khou. She rubbed herself, taking away the smell of the ||khou. Around her the older women came to burn horns, because the smell of the horns might stop the Rain becoming angry with the People.

King Mpande's Snake Charmer

This story has been edited and adapted from Levine Henrietta Samuelson's book, Some Zulu Customs and Folk-lore, originally published in 1905 by The Church Printing Company, London.

During King Mpande's reign there lived in his chief kraal a most noted and wonderful snake-charmer, who was spoken of far and wide with great awe. He was looked upon as one who was in constant communication with the spirits, as all snakes obeyed him. He was tall and slim, with a withered right arm and a crooked forefinger. It was quite an easy task for him to catch snakes in bushes, and he could even draw them out of their holes with his crooked finger. He said he had certain kinds of medicines which he always took, and also injected into his right arm and finger before setting out snake-catching in the mornings, and these prevented snake bites having any effect on him. In fact, he felt quite safe anywhere. He would sometimes take long journeys in search of various kinds of snakes, and on his return would call on people living near the roadside that he might exhibit them. He generally took two or three boys with him to carry them, and they had special bags made for them of water-broom rushes.

I shall never forget the day when the snake-charmer called at our house and asked whether we should like to see two big snakes he had caught that day. At first we felt rather scared, although, at the same time, we were curious to see them, for we had heard a great deal about this snake-charmer. So we allowed him to get them out and show us what he could do with them. He ordered the boys to open the bags, then gave two or three whistles, and the snakes came crawling out very slowly and carefully. He then drew a winding mark on the ground with his rod, which they most obediently followed, hissing and sticking out their tongues now and then, and looking about to see which way they were to go next, and he said that this was all he had been able to teach them that morning.

He put down his rod a moment, then one of the snakes made for the kitchen door, where three native girls were standing, and it went part of the way in before he could stop it. The girls were half mad with fright. One climbed on the table, another on the shelf, and the third went up the chimney, and there was a terrible scrimmage, but the man soon made the snake go into the bag again.

I then thought I would have some fun, so I went into my room to fetch a big toy snake which I kept in the window to prevent the natives from standing about there and using it as a mirror. When I brought it out, moving and wriggling about in my hand, the charmer took to flight. It was an ugly green and yellow thing, with an open red mouth. The man said his medicines would be no preventive against a bite from this strange kind of snake, of which he knew nothing. But when I told him it was only a toy, he had a good laugh over his fright.

Soon after his return to his hut at the king's kraal we heard that some gentlemen had gone up to pay him a visit and to ask him to let them see his snakes. When he went away his hut would be quite safe, for the snakes were always on the lookout for strangers. The gentlemen thought it prudent to keep at a good distance until the owner of the hut and snakes appeared. After the usual greetings and introductions had been gone through, the man said, "I hear you would like to see my pets, how much will you pay me for it?"

They answered that they were travellers, and had not much with them, but that they would give him a blanket each. So he made them go into a corner of his hut and sit down on a mat. Presently he called out "Ngqabitani". His chief snake came out with a majestic twist of satisfaction. Then he whistled for another, grunted for another, groaned for a third, hissed for a fourth, and then rattled for the whole lot. They came out by the dozen and the visitors found themselves surrounded by snakes of all sorts and sizes, the great python wriggling and twisting impatiently, with a look as much as to say, "I could swallow the whole of you if only my master would allow me."

The man sat coolly at the door of his hut enjoying the fun. The gentlemen called out, "Enough! Enough! We have seen your pets, do for pity's sake call them back!"

The man said, "How much will you give me?"

The answer was, "Ten blankets each! Anything you like! All we possess, only clear off your pets and let us out of this trap!"

He answered, "You shall have your wish my good friends," and then made the usual noises, when the snakes all promptly returned to their holes. The gentlemen heaved a sigh of relief, paid the man, but never will they ask to see his pets again. They were quite satisfied.

The Girl's Story, The Frogs' Story

This story has been edited and adapted from Specimens of Bushman Folklore, produced by Wilhelm Heinrich Immanuel Bleek and Lucy Lloyd, originally published in 1911 by George Allen and Company, London.

A girl once lay in her hut being quite ill. She did not eat the food which her mother gave her. Instead, she would only eat the children of the Water. Her mother did not know this.

Her mother and the other women went out to seek Bushman rice. The women ordered one of their children to stay at home while they were away to watch and see what her elder sister was eating. The girl who was ill did not know about this child.

When the women had gone, the ill young woman went out from the hut and descended to the spring, as she intended to kill a Water-child once again. The child waited in the hut. The young woman killed a Water-child and carried the Water-child home.

The younger girl watched as her older sibling boiled the Water-child's flesh, and ate it. Then she lay down again, all the while watched by the hidden child.

Eventually the mother returned, and the child told her how her elder sister had gone to kill a handsome thing at the water. Her mother said, "It is a Water-child!" Then the mother would speak no more. Instead, she again went out to search for Bushman rice.

When she was searching for the food, the clouds came up. And she spoke, saying, "Something is not right at home, for a whirlwind is bringing things to the spring. Something is not going on well at home."

As she watched she saw the young woman fly through the air on the whirlwind and she knew that she had killed Water-children and was being punished. The girl went into the spring, and then she became a frog. Then the women were blown into the spring by the whirlwind, and they too became frogs.

The young woman's father also fell into the spring and became a frog, Her father's arrows altogether grew out by the spring, for the great whirlwind had brought them to the spring as well. At last the mother was also thrown into the spring to become a frog. After that all of the People's things, their mats and arrows, were blown into the spring.

Why The Heron Has A Crooked Neck

This story has been edited and adapted from Sanni Metelerkamp's book, Outa Karel's Stories, originally published in 1914 by MacMillan and Company, London.

The flames leapt gaily upward in the wide fireplace, throwing strange shadows on the painted walls and gleaming on the polished wood of floor and beam and cupboard. Little Jan basked contentedly in the warmth, almost dozing - now absently stroking the terrier curled up beside him, now running his fingers through the softer fur of the rug on which he lay. It was made of silver-jackal skins - a dozen of them, to judge from the six bushy tails spread out on either side, and as Outa Karel's gaze rested on them, he remarked reminiscently, "Arré! But Oom Jakhals was a slim kerel! No one ever got the better of him without paying for it."

In an instant little Jan was sitting bolt upright, every symptom of sleep banished from his face, the book from which Willem had been laboriously trying to gain some idea of the physical features of Russia was flung to the far end of the rustbank, while Pietie, suspending for a brief moment his whittling of a catapult stick, slid along the floor to get within better sight and sound of the story-teller.

"Yes, my little masters, sometimes it was Oom Leeuw he cheated, sometimes it was Oubaas Babiaan or Oom Wolf, and once it was the poor little Dove, and that is what made me think of how he was cheated himself."

"Did the little Dove cheat him?" asked Pietie eagerly.

"No, baasje, the Dove is too frightened - not stupid, baasje, but like people are when they are too gentle and kind and believe everything other people tell them. She was sitting on her nest one day singing to her little children, 'Coo-oo, coo-oo coo-oo,' when Oom Jakhals prowled along under the tree and heard her.

"'Alla wereld! Now I'll have a nice breakfast,' he thought, and he called out, 'Good morning, Tante. I hear you have such pretty little children. Please bring them down for me to see.'

"But the Tante was frightened of Jakhals, and said, 'I'm sorry, Oom, they are not well today, and I must keep them at home.'

"Then Jakhals lost his temper, and called out, 'Nonsense, I'm hungry and want something to eat, so throw down one of your little children at once.'

"Baasjes know, sometimes crossness drives away frightenness, and Tante was so cross with Oom Jakhals for wanting to eat one of her little children that she called out, 'No, no, you bad Jakhals, I shall do nothing of the sort. Go away and look for other food.'

"'If you don't, I'll fly up and eat them all,' said Jakhals. 'Throw one down at once.' And he stamped about and made such a horrible noise that the poor Tante thought he was really flying up. She looked at her babies, there wasn't one she wanted to give, but it was better to lose one than have them all eaten, so she shut her eyes and fluttered about the nest till one of them fell out, and Jakhals caught it in his mouth and carried it off to his hole to eat.

"Ach, but the poor Tante was sad! She spread her wings over her other children and never slept all night, but looked about this way and that way with her soft eyes, thinking every little noise she heard was Oom Jakhals trying to fly up to her nest to gobble up all her babies.

"The next morning there was Oom Jakhals again. 'Tante, your child was a nice, juicy mouthful. Throw me down another. And make haste, do you hear, or I'll fly up and eat you all.'

"'Coo-oo, coo-oo, coo-oo,' said Tante, crying, 'no, I won't give you one.' But it was no use, and in the end she did what she had done before - just shut her eyes and fluttered round and round till a baby fell out of the nest. She thought there was no help for it, and, like some people are, she thought what the eye didn't see the heart wouldn't feel, but her heart was very sore, and she cried more sadly than ever, and this time she said, 'Oo-oo, oo-oo, oo-oo!' It was very sad and sorrowful to listen to 'Oo-oo, oo-oo, oo-oo!'

"Here came old Oom Reijer. He is a kind old bird, though he holds his neck so crooked and looks like there was nothing to smile at in the whole wide world.

"'Ach, why do you cry so sadly, Tante? It nearly gives me a stitch in my side.'

"'Oo-oo! I'm very miserable. Oom Jakhals has eaten two of my little children, and tomorrow he will come for another, and soon I shall have none left.'

"'But why did you let him eat them?'

"'Because he said if I didn't give him one he would fly up and eat them all. Oo-oo-oo!'

"Then Oom Reijer was very angry. He flapped his wings, and stretched out his long neck - so, my baasjes, just so" (the children hugged themselves in silent delight at Outa's fine acting) - "and he opened and shut his long beak to show how he would like to peck out Oom Jakhals's wicked eyes if he could only catch him.

"'That vervlakste Jakhals!' he said. 'To tell such lies! But, Tante, you are stupid. Don't you know Oom Jakhals can't fly? Now listen to me. When he comes again, tell him you know he can't fly, and that you won't give him any more of your children.'

"The next day there came Oom Jakhals again with his old story, but Tante just laughed at him.

"'Ach, no! You story-telling Bushytail!' she said, 'I won't give you any more of my little children, and you needn't say you'll fly up and eat them, because I know you can't.'

"'Nier-r-r, nier-r-r!' said Oom Jakhals, growling, 'how do you know that?'

"'Oom Reijer told me, so there!' said Tante. 'And you can just go to your mother!'

"My, but Tante was getting brave now that she knew she and her little children were safe. That was the worst insult you can ever give a grown-up jakhals, and Oom Jakhals growled more than ever.

"'Never mind,' he said at last, 'Tante is only a vrouwmens, I won't bother with her anymore. But wait till I catch Oom Reijer. He'll be sorry he poked his long nose into my business, the old meddler,' and he trotted off to look for him.

"He hunted and hunted, and at last he found him standing on one leg at the side of the river, with his long neck drawn in and his head resting on his shoulders.

"'Good day, Oom Reijer,' he said politely. 'How is Oom today?'

"'I'm all right,' answered Oom Reijer shortly, without moving an inch.

"Jakhals spoke in a little small voice – ach, toch so humble. 'Oom, please come this way a little, I'm so stupid, but you are so wise and clever, and I want to ask your advice about something.'

"Oom Reijer began to listen. It is maar so when people hear about themselves. He put down his other leg, stretched out his neck, and asked over his shoulder, 'What did you say, eh?'

"'Come toch this way a little, the mud over there is too soft for me to stand on. I want your valuable advice about the wind. The other people all say I must ask you, because no one is as wise as you.'

"Truly Jakhals was a slim kerel! He knew how to stroke Oom Reijer's feathers the right way.

"Oom Reijer came slowly over the mud - a person mustn't show he is too pleased, he even stopped to swallow a little frog on the way, and then he said, careless like, 'Yes, I can tell you all about the wind and weather. Ask what you like, Jakhals.' His long neck twisted about with pride.

"Oom, when the wind is from the west, how must one hold one's head?'

"'Is that all?' said Oom Reijer. 'Just so.' And he turned his head to the east.

"'Thank you, Oom. And when the wind is from the east?'

"'So,' Oom Reijer bent his neck the other way.

"'Thank you, Oom,' said the little, small voice, so grateful and humble. 'But when there is a storm and the rain beats down?'

"'So!' said Oom Reijer, and he bent his neck down till his head nearly touched his toes.

"My little masters, just as quickly as a whip-snake shoots into his hole, so Jakhals shot out his arm and caught Oom Reijer on the bend of his neck - crack! - and in a minute the poor old bird was rolling in the mud with his neck nearly broken, and so weak that he couldn't even lift his beak to peck at the false wicked eyes that were staring at him.

"How glad was cruel Jakhals! He laughed till he couldn't anymore. He screamed and danced with pleasure. He waved his bushy tail, and the silver mane on his back bristled as he jumped about.

"'Ha, ha, ha! Oom thought to do me a bad turn, but I'll teach people not to interfere with me. Ha, ha, ha! No one is as wise as Oom Reijer, eh? Then he will soon find out how to mend his broken neck. Ha, ha, ha!'

"Jakhals gave one last spring right over poor Oom Reijer, and danced off to his den in the kopjes to tell Tante Jakhals and the little Jakhalsjes how he had cheated Oom Reijer.

"And from that day, baasjes, Oom Reijer's neck is crooked, he can't hold it straight, and it's all through trying to interfere with Jakhals. That is why I said Jakhals is a slim kerel. Whether he walks on four legs or on two, the best is maar to leave him alone because he can always make a plan, and no one ever gets the better of him without paying for it in the end."

The Story Of The Hero Makoma

This story has been edited and adapted from Andrew Lang's Strange Story Book, originally published in 1913 by Longmans, Green and Company, London and New York. The original was adapted from a native Zimbabwean tale told by the Sena.

Once upon a time, at the town of Senna on the banks of the Zambesi, was born a child. He was not like other children, for he was very tall and strong, over his shoulder he carried a big sack, and in his hand an iron hammer. He could also speak like a grown man, but usually he was very silent.

One day his mother said to him, "My child, by what name shall we know you?"

And he answered, "Call all the head men of Senna here to the river's bank."

And his mother called the head men of the town, and when they had come he led them down to a deep black pool in the river where all the fierce crocodiles lived.

"O great men!" he said, while they all listened, "Which of you will leap into the pool and overcome the crocodiles?"

But no one would come forward. So he turned and sprang into the water and disappeared. The people held their breath, for they thought, "surely the boy is bewitched and throws away his life, for the crocodiles will eat him!"

Then suddenly the ground trembled, and the pool, heaving and swirling, became red with blood, and presently the boy rising to the surface swam on shore. But he was no longer just a boy! He was stronger than any man and very tall and handsome, so that the people shouted with gladness when they saw him.

"Now, O my people!" he cried, waving his hand, "You know my name. I am Makoma, 'the Greater", for have I not slain the crocodiles in the pool where none would venture?"

Then he said to his mother, "Rest gently, my mother, for I go to make a home for myself and become a hero."

Then, entering his hut he took Nu-endo, his iron hammer, and throwing the sack over his shoulder, he went away. Makoma crossed the Zambesi, and for many moons he wandered towards the north and west until he came to a very hilly country where, one day, he met a huge giant making mountains.

"Greeting," shouted Makoma, "who are you?"

"I am Chi-eswa-mapiri, who makes the mountains," answered the giant, "and who are you?"

"I am Makoma, which signifies "greater,"" answered he.

"Greater than who?" asked the giant.

"Greater than you!" answered Makoma.

The giant gave a roar and rushed upon him. Makoma said nothing, but swinging his great hammer, Nu-endo struck the giant upon the head.

He struck him so hard a blow that the giant shrank into quite a little man, who fell upon his knees saying, "You are indeed greater than I, O Makoma, take me with you to be your slave!" So Makoma picked him up and dropped him into the sack that he carried upon his back.

He was greater than ever now, for all the giant's strength had gone into him, and he resumed his journey, carrying his burden with as little difficulty as an eagle might carry a hare.

Before long he came to a country broken up with huge stones and immense clods of earth. Looking over one of the heaps he saw a giant wrapped in dust dragging out the very earth and hurling it in handfuls on either side of him.

"Who are you," cried Makoma, "that pulls up the earth in this way?"

"I am Chi-dubula-taka," said he, "and I am making the river-beds."

"Do you know who I am?" said Makoma. "I am he that is called "greater"!"

"Greater than who?" thundered the giant.

"Greater than you!" answered Makoma.

With a shout, Chi-dubula-taka seized a great clod of earth and launched it at Makoma. But the hero had his sack held over his left arm and the stones and earth fell harmlessly upon it, and, tightly gripping his iron hammer, he rushed in and struck the giant to the ground. Chi-dubula-taka grovelled before him, all the while growing smaller and smaller, and when he had become a convenient size Makoma picked him up and put him into the sack beside Chi-eswa-mapiri.

He went on his way even greater than before, as all the river-maker's power had become his, and at last he came to a forest of baobabs and thorn trees. He was astonished at their size, for every one of them was full grown and larger than any trees he had ever seen, and close by he saw Chi-gwisa-miti, the giant who was planting the forest.

Chi-gwisa-miti was taller than either of his brothers, but Makoma was not afraid, and called out to him, "Who are you, O Big One?"

"I," said the giant, "am Chi-gwisa-miti, and I am planting these baobabs and thorns as food for my children the elephants."

"Leave off!" shouted the hero, "for I am Makoma, and would like to exchange a blow with you!"

The giant, plucking up a monster baobab by the roots, struck heavily at Makoma, but the hero sprang aside, and as the weapon sank deep into the soft earth, whirled Nu-endo the hammer round his head and felled the giant with one blow.

So terrible was the stroke that Chi-gwisa-miti shrivelled up as the other giants had done, and when he had got back his breath he begged Makoma to take him as his servant. "For," said he, "it is honourable to serve a man so great as you."

Makoma, after placing him in his sack, proceeded upon his journey, and travelling for many days he at last reached a country so barren and rocky that not a single living thing grew upon it. Everywhere reigned grim desolation. And in the midst of this dead region he found a man eating fire.

"What are you doing?" demanded Makoma.

"I am eating fire," answered the man, laughing, "and my name is Chi-idea-moto, for I am the flame-spirit, and can waste and destroy what I like."

"You are wrong," said Makoma, "for I am Makoma, who is "greater" than you, and you cannot destroy me!"

The fire-eater laughed again, and blew a flame at Makoma. But the hero sprang behind a rock, just in time, for the ground upon which he had been standing was turned to molten glass, like an overbaked pot, by the heat of the flame-spirit's breath.

Then the hero flung his iron hammer at Chi-idea-moto, and, striking him, it knocked him helpless, so Makoma placed him in the sack, Woro-nowu, with the other great men that he had overcome.

And now, truly, Makoma was a very great hero, for he had the strength to make hills, the industry to lead rivers over dry wastes, foresight and wisdom in planting trees, and the power of producing fire when he wished.

Wandering on he arrived one day at a great plain, that was well watered and full of game, and in the very middle of it, close to a large river, was a grassy spot, very pleasant to make a home upon.

Makoma was so delighted with the little meadow that he sat down under a large tree and removing the sack from his shoulder, took out all the giants and set them before him. "My friends," said he, "I have travelled far and am weary. Is not this such a place as would suit a hero for his home? Let us then go, tomorrow, to bring in timber to make a kraal."

So the next day Makoma and the giants set out to get poles to build the kraal, leaving only Chi-eswa-mapiri to look after the place and cook some venison which they had killed. In the evening, when they returned, they found the giant helpless and tied to a tree by one enormous hair!

"How is it," said Makoma, astonished, "that we find you thus bound and helpless?"

"O Chief," answered Chi-eswa-mapiri, "at mid-day a man came out of the river, he was of immense stature, and his grey moustaches were of such length that I could not see where they ended! He demanded of me 'Who is your master?' And I answered, 'Makoma, the greatest of heroes.' Then the man seized me, and pulling a hair from his moustache, tied me to this tree, even as you see me."

Makoma was very wroth, but he said nothing, and drawing his finger-nail across the hair, which was as thick and strong as palm rope, cut it, and set free the mountain-maker.

The three following days exactly the same thing happened, only each time with a different one of the party, and on the fourth day Makoma stayed in camp when the others went to cut poles, saying that he would see for himself what sort of man this was that lived in the river and whose moustaches were so long that they extended beyond men's sight.

So when the giants had gone he swept and tidied the camp and put some venison on the fire to roast. At midday, when the sun was right overhead, he heard a rumbling noise from the river, and looking up he saw the head and shoulders of an enormous man emerging from it. And behold! Right down the river-bed and up the river-bed, till they faded into the blue distance, stretched the giant's grey moustaches!

"Who are you?" bellowed the giant as soon as he was out of the water.

"I am he that is called Makoma," answered the hero, "and, before I slay you, tell me, what is your name and what are you doing in the river?"

"My name is Chin-debou Mau-giri," said the giant. "My home is in the river, for my moustache is the grey fever-mist that hangs above the water, and with which I bind all those that come unto me so that they die."

"You cannot bind me!" shouted Makoma, rushing upon him and striking with his hammer. But the river giant was so slimy that the blow slid harmlessly off his green chest, and as Makoma stumbled and tried to regain his balance, the giant swung one of his long hairs around him and tripped him up.

For a moment Makoma was helpless, but remembering the power of the flame-spirit which had entered into him, he breathed a fiery breath upon the giant's hair and cut himself free.

As Chin-debou Mau-giri leaned forward to seize him the hero flung his sack Woro-nowu over the giant's slippery head, and gripping his iron hammer, struck him again. This time the blow alighted upon the dry sack and Chin-debou Mau-giri fell dead.

When the four giants returned at sunset with the poles, they rejoiced to find that Makoma had overcome the fever-spirit, and they feasted on the roast venison till far into the night, but in the morning, when they awoke, Makoma was already warming his hands to the fire, and his face was gloomy.

"In the darkness of the night, O my friends," he said presently, "the white spirits of my fathers came upon me and spoke, saying, 'Get away, Makoma, for you shall have no rest until you have found and fought with Sakatirina, who had five heads, and is very great and strong, so take leave of your friends, for you must go alone.'"

Then the giants were very sad, and bewailed the loss of their hero, but Makoma comforted them, and gave back to each the gifts he had taken from them. Then bidding them "Farewell," he went on his way.

Makoma travelled far towards the west, over rough mountains and water-logged morasses, fording deep rivers, and tramping for days across dry deserts where most men would have died, until at length he arrived at a hut standing near some large peaks, and inside the hut were two beautiful women.

"Greeting!" said the hero. "Is this the country of Sakatirina of five heads, whom I am seeking?"

"We greet you, O Great One!" answered the women. "We are the wives of Sakatirina. Your search is at an end, for there stands he whom you seek!" And they pointed to what Makoma had thought were two tall mountain peaks. "those are his legs," they said, "his body you cannot see, for it is hidden in the clouds."

Makoma was astonished when he beheld how tall the giant was, but, nothing daunted, he went forward until he reached one of Sakatirina's legs, which he struck heavily with Nu-endo. Nothing happened, so he hit again and then again until, presently, he heard a tired, far-away voice saying, "Who is it that scratches my feet?"

And Makoma shouted as loud as he could, answering, "It is I, Makoma, who is called 'Greater'!" And he listened, but there was no answer.

Then Makoma collected all the dead brushwood and trees that he could find, and making an enormous pile round the giant's legs, set a light to it.

This time the giant spoke, and his voice was very terrible, for it was the rumble of thunder in the clouds. "Who is it," he said, "making that fire smoulder around my feet?"

"It is I, Makoma!" shouted the hero. "And I have come from far away to see you, O Sakatirina, for the spirits of my fathers bade me go seek and fight with you, lest I should grow fat, and weary of myself."

There was silence for a while, and then the giant spoke softly, "It is good, O Makoma!" he said. "For I too have grown weary. There is no man so great as I, therefore I am all alone. Guard yourself!"

Bending suddenly he seized the hero in his hands and dashed him upon the ground. And lo! Instead of death, Makoma had found life, for he sprang to his feet mightier in strength and stature than before, and rushing in, he gripped the giant by the waist and wrestled with him.

Hour by hour they fought, and mountains rolled beneath their feet like pebbles in a flood. Now Makoma would break away, and summoning up his strength, strike the giant with Nu-endo his iron hammer, and Sakatirina would pluck up the mountains and hurl them upon the hero, but neither one could slay the other. At last, upon the second day, they grappled so strongly that they could not break away, but their strength was failing, and, just as the sun was sinking, they fell together to the ground, insensible.

In the morning when they awoke, Mulimo the Great Spirit was standing by them, and he said, "O Makoma and Sakatirina! You are heroes so great that no man may come against you. Therefore you will leave the world and take up your home with me in the clouds."

And as he spoke the heroes became invisible to the people of the Earth, and were no more seen among them.

The Man Who Ordered His Wife To Cut Off His Ears

This story has been edited and adapted from Specimens of Bushman Folklore, produced by Wilhelm Heinrich Immanuel Bleek and Lucy Lloyd, originally published in 1911 by George Allen and Company, London.

!Xwe-|na-sse-!k'e is the name of the Bushmen who lived first in the land. They were men of the early race, therefore, they did foolish things on account of their inexperience of the world.

One such man heard that his younger brother's head had been skinned by the brother's wife. He decided that he wanted his younger brothers skin, so he insisted that his own wife should cut off his ears so that he could wear his younger brother's skin. His wife at first refused, but he insisted that she do it.

So, his wife cut off his ears, and he screamed on account of the pain and the cutting of his skin, even though he was the one who wished his wife to do so on account of his younger brother's head having surely been skinned.

However, the younger brother's wife had only shaved the brother's head, removing just the old hair.

The #Nerru And Her Husband

This story has been edited and adapted from Specimens of Bushman Folklore, produced by Wilhelm Heinrich Immanuel Bleek and Lucy Lloyd, originally published in 1911 by George Allen and Company, London.

A man of the early race once married a #nerru. The #nerru put the dusty Bushman rice into a bag when her husband had dug out Bushman rice. She went to wash the Bushman rice, and they returned home.

The next day they went out early to seek for food. The husband dug out Bushman rice and he put the Bushman rice into the bag. And the husband again dug out other Bushman rice, which he also put in the bag on top of the other rice. He again arose, he sought for other Bushman rice. He found other Bushman rice, dug it out, and put it on top of the other rice in the bag.

He worked on and looked for more Bushman rice, which he soon found. He exclaimed, "Give me your little kaross, so that I may put the Bushman rice upon it."

And the wife said, "We are not accustomed to put Bushman rice covered with earth into our kaross. We are of the house of #nerru."

And he exclaimed, "Give me the little kaross, so that I may put the Bushman rice upon it."

And the wife said, "You should put the Bushman rice back on the ground, for we are not accustomed to put Bushman rice covered with earth into our kaross."

He exclaimed again, "Give me the little kaross, so that I may put the Bushman rice upon it."

And yet again the wife said, "You should put the Bushman rice back on the ground, for we are not accustomed to put Bushman rice covered with earth into our kaross."

The man became frustrated. He said, "Give me the kaross, so that I may put the Bushman rice upon it!". With that he away his wife's the kaross. As he made this violent act, his wife's entrails spilled onto the ground.

He cried, "Oh dear! O my wife! What shall I do?"

His wife rose up and sang:

"We, who are of the house of #nerru,

We are not used to put earthy Bushman rice

Into our back's kaross,

We, who are of the house of #nerru,

We are not used to put earthy Bushman rice

Into our back's kaross."

As she sang she walked on, putting her entrails back in place. All the while she sang:

"We, who are of the house of #nerru,

We are not used to put earthy Bushman rice

Into our back's kaross."

Back at their home the wife's mother exclaimed, "Look over to the place where your elder sister went to seek food, for the noise of the wind sounds like a person. That is because your elder sisters' husband does not act rightly. The noise of the wind sounds like a person singing."

Her daughter stood up and looked. She exclaimed, "Your daughter, my sister, comes here but she is falling."

Then her mother said, "I want you to see what your elder sister's husband does."

Then she ran to meet her daughter. When she reached her daughter she put a little kaross upon her daughter, and put her daughter's entrails upon the little kaross, and she bound up her daughter. Then she slowly conducted her daughter home, and took her into her hut.

The mother was angry about her daughter, and when her daughter's husband wanted to come to see his wife, she was even more angry. Therefore, her daughter's husband went back to his own people, for his people did not understand the ways of the house of #nerru. The husband went back to his homeland, while the mother and her daughters continued to dwell there.

The #Nerru, As A Bird

This story has been edited and adapted from Specimens of Bushman Folklore, produced by Wilhelm Heinrich Immanuel Bleek and Lucy Lloyd, originally published in 1911 by George Allen and Company, London.

The #nerru's bill is very short. The male #nerru is the one whose plumage resembles that of the ostrich. It is black like the male ostrich. The female #nerru is the one whose plumage is white like that of the female ostrich. Thus, they resemble the ostriches, because the male #nerru are black, and the female #nerru white.

They eat the things which little birds usually eat, which they pick up on the ground. They make grass nests on the ground, by the root of a bush.

When not breeding, they are found in large numbers.

The Jackal And The Wolf

This story has been edited and adapted from James A. Honey's South-African Folk Tales, originally published in 1910 by The Baker and Taylor Company.

Once on a time Jackal, who lived on the borders of the colony, saw a wagon returning from the seaside laden with fish. He tried to get into the wagon from behind, but he could not, so then he ran on in front of the wagon and lay in the road as if dead. The wagon came up to him, and the leader cried to the driver, "Here is a fine kaross for your wife!

"Throw it into the wagon," said the driver, and Jackal was thrown in.

The wagon travelled on, through a moonlight night, and all the while Jackal was throwing out the fish into the road. He then jumped out himself and secured a great prize. But stupid old Hyena, coming by, ate more than his share, for which Jackal owed him a grudge, and he said to him, "You can get plenty of fish, too, if you lie in the way of a wagon as I did, and keep quite still whatever happens."

"So!" mumbled Hyena.

Accordingly, when the next wagon came from the sea, Hyena stretched himself out in the road. "What ugly thing is this?" cried the leader, and kicked Hyena. He then took a stick and thrashed him within an inch of his life. Hyena, according to the directions of Jackal, lay quiet as long as he could, he then got up and hobbled off to tell his misfortune to Jackal, who pretended to comfort him.

"What a pity," said Hyena, "I have not got such a handsome skin as you have!"

The Lion, The Jackal, And The Man

This story has been edited and adapted from James A. Honey's South-African Folk Tales, originally published in 1910 by The Baker and Taylor Company.

It so happened one day that Lion and Jackal came together to converse on affairs of land and state. Jackal, let me say, was the most important adviser to the king of the forest, and after they had spoken about these matters for quite a while, the conversation took a more personal turn.

Lion began to boast and talk big about his strength. Jackal had, perhaps, given him cause for it, because by nature he was a flatterer. But now that Lion began to assume so many airs, Jackal said, "See here, Lion, I will show you an animal that is still more powerful than you are."

They walked along, Jackal leading the way, and met first a little boy.

"Is this the strong man?" asked Lion.

"No," answered Jackal, "he must still become a man, O king."

After a while they found an old man walking with bowed head and supporting his bent figure with a stick.

"Is this the wonderful strong man?" asked Lion.

"Not yet, O king," was Jackal's answer, "he has been a man."

Continuing their walk a short distance farther, they came across a young hunter, in the prime of youth, and accompanied by some of his dogs.

"There you have him now, O king," said Jackal. "Pit your strength against his, and if you win, then truly you are the strength of the earth."

Then Jackal made tracks to one side toward a little rocky kopje from which he would be able to see the meeting.

Growling, growling, Lion strode forward to meet the man, but when he came close the dogs beset him. He, however, paid but little attention to the dogs, and he pushed and separated them on all sides with a few sweeps of his front paws. They howled aloud, beating a hasty retreat toward the man.

Thereupon the man fired a charge of shot, hitting Lion behind the shoulder, but even to this Lion paid but little attention. Thereupon the hunter pulled out his steel knife, and gave him a few good jabs. Lion retreated, followed by the flying bullets of the hunter.

"Well, are you strongest now?" was Jackal's first question when Lion arrived at his side.

"No, Jackal," answered Lion. "Let that fellow there keep the name and welcome. Such as he I have never before seen. In the first place he had about ten of his bodyguard storm me. I really did not bother myself much about them, but when I attempted to turn him to chaff, he spat and blew fire at me, mostly into my face, and that burned just a little but not very badly. And when I again endeavoured to pull him to the ground he jerked out from his body one of his ribs with which he gave me some very ugly wounds, so bad that I had to make chips fly, and as a parting he sent some warm bullets after me. No, Jackal, give him the name."

The Stars And The Stars' Road

This story has been edited and adapted from Sanni Metelerkamp's book, Outa Karel's Stories, originally published in 1914 by MacMillan and Company, London.

Darkly-blue and illimitable, the arc of the sky hung over the great Karroo like a canopy of softest velvet, making a deep, mysterious background for the myriad stars, which twinkled brightly at a frosty world. The three little boys, gathered at the window, pointed out to each other the constellations with which Cousin Minnie had made them familiar, and were deep in a discussion as to the nature and number of the stars composing the Milky Way when Outa shuffled in.

"Outa, do you think there are a billion stars up there in the Milky Way?" asked Willem.

"A billion, you know," explained Pietie, "is a thousand million, and it would take months to count even one million."

"Aja, baasje," said the old man readily, seizing, with native adroitness, the unknown word and making it his own, "then there will surely be a billion stars up there. Perhaps," he added, judicially considering the matter, "two billion, but no one knows, because no one can ever count them. They are too many. And to think that the bright road in the sky is made of wood ashes, after all."

He settled himself on his stool, and his little audience came to attention.

"Yes, my baasjes," he went on, "long, long ago, the sky was dark at night when the Old Man with the bright armpits lay down to sleep, but people learned in time to make fires to light up the darkness. One night a girl, who sat warming herself by a wood fire, played with the ashes. She took the ashes in her hands and threw them up to see how pretty they were when they floated in the air. And as they floated away she put green bushes on the fire and stirred it with a stick. Bright sparks flew out and went high, high, mixing with the silver ashes, and they all hung in the air and made a bright road across the sky. And there it is to this day. Baasjes call it the Milky Way, but Outa calls it the Stars' Road.

"Ai, but the girl was pleased! She clapped her hands and danced, shaking herself like Outa's people do when they are happy, and singing:

"The little stars! The tiny stars!

They make a road for other stars.

Ash of wood-fire! Dust of the Sun!

They call the Dawn when Night is done!'

"Then she took some of the roots she had been eating and threw them into the sky, and there they hung and turned into large stars.

The old roots turned into stars that gave a red light, and the young roots turned into stars that gave a golden light. There they all hung, winking and twinkling and singing. Yes, singing, my baasjes, and this is what they sang:

"We are children of the Sun!

It's so! It's so! It's so!

Him we call when Night is done!

It's so! It's so! It's so!

Bright we sail across the sky

By the Stars' Road, high, so high;

And we, twinkling, smile at you,

As we sail across the blue!

It's so! It's so! It's so!'

"Baasjes know, when the stars twinkle up there in the sky they are like little children nodding their heads and saying, 'It's so! It's so! It's so!'"

At each repetition Outa nodded and winked, and the children, with antics of approval, followed suit.

"Baasjes have sometimes seen a star fall?"

Three little heads nodded in concert.

"When a star falls," said the old man impressively, "it tells us someone has died. For the star knows when a person's heart fails and the person dies, and it falls from the sky to tell those at a distance that someone they know has died.

"One star grew and grew till he was much larger than the others. He was the Great Star, and, singing, he named the other stars. He called each one by name, till they all had their names, and in this way they knew that he was the Great Star. No other could have done so. Then when he had finished, they all sang together and praised the Great Star, who had named them.

"Now, when the day is done, they walk across the sky on each side of the Stars' Road. It shows them the way. And when Night is over, they turn back and sail again by the Stars' Road to call the Daybreak, that goes before the Sun. The Star that leads the way is a big bright star. He is called the Dawn's-Heart Star, and in the dark, dark hour, before the Stars have called the Dawn, he shines.

"Ach, baasjes, he is beautiful to behold! The wife and the child of the Dawn's-Heart Star are pretty, too, but not so big and bright as he. They sail on in front, and then they wait. They wait for the other Stars to turn back and sail along the Stars' Road, calling, calling the Dawn, and for the Sun to come up from under the world, where he has been lying asleep.

"They call and sing, twinkling as they sing:

"We call across the sky,

Dawn! Come, Dawn!

You, that are like a young maid newly risen,

Rubbing the sleep from your eyes!

You, that come stretching bright hands to the sky,

Pointing the way for the Sun!

Before whose smile the Stars faint and grow pale,

And the Stars' Road melts away.

Dawn! Come Dawn!

We call across the sky,

And the Dawn's-Heart Star is waiting.

It's so! It's so! It's so!"

"So they sing, baasjes, because they know they are soon going out.

"Then slowly the Dawn comes, rubbing her eyes, smiling, stretching out bright fingers, chasing the darkness away. The Stars grow faint and the Stars' Road fades, while the Dawn makes a bright pathway for the Sun. At last he comes with both arms lifted high, and the brightness, streaming from under them, makes day for the world, and wakes people to their work and play.

"But the little Stars wait till he sleeps again before they begin their singing. Summer is the time when they sing best, but even now, if baasjes look out of the window they will see the Stars, twinkling and singing."

The children ran to the window and gazed out into the starlit heavens. The last sight Outa had, as he drained the soopje glass the Baas was just in time to hand him, was of three little heads bobbing up and down in time to the immemorial music of the Stars, while little Jan's excited treble rang out, "Yes, it's quite true, Outa. They do say, 'It's so! It's so! It's so!"

Lion And Jackal #1

This story has been edited and adapted from James A. Honey's South-African Folk Tales, originally published in 1910 by The Baker and Taylor Company.

Not because he was exactly the most capable or progressive fellow in the neighbourhood, but because he always gave that idea - that is why Jackal slowly acquired among the neighbours the name of a "progressive man." The truly well-bred people around him, who did not wish to hurt his feelings, seemed to apply this name to him, instead of, for instance, "cunning scamp," or "all-wise rat-trap," as so many others often dubbed him. He obtained this name of "a progressive man" because he spoke English most of the time, especially if he thought some of them were present who could not understand it, and also because he could always hold his body so much like a judge on public occasions.

He had a smooth tongue, could make quite a favourable speech, and especially with good effect could he expatiate on the backwardness of others. Underneath he really was the most unlettered man in the vicinity, but he had perfect control over his inborn cunningness, which allowed him for a long time to go triumphantly through life as a man of great ability.

One time, for instance, he lost his tail in an iron trap. He had long attempted to reach the Boer's goose pen, and had framed many good plans, but when he came to his senses, he was sitting in front of the goose pen with his tail in the iron trap, the dogs all the time coming for him. When he realized what it meant, he mustered together all his strength and pulled his tail, which he always thought so much of, clean off.

This would immediately have made him the butt of the whole neighbourhood had he not thought of a plan. He called together a meeting of the jackals, and made them believe that Lion had issued a proclamation to the effect that all jackals in the future should be tailless, because their beautiful tails were a thorn in the eyes of more unfortunate animals.

In his smooth way he told them how he regretted that the king should have the barbaric right to interfere with his subjects. But so it was, and he thought the sooner he paid attention to it the safer. Therefore he had had his tail cut off already and he should advise all his friends to do the same. And so it happened that once all jackals for a long time were without tails. Later on they grew again.

It was about the same time that Leopard hired Jackal as a schoolmaster. Leopard was in those days the richest man in the surrounding country, and as he had had to suffer a great deal himself because he was so untutored, he wanted his children to have the best education that could be obtained.

It was shortly after a meeting, in which it was shown how important a thing an education was, that Leopard approached Jackal and asked him to come and teach his children.

Jackal was very ready to do this. It was not exactly his vocation, he said, but he would do it to pass time and just out of friendship for his neighbour. His and Leopard's farmlands lay next each other.

That he did not make teaching his profession and that he possessed no degree was of no account in the eyes of Leopard.

"Do not praise my goodness so much, Cousin Jackal," laughed he. "We know your worth well enough. Much rather would I intrust my offspring to you than to the many so-called schoolmasters, for it is especially my wish, as well as that of their mother, to have our children obtain a progressive education, and to make such men and women of them that with the same ability as you have they can take their lawful places in this world."

"One condition," said Jackal, "I must state. It will be very inconvenient for me, almost impossible, to come here to your farm and hold school. My own farm would in that case go to pieces, and that I cannot let happen. It would never pay me."

Leopard answered that it was not exactly necessary either. In spite of their attachment to the little ones, they saw that it would probably be to their benefit to place them for a while in a stranger's house.

Jackal then told of his own bringing up by Wolf. He remembered well how small he was when his father sent him away to study with Wolf. Naturally, since then, he had passed through many schools, Wolf was only his first teacher. And only in his later days did he realize how much good it had done him.

"A man must bend the sapling while it is still young," said he. "There is no time that the child is so open to impressions as when he is plastic, about the age that most of your children are at present, and I was just thinking you would be doing a wise thing to send them away for quite a while."

He had, fortunately, just then a room in his house that would be suited for a schoolroom, and his wife could easily make some arrangement for their lodging, even if they had to enlarge their dwelling somewhat.

It was then and there agreed upon. Leopard's wife was then consulted about one thing and another, and the following day the children were to leave.

"I have just thought of one more thing," remarked Jackal, 'seven children, besides my little lot, will be quite a care on our hands, so you will have to send over each week a fat lamb, and in order not to disturb their progress, the children will have to relinquish the idea of a vacation spent with you for some time. When I think they have become used to the bit, I will inform you, and then you can come and take them to make you a short visit, but not until then.

"It is also better," continued he, 'that they do not see you for the first while, but your wife can come and see them every Saturday and I will see to all else."

On the following day there was an unearthly howling and wailing when the children were to leave. But Leopard and their mother showed them that it was best and that someday they would see that it was all for their good, and that their parents were doing it out of kindness. Eventually they were gone.

The first Saturday dawned, and early that morning Mrs. Leopard was on her way to Jackal's dwelling, because she could not defer the time any longer.

She was still a long way off when Jackal caught sight of her. He always observed neighbourly customs, and so stepped out to meet her.

After they had greeted each other, Mrs. Leopard's first question was, "Well, Cousin Jackal, how goes everything with the small team? Are they still all well and happy, and do they not trouble you, Cousin Jackal, too much?"

"Oh, my goodness, no, Mrs. Leopard," answered Jackal enthusiastically, "but don't let us talk so loud, because if they heard you, it certainly would cause them many heartfelt tears and they might also want to go back with you and then all our trouble would have been for nothing."

"But I would like to see them, Cousin Jackal," said Mrs. Leopard a little disturbed.

"Why certainly, Mrs. Leopard," was his answer, "but I do not think it is wise for them to see you. I will lift them up to the window one by one, and then you can put your mind at rest concerning their health and progress."

After Mr. and Mrs. Jackal and Mrs. Leopard had sat together for some time drinking coffee and talking over one thing and another, Jackal took Leopard's wife to a door and told her to look through it, out upon the back yard. There he would show her the children one by one, while they would not be able to see her. Everything was done exactly as Jackal had said, but the sixth little leopard he picked up twice, because the firstborn he had the day before prepared in pickle for their Sunday meal.

And so it happened every Saturday until the last little leopard, which was the youngest, had to be lifted up seven times in succession.

And when Mrs. Leopard came again the following week all was still as death and everything seemed to have a deserted appearance on the estate. She walked straight to the front door, and there she found a letter in the poll grass near the door, which read thus:

"We have gone for a picnic with the children. From there we will ride by Jackalsdance for New Year. This is necessary for the completion of their progressive education."

Lion And Jackal #2

This story has been edited and adapted from James A. Honey's South-African Folk Tales, originally published in 1910 by The Baker and Taylor Company.

Lion had now caught a large eland which lay dead on the top of a high bank. Lion was thirsty and wanted to go and drink water. "Jackal, look after my eland, I am going to get a drink. Don't you eat any."

"Very well, Uncle Lion."

Lion went to the river and Jackal quietly removed a stone on which Lion had to step to reach the bank on his return. After that Jackal and his wife ate heartily of the eland. Lion returned, but could not scale the bank. "Jackal, help me," he shouted.

"Yes, Uncle Lion, I will let down a rope and then you can climb up."

Jackal whispered to his wife, "Give me one of the old, thin hide ropes." And then aloud he added, "Wife, give me one of the strong, buffalo ropes, so Uncle Lion won't fall."

His wife gave him an old rotten rope. Jackal and his wife first ate ravenously of the meat, then gradually let the rope down. Lion seized it and struggled up. When he neared the brink Jackal gave the rope a jerk. It broke and down Lion began to roll, and he rolled the whole way down, and finally lay at the foot near the river.

Jackal began to beat a dry hide that lay there as he howled, cried, and shouted, "Wife, why did you give me such a bad rope that caused Uncle Lion to fall?"

Lion heard the row and roared, "Jackal, stop beating your wife. I will hurt you if you don't cease. Help me to climb up."

"Uncle Lion, I will give you a rope."

He whispered again to his wife, "Give me one of the old, thin hide ropes," and shouting aloud again, "Give me a strong, buffalo rope, wife, that will not break again with Lion."

Jackal gave out the rope, and when Lion had nearly reached the top, he cut the rope through. Snap! And Lion began to roll to the bottom. Jackal again beat on the hide and shouted, "Wife, why did you give me such a rotten rope? Didn't I tell you to give me a strong one?"

Lion roared, "Jackal, stop beating your wife at once. Help me instantly or you will be sorry."

"Wife," Jackal said aloud, "give me now the strongest rope you have," and aside to her, "Give me the worst rope of the lot."

Jackal again let down a rope, but just as Lion reached the top, Jackal gave a strong tug and broke the rope. Poor old Lion rolled down the side of the hill and lay there roaring from pain. He had been fatally hurt.

Jackal inquired, "Uncle Lion, have you hurt yourself? Have you much pain? Wait a while, I am coming directly to help you."

Jackal and his wife slowly walked away.

Lion And Jackal #3

This story has been edited and adapted from James A. Honey's South-African Folk Tales, originally published in 1910 by The Baker and Taylor Company.

The Lion and the Jackal agreed to hunt on shares, for the purpose of laying in a stock of meat for the winter months for their families.

As the Lion was by far the more expert hunter of the two, the Jackal suggested that he, Jackal, should be employed in transporting the game to their dens, and that Mrs. Jackal and the little Jackals should prepare and dry the meat, adding that they would take care that Mrs. Lion and her family should not want.

This was agreed to by the Lion, and the hunt commenced.

After a very successful hunt, which lasted for some time, the Lion returned to see his family, and also to enjoy, as he thought, a plentiful supply of his spoil, when, to his utter surprise, he found Mrs. Lion and all the young Lions on the point of death from sheer hunger, and in a mangy state. The Jackal, it appeared, had only given them a few entrails of the game, and in such limited quantities as barely to keep them alive, always telling them that he and Lion had been most unsuccessful in their hunting. All the while, of course, his own family was revelling in abundance, and each member of it was sleek and fat.

This was too much for the Lion to bear. He immediately started off in a terrible fury, vowing certain death to the Jackal and all his family, wherever he should meet them. The Jackal was more or less prepared for a storm, and had taken the precaution to remove all his belongings to the top of a Krantz, which is a cliff, accessible only by a most difficult and circuitous path, which he alone knew.

When the Lion saw him on the Krantz, the Jackal immediately greeted him by calling out, "Good morning, Uncle Lion."

"How dare you call me uncle, you impudent scoundrel," roared out the Lion, in a voice of thunder, "after the way in which you have behaved to my family?"

"Oh, Uncle! How shall I explain matters? That beast of a wife of mine!"

Whack, whack was heard, as he beat with a stick on dry hide, which was a mere pretence for Mrs. Jackal's back, while that lady was pre-instructed to scream whenever he operated on the hide, which she did with a vengeance, joined by the little Jackals, who set up a most doleful chorus.

"That wretch!" said the Jackal. "It is all her doing. I shall kill her straight off," and away he again belaboured the hide, while his wife and children uttered such a dismal howl that the Lion begged of him to leave off flogging his wife.

After cooling down a little, he invited Uncle Lion to come up and have something to eat. The Lion, after several ineffectual attempts to scale the precipice, had to give it up.

The Jackal, always ready for emergencies, suggested that a reim should be lowered to haul up his uncle. This was agreed to, and when the Lion was drawn about halfway up by the whole family of Jackals, the reim was cleverly cut, and down went the Lion with a tremendous crash which hurt him very much.

Upon this, the Jackal again performed upon the hide with tremendous force, for their daring to give him such a rotten reim, and Mrs. Jackal and the little ones responded with some fearful screams and yells. He then called loudly out to his wife for a strong buffalo reim which would support any weight. This again was lowered and fastened to the Lion, when all hands pulled away at their uncle, and, just when he had reached so far that he could look over the precipice into the pots to see all the fat meat cooking, and all the biltongs hanging out to dry, the reim was again cut, and the poor Lion fell with such force that he was fairly stunned for some time.

After the Lion had recovered his senses, the Jackal, in a most sympathizing tone, suggested that he was afraid that it was of no use to attempt to haul him up onto the precipice, and recommended, instead, that a nice fat piece of eland's breast be roasted and dropped into the Lion's mouth. The Lion, half famished with hunger, and much bruised, readily accepted the offer, and sat eagerly awaiting the fat morsel.

In the meantime, the Jackal had a round stone made red-hot, and wrapped inside a quantity of fat, or suet, to make it appear like a ball of fat. When the Lion saw it held out above him, he opened his capacious mouth to the utmost extent, and the wily Jackal cleverly dropped the hot ball right into it, which ran through the poor old beast, killing him on the spot.

It need hardly be told that there was great rejoicing on the precipice that night.

236

The Hunt Of Lion And Jackal

This story has been edited and adapted from James A. Honey's South-African Folk Tales, originally published in 1910 by The Baker and Taylor Company. This is clearly derived from a Bushman tale,

Lion and Jackal, it is said, were one day lying in wait for Eland. Lion shot with a bow and missed, but Jackal hit and sang out, "Hah! Hah!"

Lion said, "No, you did not shoot anything. It was I who hit."

Jackal answered, "Yea, my father, you have hit Eland."

Then they went home meaning to return when Eland was dead, and cut him up. Jackal, however, turned back, unknown to Lion, in order to cheat Lion. Jackal hit his own nose so that the blood ran on the spoor of the eland, and marked what was supposed to be their track,. When he had gone some distance, he returned by another way to the dead eland, and creeping into its carcass, cut out all the fat.

Meanwhile Lion followed the blood-stained spoor of Jackal, thinking that it was eland blood, and only when he had gone some distance did he find out that he had been deceived. He then returned on Jackal's spoor, and reached the dead eland, where, finding Jackal in its carcass, he seized him by his tail and drew him out with a swing.

Lion upbraided Jackal with these words, "Why do you cheat me?"

Jackal answered, "No, my father, I do not cheat you, you may know it, I think. I prepared this fat for you, father."

Lion said, "Then take the fat and carry it to your mother, my lioness", and he gave him the lungs to take to his own wife and children.

When Jackal arrived, he did not give the fat to Lion's wife, but to his own wife and children. He gave, however, the lungs to Lion's wife, and he pelted Lion's little children with the lungs, saying, "You children of the big-pawed one! You big-pawed ones!"

He said to Lioness, "I go to help my father, the lion", but he went far away with his wife and children.

Who Was King?

This story has been edited and adapted from Sanni Metelerkamp's book, Outa Karel's Stories, originally published in 1914 by MacMillan and Company, London.

"Once upon a time," began Outa Karel, and his audience of three looked up expectantly.

"Once upon a time, Oom Leeuw roared and the forest shook with the dreadful sound. Then, from far away over the vlakte, floated another roar, and the little lion cubs jumped about and stood on their heads, tumbling over each other in their merriment.

"'Hear,' they said, 'it is Volstruis, old Three Sticks. He tries to imitate the King, our father. He roars well. Truly there is no difference.'

"When Leeuw heard this he was very angry, so he roared again, louder than ever. Again came back the sound over the veld, as if it had been an echo.

"'Ach, no! This will never do,' thought Leeuw. 'I must put a stop to this impudence. I alone am King here, and imitators - I want none.'

"So he went forth and roamed over the vlakte till he met old Three Sticks, the Ostrich. They stood glaring at each other.

"Leeuw's eyes flamed, his mane rose in a huge mass and he lashed his tail angrily. Volstruis spread out his beautiful wings and swayed from side to side, his beak open and his neck twisting like a whip-snake. Ach, it was pretty, but if baasjes could have seen his eyes! Baasjes know, Volstruis's eyes are very soft and beautiful - like Nonnie's when she tells the Bible stories, but now there was only fierceness in them, and yellow lights that looked like fire.

"But there was no fight - yet. It was only their way of meeting. Leeuw came a step nearer and said, 'We must see who is baas. You, Volstruis, please roar a little.'

"So Volstruis roared, blowing out his throat, so, 'Hoo-hoo-hoor-r-r-r!'

It was a fearsome sound - the sort of sound that makes you feel streams of cold water running down your back when you hear it suddenly and don't know what it is. Yes, baasjes, if you are in bed you curl up and pull the blankets over your head, and if you are outside you run in and get close to the Nooi or Nonnie."

A slight movement, indicative of contradiction, passed from one to another of his small hearers, but - unless it was a free and easy, conversational evening - they made it a point of honour never to interrupt Outa in full career. This, like other things, could await the finish of the story.

"Then Leeuw roared, and truly the voices were the same. No one could say, 'This is a bigger voice,' or 'That is a more terrifying voice.' No, they were just equal.

"So Leeuw said to Volstruis, 'Our voices are alike. You are my equal in roaring. Let it then be so. You will be King of the Birds as I am King of the Beasts. Now let us go hunting and see who is baas there.'

"Out in the vlakte some sassaby were feeding, big fat ones, a nice klompje, so Leeuw started off in one direction and Volstruis in the other, but both kept away from the side the wind came from. Wild bucks can smell - ach toch, so good. Just one little puff when a hunter is creeping up to them, and at once all the heads are in the air - sniff, sniff, sniff - and they are off like the wind. Dust is all you see, and when that has blown away - ach no, there are no bucks, the whole veld is empty, empty!"

Outa stretched out his arms and waved them from side to side with an exaggerated expression of finding nothing but empty space, his voice mournful with a sense of irreparable loss.

"But" - he took up his tale with renewed energy - "Leeuw and Volstruis were old hunters. They knew how to get nearer and nearer without letting the bucks know. Leeuw trailed himself along slowly, slowly, close to the ground, and only when he was moving could you see which was Leeuw and which was sand, the colour was just the same.

"He picked out a big buck, well-grown and fat, but not too old to be juicy, and when he got near enough he hunched himself up very quietly - so, my little masters, just so - ready to spring, and then before you could whistle, he shot through the air like a stone from a catapult, and fell, fair and square, on to the sassaby's back, his great tearing claws fastened on its shoulders and his wicked teeth meeting in the poor thing's neck.

"Ach, the beautiful big buck! Never again would his pointed horns tear open his enemies! Never again would he lead the herd, or pronk in the veld in mating time! Never again would his soft nostrils scent danger in the distance, nor his quick hoofs give the signal for the stampede! No, it was really all up with him this time! When Oom Leeuw gets hold of a thing, he doesn't let go till it is dead.

"The rest of the herd - ach, but they ran! Soon they were far away, only specks in the distance, all except those that Volstruis had killed. Truly Volstruis was clever! Baasjes know, he can run fast - faster even than the sassaby. So when he saw Leeuw getting ready to spring, he raced up-wind as hard as he could, knowing that was what the herd would do. So there he was waiting for them, and didn't he play with them! See, baasjes, he stood just so" - in his excitement Outa rose and struck an attitude - "and when they streaked past him he jumped like this, striking at them with the hard, sharp claws on his old two toes."

Outa hopped about like a fighting bantam, while the children hugged themselves in silent delight.

"Voerts! There was one dead!" - Outa kicked to the right. "Voerts! there was another!" - he kicked to the left - 'till there was a klomp of bucks lying about the veld giving their last blare. Yes, old Two Toes did his work well that day.

"When Leeuw came up and saw that Volstruis had killed more than he had, he was not very pleased, but Volstruis soon made it all right.

"Leeuw said, 'You have killed most, so you rip open and begin to eat.'

"'Oh no!' said Volstruis, 'you have cubs to share the food with, so you rip open and eat. I shall only drink the blood.'

"This put Leeuw in a good humour, he thought Volstruis a noble, unselfish creature. But truly, as I said before, Volstruis was clever. Baasjes see, he couldn't eat meat, he had no teeth. But he didn't want Leeuw to know. Therefore he said, 'You eat, I will only drink the blood.'

"So Leeuw ripped open - sk-r-r-r-r, sk-r-r-r-r - and called the cubs, and they all ate till they were satisfied. Then Volstruis came along in a careless fashion, pecking, pecking as he walked, and drank the blood. Then he and Leeuw lay down in the shade of some trees and went to sleep.

"The cubs played about, rolling and tumbling over each other. As they played they came to the place where Volstruis lay.

"'Aha!' said one, 'he sleeps with his mouth open.'

"He peeped into Volstruis's mouth. 'Aha!' he said again, 'I see something.'

"Another cub came and peeped.

"'Alle kracht!' he said, 'I see something too. Let us go and tell our father.'

"So they ran off in great excitement and woke Leeuw. 'Come, come quickly,' they said. 'Volstruis insults you by saying he is your equal. He lies sleeping under the trees with his mouth wide open, and we have peeped into it, and behold, he has no teeth! Come and see for yourself.'

"Leeuw bounded off quick-quick with the cubs at his tail.

"'Nier-r-r-r,' he growled, waking Volstruis. 'Nier-r-r-r. What is the meaning of this? You pretend you are my equal, and you haven't even got teeth.'

"'Teeth or no teeth,' said Volstruis, standing up wide awake, 'I killed more bucks than you did today. Teeth or no teeth, I'll fight you to show who's baas.'

"'Come on,' said Leeuw. 'Who's afraid? I'm just ready for you. Come on!'

"'No, wait a little,' said Volstruis. 'I've got a plan. You see that ant-heap over there? Well, you stand on one side of it, and I'll stand on the other side, and we'll see who can push it over first. After that we'll come out into the open and fight.'

"'That seems an all-right plan,' said Leeuw, and he thought to himself, 'I'm heavier and stronger, I can easily send the ant-heap flying on to old Three Sticks, and then spring over and kill him.'

"But wait a bit! It was not as easy as he thought. Every time he sprang at the ant-heap he clung to it as he was accustomed to cling to his prey. He had no other way of doing things. And then Volstruis would take the opportunity of kicking high into the air, sending the sand and stones into Leeuw's face, and making him howl and splutter with rage.

"Sometimes he would stand still and roar, and Volstruis would send a roar back from the other side.

"So they went on till the top of the ant-heap was quite loosened by the kicks and blows. Leeuw was getting angrier and angrier, and he could hardly see - his eyes were so full of dust. He gathered himself together for a tremendous spring, but, before he could make it, Volstruis bounded into the air and kicked the whole top off the ant-heap. Arré, but the dust was thick!

"When it cleared away, there lay Leeuw, groaning and coughing, with the great heap of earth and stones on top of him.

"'Ohé! Ohé!' wailed the cubs, 'Get up, my father. Here he comes, the Toothless One! He who has teeth only on his feet! Get up and slay him.'

"Leeuw shook himself free of the earth and sprang at Volstruis, but his eyes were full of sand, he could not see properly, so he missed. As he came down heavily, Volstruis shot out his strong right leg and caught Leeuw in the side. Sk-r-r-r-r! went the skin, and goops, goops! Over fell poor Oom Leeuw, with Volstruis's terrible claws - the teeth of old Two Toes - fastened into him.

"Volstruis danced on him, flapping and waving his beautiful black and white wings, and tearing the life out of Oom Leeuw.

"When it was all over, he cleaned his claws in the sand and waltzed away slowly over the veld to where his mate sat on the nest.

"Only the cubs were left wailing over the dead King of the Forest."

The usual babel of question and comment broke out at the close of the story, till at last Pietie's decided young voice detached itself from the general chatter.

"Outa, what made you say that about pulling the blankets over one's head and running to get near Mammie if one heard Volstruis bellowing at night? You know quite well that none of us would ever do it."

"Yes, yes, my baasje, I know," said Outa, soothingly. "I never meant anyone who belongs to the land of Volstruise. But other little masters, who did not know the voice of old Three Sticks - they would run to their mammas if they heard him."

"Oh, I see," said Pietie, accepting the apology graciously. "I was sure you could not mean a karroo farm boy."

"Is your story a parable, Outa?" asked little Jan, who had been doing some hard thinking for the last minute.

"Ach! And what is that, my little master?"

"A kind of fable, Outa."

"Yes, that's what it is, baasje," said Outa, gladly seizing on the word he understood, "a fable, a sort of nice little fable."

"But a parable is an earthly story with a heavenly meaning, and when Cousin Minnie tells us parables she always finds the meaning for us. What is the heavenly meaning of this, Outa?"

Little Jan's innocent grey eyes were earnestly fixed on Outa's face, as though to read from it the explanation he sought. For once the old native was nonplussed. He rubbed his red kopdoek, laid a crooked finger thoughtfully against his flat nose, scratched his sides, monkey-fashion, and finally had recourse once more to the kopdoek. But all these expedients failed to inspire him with the heavenly meaning of the story he had just told. Ach! These dear little ones, to think of such strange things! There they all were, waiting for his next words. He must get out of it somehow.

"Baasjes," he began, smoothly, 'there is a beautiful meaning to the story, but Outa hasn't got time to tell it now. Another time..."

"Outa," broke in Willem, reprovingly, "you know you only want to get away so that you can go to the old tramp-floor, where the volk are dancing tonight."

"No, my baasje, truly no!"

"And I wouldn't be surprised to hear that you had danced, too, after the way you have been jumping about here."

"Yes, that was fine," said Pietie, with relish. "'Voerts! There is one dead! Voerts! There is another!' Outa, you always say you are so stiff, but you can still kick well."

"Aja, baasje," returned Outa, modestly, "in my day I was a great dancer. No one could do the Vastrap better - and the Hondekrap - and the Valsrivier. Arré, those were the times!"

He gave a little hop at the remembrance of those mad and merry days, and yet another and another, always towards the passage leading to the kitchen.

"But the meaning, Outa, the heavenly meaning!" cried little Jan. "You haven't told us."

"No, my little baas, not tonight. Ask the Nonnie, she will tell you. Here she comes."

And as Cousin Minnie entered the room, the wily old native, with an agility not to be expected from his cramped and crooked limbs, skipped away, leaving her to bear the brunt of his inability to explain his own story.

The Famine

This story has been edited and adapted from Minnie Martin's book, Basutoland, Its Legends And Customs, originally published in 1903 by Nichols and Company, London.

In the years when the locusts visited the lands of the chief Makaota, and devoured all the food, the people grew thin and ill from starvation, and many of them died. When their food was all gone, they wandered in the lands and up the mountains, searching for roots upon which to feed. Now as they searched, Mamokete, the wife of the Chief Makaota, chanced to wander near some bushes, when suddenly she heard the most exquisite singing. She stopped to listen, but could see nothing. So she walked up to the bushes and looked in, and there she saw the most beautiful bird she had ever seen.

"Oh! ho! little bird," she cried, "help me, for I and my husband and children are starving. Our cattle are all dead, and we know not where to find food."

"Take me," sang the bird, "and I will be your food. Keep me safely, guard me well, and you shall never starve as long as I remain with you."

Thankfully the poor woman took the bird and hurried home with it. She placed it in an earthen pitcher and went to call her husband. When they returned, they opened the pitcher to look at the bird, when milk poured from the mouth of the pitcher, and the hungry people drank. How their hearts rejoiced over the gift which had been given them!

One day Makaota and his wife were going out to the lands to work, but before leaving they called their children, and bade them be good, and guard the pitcher well. The children promised to obey, but soon began to quarrel. Each wished to drink out of the pitcher first, and in their greediness they upset and broke the pitcher, and the bird flew out of the open door. Terrified at what they had done, the children ran after it, but when they got outside, there was no sign of the beautiful bird. It had completely vanished.

What grief now filled their hearts and the hearts of Makaota and Mamokete his wife! Hunger seized once more upon them, and despair filled their hearts. Day by day they sought the wonderful bird, but did not find her. At length, when the two children lay sick for want of food, and the parents' hearts were heavy with grief, there came again the wonderful singing, borne upon the evening wind. Nearer and nearer it came, and then they saw the lovely bird.

"I have come back," she said, "because the punishment has been enough. Take me, and your house shall prosper."

Gladly they took the beautiful bird in their hands, and vowed never again to let anger and greed drive her away from them, and so their house thrived, and peace and plenty dwelt not only in the house of Makaota, but in the whole village for ever after.

Jackal And Monkey

This story has been edited and adapted from James A. Honey's South-African Folk Tales, originally published in 1910 by The Baker and Taylor Company.

Every evening Jackal went to the Boer's kraal. He crept through the sliding door and stole a fat young lamb. This, clever Jackal did several times in succession. Boer set a trap for him at the door. Jackal went again and zip - there he was caught around the body by the noose. He swung and swayed high in the air and couldn't touch ground. The day began to dawn and Jackal became uneasy.

Monkey sat on a stone kopje. When it became light he could see the whole affair, and descended hastily to mock Jackal. He went and sat on the wall. "Ha, ha, good morning. So there you are hanging now, eventually caught."

"What? I caught? I am simply swinging for my pleasure, it is enjoyable."

"You fibber. You are caught in the trap."

"If you but realized how nice it was to swing and sway like this, you wouldn't hesitate. Come, try it a little. You feel so healthy and strong for the day, and you never tire afterwards."

"No, I won't. You are caught."

After a while Jackal convinced Monkey. He sprang from the kraal wall, and freeing Jackal, adjusted the noose around his own body. Jackal quickly let go and began to laugh, as Monkey was now swinging high in the air.

"Ha, ha, ha," he laughed. "Now Monkey is in the trap."

"Jackal, free me," he screamed.

"There, Boer is coming," shouted Jackal.

"Jackal, free me of this, or I'll break your playthings."

"No, Boer is coming with his gun, so you rest a while in the trap."

"Jackal, quickly make me free."

"No, here's Boer already, and he's got his gun. Good morning."

And with these parting words he ran away as fast as he could.

Boer came and saw Monkey in the trap. "So, so, Monkey, now you are caught. You are the fellow who has been stealing my lambs, hey?"

"No, Boer, no," screamed Monkey, "not I, but Jackal."

"No, I know you, you aren't too good for that.

"No, Boer, no, not I, but Jackal," Monkey stammered.

"Oh, I know you. Just wait a little," and Boer, raising his gun, aimed and shot poor Monkey dead.

The Chief And The Tigers

This story has been edited and adapted from Minnie Martin's book, Basutoland, Its Legends And Customs, originally published in 1903 by Nichols and Company, London.

There lived long ago a chief whose wife was as beautiful as the morning sun. Dear was she to the heart of her lord, and great was his sorrow when she grew sick. Many doctors and wise women tried to cure her, but in vain. Worse and worse she grew, till the people said she would surely die, and the heart of the chief became as water within him.

One day, as the shadows grew long on the ground, an old, old man came slowly to the village, and asked to see the chief. "Morena, my Master," he said, "I have heard of your trouble, and have come to help you. Your wife is ill of a great sickness, and she will die unless you can get a leopard's heart with which to make medicine for her to drink. See, I have here a wonderful stone which will help you, and some medicine for you to drink. Now wrap yourself in a leopard-skin. The medicine will make you wise to understand and to speak their tongue, so shall they look upon you as a brother. When you have drunk the medicine, take the stone in your hand,

and set out on your journey. When you come to the home of the leopards, you must live among them as one of themselves, until you can find yourself alone with one. Him must you quickly kill, and tear from his warm body his heart unbroken, and then, throwing away your leopard skin, you must flee to your home. The leopards will chase you, but when they come too near, you must throw down the stone in front of you and jump upon it, when it will become a great rock, from whose sides fire will dart forth, and burn any who try to climb it. Thus will you be saved from the power of the leopards, and your wife be restored to health."

Gratefully the chief did as the old man desired, and set off to seek the home of the leopards. Many days he wandered across the plains and over the mountains, into the unknown valleys beyond, and there he found those he sought. They greeted him joyfully, welcoming him as a brother

All except one, a young leopard of great beauty, who held back, and muttered, "This is no leopard but a man. He will bring misfortune upon us. Slay him, my brothers, before it be too late." But they heeded him not.

Not many days had passed, when all the leopards scattered themselves over the valley, and the chief found himself alone with the angry young leopard. Watching him patiently, he soon found the opportunity he sought, and, hastily killing him, he tore the still warm heart from the lifeless body, and throwing off his disguise, set off towards his home.

On, on he went, and still no sign of the leopards, but, as the sun sank to rest, they appeared in the distance, and he knew they would soon overtake him. When they were so close behind him that he heard the angry snap of their teeth, he threw down the stone the old man had given him, and sprang on to it. Instantly it became a great rock, even as the old man had said. Up came the leopards, each striving to be the first to tear the heart out of the chief, even as he had torn out their brother's heart, but the first one that reached the rock, sprang back with a howl of agony, and rolled over on his side - dead. The others all drew up in alarm, and dared not approach the stone, but spent many hours in wandering round and round the rock, and grinding their teeth at the chief, who calmly watched them from his seat on the top of the rock.

Just before dawn the leopards, now thoroughly tired, lay down, and soon were fast asleep. Carefully, silently, the chief crawled down from the rock, which immediately became again a small stone. Taking the stone in his hand, and holding close the precious heart, which was to restore his wife to health, he fled like a deer towards his village, which he now saw in the plain below. Should he reach it before the leopards caught him? The perspiration streamed from his body, his ears rang with strange noises, and his breath came in great gasps, but still he hurried on.

Presently he heard the leopards coming. There was no time even to look behind. He *must* reach the village before they overtook him. On, on, stumbling blindly over every obstacle, he staggered. How far away it still looked! Would his people *never* see him? Yes, at last he was seen. He could hear the shout of his men as they rushed to help him. Only a few more steps now and he would be safe. Bravely he tottered on, then stumbled and fell helpless, exhausted, as his men arrived, and carried him in triumph into the village, while the leopards, baffled and furious, retreated to their home beyond the mountains.

With song and dance the people kept festival, for their chief had returned in safety, and his beautiful wife, restored to perfect health, sat smiling by his side, receiving the loving congratulations of old and young, but the old man came not to join the throng, nor was he ever seen in their land again. Quietly as he had come, so he had gone, leaving no sign behind him.

Jackal's Bride

This story has been edited and adapted from James A. Honey's South-African Folk Tales, originally published in 1910 by The Baker and Taylor Company.

Jackal, it is said, married Hyena, and carried off a cow belonging to the ants, to slaughter for the wedding, and when he had slaughtered her, he put the cowskin over his bride, and when he had fixed a pole on which to hang the flesh, he placed on the top of the forked pole the hearth for the cooking, in order to cook upon it all sorts of delicious food.

Lion also came and he wished to go up. Jackal, therefore, asked his little daughter for a thong with which he could pull Lion up, and he began to pull him up, and when his face came near to the cooking-pot, he cut the thong in two, so that Lion tumbled down.

Then Jackal upbraided his little daughter with these words, "Why do you give me such an old thong?" And he added, "Give me a fresh thong."

She gave him a new thong, and he pulled Lion up again, and when his face came near the pot, which stood on the fire, he said, "open your mouth." Then he put into his mouth a hot piece of quartz which had been boiled together with the fat, and the stone went down, burning his throat. Thus Lion died.

Then the ants came running after the cow, and when Jackal saw them he fled. Then the ants beat the bride in her brookaross dress. Hyena, the bride, believing that it was Jackal, said, "You tawny rogue! Have you not played at beating long enough? Have you no more loving game than this?"

But when she had bitten a hole through the cowskin, and she saw that they were other people, then she fled, falling here and there, yet made her escape.

Lion's Illness

This story has been edited and adapted from James A. Honey's South-African Folk Tales, originally published in 1910 by The Baker and Taylor Company.

Lion, it is said, was ill, and they all went to see him in his suffering. But Jackal did not go, because the traces of the people who went to see him did not turn back. Thereupon, he was accused by Hyena, who said, "Though I go to look, yet Jackal does not want to come and look at the man's sufferings."

Then Lion let Hyena go, in order that she might catch Jackal, and she did so, and brought him.

Lion asked Jackal, "Why did you not come here to see me?"

Jackal said, "Oh, no! When I heard that my uncle was so very ill, I went to the witch doctor to consult him, whether and what medicine would be good for my uncle against the pain. The doctor said to me, 'Go and tell your uncle to take hold of Hyena and draw off her skin, and put it on while it is still warm. Then he will recover.' Hyena is one who does not care for my uncle's sufferings."

Lion followed his advice, got hold of Hyena, drew the skin over her ears and put it on, whilst she howled with all her might.

Jackal, Dove, And Heron

This story has been edited and adapted from James A. Honey's South-African Folk Tales, originally published in 1910 by The Baker and Taylor Company.

Jackal, it is said, came once to Dove, who lived on the top of a rock, and said, "Give me one of your little ones."

Dove answered, "I shall not do anything of the kind."

Jackal said, "Give me it at once! Otherwise, I shall fly up to you."

Then she threw one down to him.

He came back another day and demanded another little one, and she gave it to him.

After Jackal had gone, Heron came, and asked, "Dove, why do you cry?"

Dove answered him, "Jackal has taken away my little ones, and it is for this that I cry."

He asked her, "In what manner did he take them?"

She answered him, "When he asked me I refused him, but when he said, 'I shall at once fly up, therefore give me it,' I threw it down to him."

Heron said, "Are you such a fool as to give your young ones to Jackal, who cannot fly?" Then, with the admonition to give no more, he went away.

Jackal came again, and said, "Dove, give me a little one."

Dove refused, and told him that Heron had told her that he could not fly up.

Jackal said, "I shall catch him."

So when Heron came to the banks of the water, Jackal asked him, "Brother Heron, when the wind comes from this side, how will you stand?"

He turned his neck towards him and said, "I stand thus, bending my neck on one side."

Jackal asked him again, "When a storm comes and when it rains, how do you stand?"

He said to him, "I stand thus, indeed, bending my neck down."

Then Jackal beat him on his neck, and broke his neck in the middle.

Since that day Heron's neck is bent.

Lelimo And The Magic Cap

This story has been edited and adapted from Minnie Martin's book, Basutoland, Its Legends And Customs, originally published in 1903 by Nichols and Company, London.

Once long ago, when giants dwelt upon the earth, there lived in a little village, far up in the mountains, a woman who had the power of making magic caps. When her daughter Siloane grew old enough to please the eyes of men, her mother made her a magic cap.

"Keep this cap safely, my child, for it will protect you from the power of Lelimo, the giant. If you lose it, he will surely seize you and carry you away to his dwelling in the mountains, where he and his children will eat you."

Siloane promised to be very careful, and for a long time always carried the magic cap with her whenever she went beyond the village.

Now it was the custom each year for the maidens of the village to go to a certain spot, where the 'tuani' or long rushes grew, there to gather great bundles with which to make new mats for the floors of the houses. When the time came, Siloane and many more maidens set out for the place. The distance was great, and as they must reach their destination at the rising of the sun, they set off from the village at midnight.

Just as the sun rose from sleep, the maidens arrived at the graves on which the rushes grew. Soon all were busy cutting rushes and making mats. Siloane laid down her cap on one of the graves by which she was working. All day the maidens worked, and at sunset they started on their homeward journey. Soon the moon arose and lighted the land, and the light-hearted maidens went gaily singing on their way.

When they had gone some way, Siloane suddenly remembered she had left the magic cap on the grave where she had been sitting. Afraid to face her mother without it, she asked her companions to wait for her while she hurried back to fetch it.

Long the maidens waited, amusing themselves by telling stories and singing songs in the moonlight, but Siloane returned not. At length two girls set out to look for her, but when they reached the spot, no trace of her was to be found. Great was their dismay. How could they tell the news to her parents? Still there was nothing else to be done, and, with heavy hearts, they all returned to the village.

When Ma-Batu, the mother of Siloane, heard their story, she immediately set to work to make another magic cap, which she gave to her younger daughter Sieng, telling her to have it always by her, in case Siloane should need her help.

Meanwhile, Siloane had been taken captive by the giant as she was making her way back to recover her magic cap. When she felt Lelimo's heavy hand on her shoulder, she struggled frantically to get away, but her strength was as water against such a man, and he soon had her securely tied up in his big bag, made out of the skin of an ox.

Now when Lelimo saw Siloane, he was returning from a feast, and was very drunk, so that he mistook his way, and wandered long and far, until, in the morning, he came to a large hut, where he threw down the sack containing Siloane, and demanded a drink of the woman who stood in the door. She gave him some very strong juala beer, which made him more drunk than before.

While he was drinking, Siloane called softly from the sack, for she had recognised her mother's voice talking to the giant, and knew that he had brought her in some wonderful way to her father's house. Again she called, and this time her sister heard her, and hastened to undo the sack. She then hid Siloane, and, by the aid of the magic cap, she filled the sack with bees and wasps and closed it firmly.

When the giant came out from the hut, he picked up the sack and started for his own home. On his arrival there he again threw down the sack, and ordered his wife to kill and cook the captive girl he imagined he had brought home. His wife began to feel the sack in order to find out how big the girl was, but the bees became angry and stung her through the sack, which frightened her, and she refused to open it. Thereupon Lelimo called his son, but he also refused. In a great rage, the giant turned them both out of the house, and closed all the openings. He then made a great fire, and prepared to roast the girl.

When he opened the sack, the bees and wasps, who were by this time thoroughly furious, swarmed upon him, and stung him till he howled with agony, and, mad with pain, he broke down the door of the hut and rushed down to the river, into which he flung himself headfirst. In this position he was afterwards found by his wife, his feet resting on a rock above the water, his head buried in the mud of the river.

Such was the end of this wicked giant, who had been the terror of that part of the country for many, many years.

Cock And Jackal

This story has been edited and adapted from James A. Honey's South-African Folk Tales, originally published in 1910 by The Baker and Taylor Company.

Cock, it is said, was once overtaken by Jackal, and caught. Cock said to Jackal, "Please, pray first before you kill me, as the white man does."

Jackal asked, "In what manner does he pray? Tell me."

"He folds his hands in praying," said Cock.

Jackal folded his hands and prayed.

Then Cock spoke again, "You ought not to look about you as you do. You had better shut your eyes."

He did so, and Cock flew away, upbraiding at the same time Jackal with these words, "You rogue! Do you really pray?"

There sat Jackal, speechless, because he had been outdone.

The Judgment Of Baboon

This story has been edited and adapted from James A. Honey's South-African Folk Tales, originally published in 1910 by The Baker and Taylor Company.

One day, it is said, the following story happened:

Mouse had torn the clothes of Itkler, the tailor, who then went to Baboon, and accused Mouse with these words, "In this manner I come to you. Mouse has torn my clothes, but will not admit anything of it, and accuses Cat. Cat protests likewise her innocence, and says, 'Dog must have done it', but Dog denies it also, and declares Wood has done it. Wood throws the blame on Fire, and says, 'Fire did it'. Fire says, 'I have not, Water did it'. Water says, 'Elephant tore the clothes', and Elephant says, 'Ant tore them.' Thus a dispute has arisen among them. Therefore, I, Itkler, come to you with this proposition, Assemble the people and try them in order that I may get satisfaction."

Thus he spoke and Baboon assembled them for trial. Then they made the same excuses which had been mentioned by Itkler, each one putting the blame upon the other.

So Baboon did not see any other way of punishing them, save through making them punish each other. So, he said, "Mouse, give Itkler satisfaction."

Mouse, however, pleaded not guilty. But Baboon said, "Cat, bite Mouse." She did so.

He then put the same question to Cat, and when she exculpated herself, Baboon called to Dog, "Here, bite Cat."

In this manner Baboon questioned them all, one after the other, but they each denied the charge. Then he addressed the following words to them, and said,

"Wood, beat Dog.

Fire, burn Wood.

Water, quench Fire.

Elephant, drink Water.

Ant, bite Elephant in his most tender parts."

They did so, and since that day they cannot any longer agree with each other. Ant enters into Elephant's most tender parts and bites him. Elephant swallows Water. Water quenches Fire. Fire consumes Wood. Wood beats Dog. Dog bites Cat. And Cat bites Mouse.

Through this judgment Itkler got satisfaction and addressed Baboon in the following manner, "Yes! Now I am content, since I have received satisfaction, and with all my heart I thank you,

Baboon, because you have exercised justice on my behalf and given me redress."

Then Baboon said, "From today I will no longer be called Jan, but Baboon shall be my name."

Since that time Baboon walks on all fours, having probably lost the privilege of walking erect through this foolish judgment.

Morena-Y-A-Letsatsi, Or The Sun Chief

This story has been edited and adapted from Minnie Martin's book, Basutoland, Its Legends And Customs, originally published in 1903 by Nichols and Company, London.

In the time of the great famine, when our fathers' fathers were young, there lived across the mountains, many days' journey, a great chief, who bore upon his breast the signs of the sun, the moon, and eleven stars. Greatly was he beloved, and marvellous was his power. When all around were starving, his people had plenty, and many journeyed to his village to implore his protection. Amongst others came two young girls, the daughters of one mother. Tall and lovely as a deep still river was the elder, gentle and timid as the wild deer, and her they called Siloane (the tear-drop.)

Of a different mould was her sister Mokete. Plump and round were her limbs, bright as the stars her eyes, like running water was the music of her voice, and she feared not man nor spirit. When the chief asked what they could do to repay him for helping them in their need, Mokete replied, "Lord, I can cook, I can grind corn, I can make 'leting,' I can do all a woman's work."

Gravely the chief turned to Siloane and asked, "And you? What can you do?"

"Alas, lord!" Siloane replied, "what can I say, seeing that my sister has taken all words out of my mouth."

"It is enough," said the chief, "you shall be my wife. As for Mokete, since she is so clever, let her be your servant."

Now the heart of Mokete burned with black hate against her sister, and she vowed to humble her to the dust, but no one must see into her heart, so with a smiling face she embraced Siloane.

The next day the marriage feast took place, amidst great rejoicing, and continued for many days, as befitted the great Sun Chief. Many braves came from far to dance at the feast, and to delight the people with tales of the great deeds they had done in battle. Beautiful maidens were there, but none so beautiful as Siloane. How happy she was, how beloved! In the gladness of her heart she sang a song of praise to her lord:

"Great is the sun in the heavens,

And great are the moon and stars,

But greater and more beautiful

In the eyes of his handmaiden is my lord.

Upon his breast are the signs of his greatness,

And by their power I swear to love him

With a love so strong, so true,

That his son shall be in his image,

And shall bear upon his breast

The same tokens of the favour

Of the heavens."

Many moons came and went, and all was peace and joy in the hearts of the Sun Chief and his bride, but Mokete smiled darkly in her heart, for the time of her revenge approached. At length came the day, when Siloane should fulfil her vow, when the son should be born. The chief ordered that the child should be brought to him at once, that he might rejoice in the fulfilment of Siloane's vow. In the dark hut the young mother lay with great content, for had not Mokete assured her the child was his father's image, and upon his breast were the signs of the sun, the moon, and eleven stars?

Why then this angry frown on the chief's face, this look of triumph in the eyes of Mokete? What was this which she was holding covered with a skin? She turned back the covering, and, with a wicked laugh of triumph, showed the chief, not the beautiful son he had looked for, but an ugly, deformed child with the face of a baboon. "Here, my lord," Mokete said, "is the long-desired son. See how well Siloane loves you, see how well she has kept her vow! Shall I tell her of your heart's content?"

"Woman," roared the disappointed chief, "speak not thus to me. Take from my sight both mother and child, and tell my headman it is my will that they be destroyed before the sun hide his head in yonder mountains."

Sore at heart, angry and unhappy, the chief strode away into the lands, while Mokete hastened to the headman to bid him carry out his master's orders, but before they could be obeyed, a messenger came from the chief to say the child alone was to be destroyed, but

Siloane should become a servant, and on the morrow should witness his marriage to Mokete.

Bitter tears rolled down Siloane's cheeks. What evil thing had befallen her, that the babe she had borne, and whom she had felt in her arms, strong and straight, should have been so changed before the eyes of his father had rested upon him? Not once did she doubt Mokete. Was she not her own sister? What reason would she have for casting the "Evil Eye" upon the child? It was hard to lose her child, hard indeed to lose the love of her lord, but he had not banished her altogether from his sight, and perhaps someday the spirits might be willing that she should once again find favour in his sight, and should bear him a child in his own image.

Meanwhile Mokete had taken the real baby to the pigs, hoping they would devour him, for each time she tried to kill him some unseen power held her hand, but the pigs took the babe and nourished him, and many weeks went by - weeks of triumph for Mokete, but of bitter sorrow for Siloane.

At length Mokete thought of the child, and wondered if the pigs had left any trace of him. When she reached the kraal, she started back in terror, for there, fat, healthy, and happy, lay the babe, while the young pigs played around him. What should she do? Had Siloane seen him? No, she hardly thought so, for the child was in every way the image of the chief. Siloane would at once have known who he was.

Hurriedly returning to her husband, Mokete begged him to get rid of all the pigs, and have their kraal burnt, as they were all ill of a terrible disease. So the chief gave orders to do as Mokete desired, but the spirits took the child to the elephant which lived in the great bush, and told it to guard him.

After this Mokete was at peace for many months, but no child came to gladden the heart of her lord, and to take away her reproach. In her anger and bitterness she longed to kill Siloane, but she was afraid.

One day she wandered far into the bush, and there she beheld the child, grown more beautiful than ever, playing with the elephant. Mad with rage, she returned home, and gave her lord no rest until he consented to burn the bush, which she told him was full of terrible wild beasts, which would one day devour the whole village if they were not destroyed. But the spirits took the child and gave him to the fishes in the great river, bidding them guard him safely.

Many moons passed, many crops were reaped and Mokete had almost forgotten about the child, when one day, as she walked by the riverbank, she saw him, a beautiful youth, playing with the fishes. This was terrible. Would nothing kill him? In her rage she tore great rocks from their beds and rolled them into the water, but the spirits carried the youth to a mountain, where they gave him a wand.

"This wand," said they, "will keep you safe. If danger threatens you from above, strike once with the wand upon the ground, and a path will be opened to you to the country beneath. If you wish to return to this upper world, strike twice with the wand, and the path will reopen."

So again they left him, and the youth, fearing the vengeance of his stepmother, struck once upon the ground with his wand. The earth opened, showing a long narrow passage. Down this the youth went, and, upon reaching the other end, found himself at the entrance to a large and very beautiful village. As he walked along, the people stood to gaze at him, and all, when they saw the signs upon his breast, fell down and worshipped him, saying, "Greetings, lord!"

At length, he was informed that for many years these people had had no chief, but the spirits had told them that at the proper time a chief would appear who should bear strange signs upon his breast, and him the people were to receive and to obey, for he would be the chosen one, and his name should be Tsepitso, or the promise.

From that day the youth bore the name of Tsepitso, and ruled over that land, but he never forgotten his mother, and often wandered to the world above, to find out how she fared and to watch over her. On these journeys he always clothed himself in old skins, and covered up his breast that none might behold the signs. One day, as he wandered, he found himself in a strange village, and as he passed the well, a maiden greeted him, saying, "Stranger, you look weary. Will you not rest and drink of this fountain?"

Tsepitso gazed into her eyes, and knew what love meant. Here, he felt, was the wife the spirits intended him to wed. He must not let her depart, so he sat down by the well and drank of the cool, delicious water, while he questioned the maid. She told him her name was Ma Thabo, or Mother of Joy, and that her father was chief of that part of the country. Tsepitso told her he was a poor youth looking for work, whereupon she took him to her father, who consented to employ him.

One stipulation Tsepitso made, which was that for one hour every day before sunset he should be free from his duties. This was agreed to, and for several moons he worked for the old chief, and grew more and more in favour, both with him and with his daughter. The hour before sunset each day he spent amongst his own people, attending to their wants and giving judgment. At length he told Ma Thabo of his love, and read her answering love in her beautiful eyes. Together they sought the old chief, to whom Tsepitso told his story, and revealed his true self. The marriage was soon after celebrated, with much rejoicing, and Tsepitso bore his bride in triumph to his beautiful home in the world beneath, where she was received with every joy.

But amidst all his happiness Tsepitso did not forget his mother, and after the feasting and rejoicing were ended, he took Ma Thabo with him, for the time had at length come when he might free his mother for ever from the power of Mokete.

When they approached his father's house, Mokete saw them, and, recognising Tsepitso, knew that her time had come. With a scream she fled to the hut, but Tsepitso followed her, and sternly demanded his mother. Mokete only moaned as she knelt at her lord's feet. The old chief arose, and said, "Young man, I know not who you are, nor who your mother is, but this woman is my wife, and I pray you speak to her not thus rudely."

Tsepitso replied, "Lord, I am your son."

"Nay now, you are a liar," said the old man sadly, "I have no son."

"Indeed, my father, I am your son, and Siloane is my mother. Do you need proof of the truth of my words? Then look," and turning to the light, Tsepitso revealed to his father the signs upon his breast, and the old chief, with a great cry, threw himself upon his son's neck and wept. Siloane was soon called, and knew that indeed she had fulfilled her vow, that here before her stood in very truth the son she had borne, and a great content filled her heart. Tsepitso and Ma Thabo soon persuaded her to return with them, knowing full well that her life would no longer be safe were she to remain near Mokete, so, when the old chief was absent, in the dusk of the evening they departed to their own home.

When the Sun Chief discovered their flight, he determined to follow, and restore his beloved Siloane to her rightful place, but Mokete followed him, though many times he ordered her to return to the village, for never again would she be his wife, and that if she continued to follow him, he would kill her. At length he thought, "If I cut off her feet she will not be able to walk," so, turning round suddenly, he seized Mokete, and cut off her feet. "Now, you will leave me in peace, woman? Take care nothing worse befalls you." So saying, he left her, and continued his journey.

But Mokete continued to follow him, till the sun was high in the heavens. Each time he saw her close behind him, he stopped and cut off more of her legs, till only her body was left, even then she was not conquered, but continued to roll after him. Thoroughly enraged, the Sun Chief seized her, and called down fire from the heavens to consume her, and a wind from the edge of the world to scatter her ashes.

When this was done, he went on his way rejoicing, for surely now she would trouble him no more. Then as he journeyed, a voice rose in the evening air, "I follow, I follow, to the edge of the world, yes, even beyond, shall I follow you."

Placing his hands over his ears to shut out the voice, the Sun Chief ran with the fleetness of a young brave, until, at the hour when the spirits visit the abodes of men, he overtook Tsepitso and the two women, and with them entered the kingdom of his son.

How he won pardon from Siloane, and gained his son's love, and how it was arranged that he and Siloane should again be married, are old tales now in the country of Tsepitso. When the marriage feast was begun, a cloud of ashes dashed against the Sun Chief, and an angry voice was heard from the midst of the cloud, saying, "Nay, you shall not wed Siloane, for I have found you, and I shall claim you for ever."

Hastily the witch doctor was called to free the Sun Chief from the power of Mokete. As the old man approached the cloud, chanting a hymn to the gods, everyone gazed in silence. Raising his wand, the wizard made some mystic signs, the cloud vanished, and only a handful of ashes lay upon the ground.

Thus was the Evil Eye of Mokete stilled for evermore, and peace reigned in the hearts of the Sun Chief and his wife Siloane.

Lion And Baboon

This story has been edited and adapted from James A. Honey's South-African Folk Tales, originally published in 1910 by The Baker and Taylor Company.

Baboon, it is said, once worked bamboos, sitting on the edge of a precipice, and Lion stole upon him. Baboon, however, had fixed some round, glistening, eye-like plates on the back of his head. When, therefore, Lion crept upon him, he thought, when Baboon was looking at him, that he sat with his back towards him, and so he crept with all his might upon him.

When, however, Baboon turned his back towards him, Lion thought that he was seen, and hid himself. Thus, when Baboon looked at him, he crept upon him. When he was near him Baboon looked up, and Lion continued to creep upon him. Baboon said to himself, "Whilst I am looking at him he steals upon me."

When at last Lion sprung at him, Baboon lay down quickly upon his face, and Lion jumped over him, falling down the precipice, and was dashed to pieces.

When Lion Could Fly

This story has been edited and adapted from James A. Honey's South-African Folk Tales, originally published in 1910 by The Baker and Taylor Company.

Lion, it is said, used once to fly, and at that time nothing could live before him. As he was unwilling that the bones of what he caught should be broken into pieces, he made a pair of White Crows watch the bones, leaving them behind at the kraal whilst he went a-hunting.

But one day Great Frog came there, broke the bones in pieces, and said, "Why can men and animals live no longer?" And he added these words, "When he comes, tell him that I live at yonder pool, if he wishes to see me, he must come there."

Lion, lying in wait for game, wanted to fly up, but found he could not fly. Then he got angry, thinking that at the kraal something was wrong, and he returned home. When he arrived he asked, "What have you done that I cannot fly?"

Then they answered and said, "Someone came here, broke the bones into pieces, and said, 'If he want me, he may look for me at yonder pool!'"

Lion went, and arrived while Frog was sitting at the water's edge, and he tried to creep stealthily upon him. When he was about to get hold of him, Frog said, "Ho!" and, diving, went to the other side of the pool, and sat there. Lion pursued him, but as he could not catch him he returned home.

From that day, it is said, Lion walked on his feet, and also began to creep upon his game, and the White Crows became entirely dumb since the day that they said, "Nothing can be said of that matter."

The Village Maiden And The Cannibal

This story has been edited and adapted from Minnie Martin's book, Basutoland, Its Legends And Customs, originally published in 1903 by Nichols and Company, London.

The village was starving. There was no running away from the fact. The men's eyes were big and hungry-looking, and even the plumpest girl was thin. What was to be done? The maidens must go out to find roots. Perhaps the spirits would take pity on their starved looks and guide them to where the roots grew, so early in the morning all the maidens, led by the chief's two daughters, left the village to seek for food. They walked two by two, a maid and a little girl, side by side. Long they journeyed, and weary were their feet, yet they found nothing, and darkness was creeping over the land. So they laid themselves down to rest under the Great Above, with no shelter or covering over them, to wait for the coming dawn.

Next day as they journeyed, behold one of the children espied a root, another, and yet another, until all were busy digging up the precious food. Now a strange thing happened, for, while the maidens only found long thin roots, the children gathered only thick large ones. At length enough had been found to last the village for a time, so the girls set off to return home. As they came near the river they saw it was terribly flooded, and an old, old woman sat crooning upon the bank. As they approached they began to distinguish the words she was chanting:

"The Water Spirit loves not the thin roots,

They are the food of swine -

There is no safety for them.

But the large root, how good it is -

It is the food of spirits, even of the

Great Water Spirit.

Safety and strength are in it;

The water flows on, flows on."

"Mother," said the elder of the chief's daughters, approaching the old woman, 'tell us of your wisdom. How we shall cross this swollen river, for we are in haste to reach our home."

Without lifting her eyes from the water, the dame replied, "To the swollen river a swollen root, in each maid's right hand a root that is large, then cross and fear not."

Accordingly the maids chose their largest root, which they threw upon the water. Then each child chose two fat roots. One she gave to one of the elder maidens, the other she held in her own right hand, then two by two they stepped into the river and in safety gained the opposite bank. But when it came to the turn of the chief's two daughters, the child refused to give her sister one of her large roots, nor were threats or entreaties of any avail. The night was fast approaching, their companions were almost out of sight, and the river rolled at their feet, dark, swift, and deep.

At length the child relented, and soon the two girls were speeding after their friends, but it was too dark to see, and they missed their road and wandered far in the darkness. When midnight was fast approaching they saw a light shining near, and upon going up to it, found themselves at the door of a hut, over which a mat hung. "Let us ask for shelter for the night," said the elder girl, and shook the mat.

"Get up! Get up! Son of mine, and see if people are at the door, for I am hungry and would eat meat." The voice was that of a man, who was seated in front of some red-hot cinders in the middle of the hut.

The little boy ran to the door, and, upon seeing the two girls standing there, implored them to run away at once, as his father was a cannibal and would eat them up, but before they had time to do so, the old man appeared and dragged them into the hut.

Early the next morning the old cannibal left the hut to call two of his friends to share his feast. Before he left he securely fastened the two girls together, and told his son to watch them carefully.

Now, as soon as he was out of sight, there appeared at the door the old woman who yesterday had been sitting on the riverbank. She at once set the girls free, but told them she must cut off all their hair. When this was done, she took a little and buried it under the floor of the hut, another bunch she buried under the refuse heap outside, another near the spring, and yet another halfway up the hill. She then returned to the hut and burnt the remaining hair.

"Now, my children," said she, "you must fly to your home. I shall follow you under the ground, but your guide shall be a bee. Follow where it leads, and you will be safe." So saying, she led them to the door and drew down the mat.

"Run!" said the boy, "Make haste! There is the bee grandmother told you of. Follow quickly, lest my father find you and kill you."

Seeing a bee hovering near, the girls followed where it led. Presently they met two men, who stopped them, and asked, "Who are you? Are you not the two girls our friend has told us of? Did you not stay last night in a hut with an old man and a boy?"

"We know not of whom you speak," replied the girls. "We have seen no old man, nor little boy."

"Ho, ho! Is that true? But yes, we see it is true. He told us his victims had plenty of hair, but you have none. No, no, these are not they, these are only people." So saying, they allowed the girls to continue their journey.

Now when the old man and his friends found the girls had escaped, they were very angry, but the little boy said he did not think they could be very far away. The old man went out and began calling, but, as he called, there answered him a voice from the hair under the hut, another voice from the hair by the spring, another from the mountain, and so on from each spot where the old woman had buried the hair, until he became mad with rage and disappointment, then, guessing that witchcraft had been used, and that the two girls his friends had spoken to were indeed his intended victims, he set off in pursuit, but when he caught sight of them, they were almost at their father's village, and a large swarm of bees was between him and them, which, when he tried to overtake the girls, stung him so terribly that he howled with agony, and dared not approach any nearer. Thus the girls escaped, and returned to bring the light of day to their parents' eyes.

Lion Who Thought Himself Wiser Than His Mother

This story has been edited and adapted from James A. Honey's South-African Folk Tales, originally published in 1910 by The Baker and Taylor Company.

It is said that when Lion and Gurikhoisip, then the only man, together with Baboon, Buffalo, and other friends, were playing one day at a certain game, there was a thunderstorm and rain at Aroxaams. Lion and Gurikhoisip began to quarrel.

"I shall run to the rain-field," said Lion.

Gurikhoisip said also, "I shall run to the rain-field."

As neither would concede this to the other, they separated angrily. After they had parted, Lion went to tell his Mother those things which they had both said.

His Mother said to him, "My son! That Man whose head is in a line with his shoulders and breast, who has pinching weapons, who keeps white dogs, who goes about wearing the tuft of a leopard's tail, beware of him!"

Lion, however, said, "Why do I need to be on my guard against those whom I know?"

Lioness answered, "My Son, take care of him who has pinching weapons!"

But Lion would not follow his Mother's advice, and the same morning, when it was still pitch dark, he went to Aroxaams, and laid himself in ambush. Gurikhoisip also went that morning to the same place. When he had arrived he let his dogs drink, and then bathe. After they had finished they wallowed. Then also Man drank, and, when he had done drinking, Lion came out of the bush. Dogs surrounded him as his Mother had foretold, and he was speared by Gurikhoisip. Just as he became aware that he was speared, the dogs drew him down again. In this manner he grew faint.

While he was in this state, Gurikhoisip said to the dogs, "Let him alone now, that he may go and be taught by his Mother."

So the dogs let him go. They left him, and went home as he lay there. The same night Lion walked towards home, but whilst he was on the way his strength failed him, and he lamented:

"Mother! take me up!

Grandmother! take me up! Oh me! Alas!"

At the dawn of day his Mother heard his wailing, and said, "My Son, this is the thing which I told you about:

"'Beware of the one who has pinching weapons,

Who wears a tuft of leopard's tail,

Of him who has white dogs!

Alas! you son of her who is short-eared,

You, my short-eared child!

Son of her who eats raw flesh,

You flesh-devourer;

Son of her whose nostrils are red from the prey,

You with blood-stained nostrils!

Son of her who drinks pit-water,

You water-drinker!'"

How Khosi Chose A Wife

This story has been edited and adapted from Minnie Martin's book, Basutoland, Its Legends And Customs, originally published in 1903 by Nichols and Company, London.

In the days of our fathers' fathers there lived a rich chief who had only one wife, whom he loved so much that he would not take even one of the beautiful daughters of any other great chief to wife, not even when, after many years, no child was born to them.

"I will wait," said the old chief, "the spirits will relent before I die, for we will offer many sacrifices to them."

Accordingly the best of the flocks and herds were sacrificed, and the woman found favour in the eyes of the gods, and a daughter, beautiful as the morning, was born. So precious was this child in the eyes of her parents that they hid her from the sight of men, wrapping her in the skin of the crocodile, the sacred beast of the people. Because of this the people called her "Polomahache", or Crocodile Scale, and very few believed in her beauty, for they thought she must be deformed or terribly ugly to be hidden away under a covering always, but the maiden grew in beauty and grace, until her parents felt they must strive to find a youth worthy of her, if one was to be had upon the earth.

Now the greatest chief had a son who was dearer to him than all his wives or his other children, or even his flocks and herds, a son tall and straight as the spear, fleet of foot as the wild deer, and brave as the mighty lion of the mountains. This youth the people called Khosi, the fleet one.

At the time when Polomahache had become old enough to marry, Khosi had begun to think of taking a wife, and had sent round to the neighbouring villages requesting the people to send the prettiest girls for his inspection, naming a certain day upon which he would receive them. Upon the day named, very early in the morning, Polomahache, enveloped in her crocodile skin and accompanied by two female attendants, set out for Khosi's village. Many other damsels passed them with jest and laughter, bidding Polomahache remain at home, as her looks were enough to frighten even the bravest lover.

Now the custom was that each damsel should wash in the pool below the village of the expectant bridegroom-elect, and accordingly the pool below Khosi's village was soon thronged with merry, laughing girls, who were quite unconscious of the fact that Khosi was hidden in the branches of a tree close by, from where he could, unseen, inspect his would-be wives. While the other girls bathed, Polomahache remained quietly in the background, but when they had departed she stepped timidly down to the water's edge, where she stood hesitatingly, as if afraid to throw off her hideous covering.

Khosi, upon seeing her, hid himself more securely in the tree, exclaiming, "Ah! What wild beast have we here? Surely she does not hope that I shall choose her?"

"My child," said one of the attendants, "why do you stand in fear? Know you not that it is the custom of our tribe for the damsels to wash before they approach their master's house. Remove your covering, then, and be not afraid, for we are alone."

Reluctantly Polomahache did so, and stepped into the clear, cold water, revealing herself in all her beauty to the enraptured gaze of the spectator in the tree.

"Ha!" exclaimed Khosi, "What beauty, what eyes, what a face! She, and she alone, shall be my bride." And he continued to gaze upon her until, her bathing completed, she once more enveloped herself in the crocodile skin and departed to the village, when Khosi descended from his hiding-place and returned by another path to his home.

When all the maidens were assembled, Khosi, accompanied by his father and mother, came out from the hut and walked slowly along, carefully studying each maid as he passed. Many bright glances were shot at him, many maiden hearts fluttered in hopeful expectation, but one by one he passed them all until he came to little Polomahache, who had hidden herself away at the end of the row of maidens.

"Ho! Hèla! What is this?" exclaimed Khosi. "Surely this is no maiden, but some wild beast?"

"Indeed, Chief Khosi," replied a gentle voice from behind the skin, "I am but a poor maid who fears she cannot hope to find favour in the eyes of the Great One."

"Now truly, mother, this is the wife for me. Send all the other maidens away, for I will have none of them." So saying, Khosi turned and re-entered the hut.

His mother trembled with rage, for she thought Polomahache had bewitched her son, so she followed him into the hut, but when she heard what he had to tell her, she promised to try to arrange the marriage on condition that Khosi would manage to let her see Polomahache without the skin. Accordingly they arranged that Khosi was to see his bride alone, and if he could persuade her to throw off the crocodile skin he was to clap three times as if in pleasure, and his mother would come in.

When the sun was low in the heavens Khosi conducted Polomahache to his father's hut, where at length he persuaded her to throw off the skin. As it fell to the ground he clapped three times, exclaiming, "Oh! Beautiful as the dawn is my beloved, her eyes are tender as the eyes of a deer, her voice is like many waters."

As he spoke his mother entered, and being quite satisfied with the maiden's beauty, the marriage was soon arranged, and Khosi and his beautiful bride dwelt long in happiness and prosperity in the land of their fathers.

Lion Who Took A Woman's Shape

This story has been edited and adapted from James A. Honey's South-African Folk Tales, originally published in 1910 by The Baker and Taylor Company.

Some Women, it is said, went out to seek roots and herbs and other wild food. On their way home they sat down and said, "Let us taste the food of the field." Now they found that the food picked by one of them was sweet, while that of the others was bitter. The latter said to each other, "Look here! This Woman's herbs are sweet."

Then they said to the owner of the sweet food, "Throw it away and seek for something else."

So she threw away the food, and went to gather more. When she had collected a sufficient supply, she returned to join the other Women, but could not find them. She went down to the river, where Hare sat lading water, and said to him, "Hare, give me some water that I may drink."

But he replied, "This is the cup out of which my uncle Lion and I alone may drink."

She asked again, "Hare, draw water for me that I may drink."

But Hare made the same reply. Then she snatched the cup from him and drank, but he ran home to tell his uncle of the outrage which had been committed.

The Woman meanwhile replaced the cup and went away. After she had departed Lion came down, and, seeing her in the distance, pursued her on the road. When she turned round and saw him coming, she sang in the following manner:

"My mother, she would not let me seek herbs,

Herbs of the field, food from the field. Hoo!"

When Lion at last came up with the Woman, they hunted each other round a shrub. She wore many beads and arm-rings, and Lion said, "Let me put them on!" So she lent them to him, but he afterwards refused to return them to her.

They then hunted each other again round the shrub, till Lion fell down, and the Woman jumped upon him, and kept him there. Lion, uttering a form of conjuration, sang:

"My Aunt! it is morning, and time to rise;

Pray, rise from me!"

She then rose from him, and they hunted after each again other round the shrub, till the Woman fell down, and Lion jumped upon her. She then addressed him:

"My Uncle! it is morning, and time to rise;

Pray, rise from me!"

He rose, of course, and they hunted each other again, till Lion fell a second time. When she jumped upon him he sang:

"My Aunt! it is morning, and time to rise;

Pray, rise from me!"

They rose again and hunted after each other. The Woman at last fell down. But this time when she repeated the above conjuration, Lion sang:

"Hè Kha! Is it morning, and time to rise?"

He then ate her, taking care, however, to leave her skin whole, which he put on, together with her dress and ornaments, so that he looked quite like a woman, and then went home to her kraal.

When this counterfeit woman arrived, her little sister, crying, said, "My sister, pour some milk out for me."

She answered, "I shall not pour you out any."

Then the Child addressed their Mother, "Mama, do pour out some for me."

The Mother of the kraal said, "Go to your sister, and let her give it to you!"

The little Child said again to her sister, "Please, pour out for me!"

She, however, repeated her refusal, saying, "I will not do it."

Then the Mother of the kraal said to the little One, "I refused to let her seek herbs in the field, and I do not know what may have happened, go therefore to Hare, and ask him to pour out for you."

So then Hare gave her some milk, but her elder sister said, "Come and share it with me."

The little Child then went to her sister with her bamboo cup, and they both sucked the milk out of it. Whilst they were doing this, some milk was spilt on the little one's hand, and the elder sister licked it up with her tongue, the roughness of which drew blood, and this, too, the Woman licked up.

The little Child complained to her Mother, "Mama, sister pricks holes in me and sucks the blood."

The Mother said, "With what Lion's nature your sister went the way that I forbade her, and returned, I do not know."

Now the Cows arrived, and the elder sister cleansed the pails in order to milk them. But when she approached the Cows with a thong in order to tie their fore-legs, they all refused to be milked by her.

Hare said, "Why do not you stand before the Cow?"

She replied, "Hare, call your brother, and you two stand before the Cow."

Her husband said, "What has come over her that the Cows refuse her? These are the same Cows she always milks."

The Mother of the kraal said, "What has happened this evening? These are Cows which she always milks without assistance. What can have affected her that she comes home as a woman with a Lion's nature?"

The elder daughter then said to her Mother, "I shall not milk the Cows." With these words she sat down.

The Mother said therefore to Hare, "Bring me the bamboos, that I may milk. I do not know what has come over the girl."

So the Mother herself milked the cows, and when she had done so, Hare brought the bamboos to the young wife's house, where her husband was, but the wife did not give him anything to eat. But when at night-time she fell asleep, they saw some of the Lion's hair, which was hanging out where he had slipped on the Woman's skin, and they cried, "Verily! This is quite another being. It is for this reason that the Cows refused to be milked."

Then the people of the kraal began to break up the hut in which Lion lay asleep. When they took off the mats, they said, conjuring them, "If you are favourably inclined to me, O Mat, give the sound 'sawa'" (meaning, making no noise).

To the poles on which the hut rested they said, "If you are favourably inclined to me, O Pole, you must give the sound 'gara.'"

They also addressed the bamboos and the bed-skins in a similar manner.

Thus gradually and noiselessly they removed the hut and all its contents. Then they took bunches of grass, put them over the Lion, and lighting them, said, "If you are favourably inclined to me, O Fire, you must flare up, 'boo boo,' before you come to the heart."

So the Fire flared up when it came towards the heart, and the heart of the Woman jumped upon the ground. The Mother of the kraal picked it up, and put it into a calabash.

Lion, from his place in the fire, said to the Mother of the kraal, "How nicely I have eaten your daughter."

The Woman answered, "You have also now a comfortable place!"

Now the Woman took the first milk of as many Cows as had calves, and put it into the calabash where her daughter's heart was. The calabash increased in size, and in proportion to this the girl grew again inside it

One day, when the Mother of the kraal went out to fetch wood, she said to Hare, "By the time that I come back you must have everything nice and clean."

But during her Mother's absence, the girl crept out of the calabash, and put the hut in good order, as she had been used to do in former days, and said to Hare, "When Mother comes back and asks, 'Who has done these things?' you must say, 'I, Hare, did them.'" After she had done all, she hid herself on the stage.

When the Mother of the kraal came home, she said, "Hare, who has done these things? They look just as they used to when my daughter did them."

Hare said, "I did the things." But the Mother would not believe it, and looked at the calabash. Seeing it was empty, she searched the stage and found her daughter. Then she embraced and kissed her, and from that day the girl stayed with her Mother, and did everything as she was wont to do in former times, but she now remained unmarried.

The Story Of Takane

This story has been edited and adapted from Minnie Martin's book, Basutoland, Its Legends And Customs, originally published in 1903 by Nichols and Company, London.

Once long ago there lived in Basutoland a chief who had many herds of cattle and flocks of sheep, and also a beautiful daughter called Takane, the joy of his heart, and her mother's pride. Takane was loved by Masilo, her cousin, who secretly sought to marry her, but she did not like him, neither would she pay heed to his entreaties. At length Masilo wearied her so, that her anger broke forth, and with scorn she said, "Masilo, I like you not. Talk not to me of marriage, for I would rather die than be your wife."

"Ho! Is that true?" asked Masilo, the evil spirit shining out of his eyes. "Wait a little while, proud daughter of our chief, I will yet repay you for those words."

Takane laughed a scornful laugh, and, taking up her pitcher, stepped blithely down to the well. How stupid Masilo was, and why did he keep on troubling her? Did he think, the great baboon, that she would ever marry him? Ho! How stupid men were, after all!

But in Masilo's heart there raged a devil prompting him to deeds of revenge. It whispered in his ear, and, as he listened, he smiled, well pleased, for already he saw the desire of his heart within his reach. Patience and a little cunning, and she should be his.

The next day Masilo obtained his uncle's consent to his giving a feast at a small village across the river for youths and maidens, as was the custom of his tribe. He then paid a visit to the old witch-doctor, who promised to send a terrible hailstorm upon the village in the middle of the feast. Next he went to all the people of the village, and, because he was a chief's son, and had power in the land, and they were afraid to offend him, he made them promise that none of them would allow Takane to enter their huts, but he said no word of the hailstorm, only he told the people the evil eye would smite them if they disobeyed him.

Early the next day all the villages were astir with excitement, the youths set out in companies by themselves, the maidens following later, singing and dancing as they went. How lovely Takane looked, her face and beautifully rounded limbs shining with fat and red clay, the bangles on her arms and ankles burnished until human endeavour could do no more. Soon all were assembled, and dancing, singing, feasting, and gladness held sway.

Suddenly the sky grew dark, the rain-god frowned upon the village, and hail poured in fury down upon the feast. Away ran old and young, seeking shelter in the friendly huts. Takane alone remained outside. As she ran from hut to hut, the people crowded to the doorway, and, when she implored them to take her in, they replied that indeed they would gladly do so, but how could they find room for even one more? Did she not see how some of them were almost outside the door already? At length she came to a hut in which there was only one old woman, sitting shivering over a small fire. "Mother," exclaimed Takane, "I pray you, let me come in, for I am nearly dead already."

The old woman placed herself in the doorway, exclaiming, "Go away, don't you see my house is full?" But the girl gently pushed her aside and entered.

After the storm had passed, the merry-makers returned to their homes, Masilo alone remaining behind, in the hope of discovering Takane's dead body, or hearing something of her fate. As he wandered here and there, he saw her coming towards him, unconscious of his presence, and evidently on her way to cross the river. Quickly he hid behind a huge boulder until she had passed, when he cautiously followed her, overtaking her just as she reached the bank of the river. Now by this time the river was getting almost too full to cross in safety, and the Water Spirit was angrily murmuring, for he wanted a sacrifice of a human being to satisfy him. Masilo went up to Takane, who stood hesitating whether to cross or not, and, seizing her by the hand, drew her into the river, until the water came up to her neck.

"Will you marry me now, Takane, or shall I let the Water Spirit have you? I know you cannot swim, so if you won't marry me, I shall take you into the deep hole by that tree and push you in. Say, now, will you marry me?"

"No, Masilo, I will never marry you, never. Let the Water Spirit take me first." She struggled to free her hand, but he was strong, and he held her fast. Again he drew her farther into the river, until the water reached her lips.

"Now, Takane, is not life with me better than death with the Water Spirit for husband? Say, will you marry me now?"

"I choose rather death in the black pool, with the cold stones for my bed and the water for my covering, than life with you as my husband. Haste, haste, for I am weary and would sleep."

Her continued refusal to marry him so infuriated Masilo, that, seizing her by the hair of her head, he swam out towards the pool, into which he pushed her with a fierce laugh, saying, "There! Go down and drown! It is too late now to change your mind." He then turned, and in a few moments reached the bank, and, without one backward glance, walked off to his hut.

Now a wonderful thing happened to Takane. When Masilo pushed her into the pool, the hungry water took her swiftly down towards the tree which grew out of the middle of the river. She did not sink, because her skin mantle was not yet wet through, and, as she passed under the tree, the mantle caught in a low branch and held her firmly. There she remained for some time, vainly trying to pull herself up into the tree. At length she succeeded in doing so, and for the moment at any rate was safe, but, as she looked at the water all round her, and realized that even when the river was low she could not reach the bank unaided, she felt that it would be better to drown at once than to die a slow death from starvation, which seemed the only fate before her if she remained in the tree. Still, something might happen. Someone might pass and see her. Yes, she would wait at least a little while. So, arranging herself as comfortably as she could, she prepared to pass the night in the tree.

The next morning Masilo came down to the river with the cows. Takane hid herself as much as possible, but his sharp eyes soon discovered her.

"Oh, ho! What strange bird is that?" he exclaimed. "How came it in the tree? I must try to catch it." Then, seeing that Takane remained motionless, he sat down on the bank and began to eat his bogobe with great enjoyment. "See what nice bread I have. Are you not hungry, Takane? Shall I send you some? But no, you do not need it. You are so fat, you will live for a long time. Well, I must go away now, but I will come again tomorrow. It is nice to see the dear little Takane so happy."

The next day Masilo came again, and ate his breakfast on the riverbank, taunting Takane all the while. This he did on several following days, until Takane became so weak that she neither heard nor saw him, and would have fallen into the water were it not that her mantle held her firmly to the tree. Meanwhile, there was mourning in her father's house and village, for all thought she had been drowned in trying to cross the river after the storm.

One day, Takane's little brother followed Masilo when he took the cattle out to graze. When they came near the river, Masilo told the child not to come any farther, saying if he was a good boy, and did what he was told, he would get a present of some little birds which were in a tree in the river. Masilo then left the child and paid his daily visit to Takane, but the little boy, full of curiosity, followed unseen, and to his great astonishment saw, not a bird's-nest, with the promised young, but his sister Takane, almost unrecognisable from starvation. He listened for a little while to the conversation, then, fearing Masilo's anger if he were discovered, he crept back to the herd. When Masilo returned, he told the child the birds were not quite big enough to leave their nest.

The little boy then went home and told his parents what he had seen. They made him promise to keep his secret, then, calling their medicine man, they hurriedly took counsel together. Late that night, when the village was wrapped in darkness, the parents of Takane and the medicine man set out for the spot where the girl was hidden. The medicine man called upon the spirit of the water to aid them, and soon Takane lay in her mother's arms, too weak even to speak. Slowly and tenderly they bore her back to her home, where for days she lay between life and death. Masilo and the other villagers were told that a sick stranger was in the hut, therefore they must not enter, and, as this is the custom of the people, they thought nothing more of it. Masilo, it is true, had been down to the river and had found Takane gone, but he only thought that at last she had fallen into the water and been drowned. Several times he went down to see if the Water Spirit had given up its victim, but no sign of Takane's real fate came to warn him.

When two moons had come and gone, the old chief saw that the time to punish Masilo had come, so, calling all his people to assemble on a certain day, he made preparations for a great feast. When the day came, the people all assembled in the open space in front of the khotla, the court-house, leaving a wide path from the chief's hut to the centre of the open space. This path was carpeted with new mats, and skin karosses were laid on the ground for the chief and his family to sit upon. Masilo, by right of his near relationship to the chief, took a prominent place in the inner circle, while, unknown to him, several warriors quietly took their stand immediately behind him.

Presently the old chief issued from his hut, followed by his chief councillor and medicine man, and behind them came Takane's mother, leading by the hand Takane herself, no longer a living skeleton, but plump, smiling, and lovely as ever. A stir like the beginning of a storm shook the people, while Masilo, with a wild cry, turned to escape, but was quickly caught by the armed warriors, who had remained motionless behind him. Briefly the old chief related the story, then, raising his hand and pointing at the terrified Masilo, he cried, "What, my children, shall be the fate of this toad?"

With one voice, the people answered, "The cruel death for him! The cruel death for him!"

A smile of approval passed over the chief's face, and, making a sign to the warriors who held Masilo, he turned his back on the trembling wretch, who was dragged off to a distance and tortured to death, while the village feasted and danced.

When darkness once again enfolded the land, the dead body of Masilo was taken to a secret spot and buried, and life at the village returned to its daily duties, but the spirit of Masilo could not rest, and still strove to possess Takane, as his body had longed for her.

One day the daughters of the village, accompanied by Takane, went forth to gather reeds for the making of mats. They wandered far in their search, and were growing weary, when one of them cried, "See! There are reeds, beautiful reeds, as many as we shall need."

They looked and saw, just as their companion had said, a small bed of beautiful reeds. Soon all were busily engaged in cutting down armfuls of the desired plant, but Takane, being a chief's daughter, was not allowed to work as hard as the other girls, and soon seated herself down to rest in the middle of the reed bed.

When the sun was low in the sky the girls prepared to return home, but Takane could not rise from the ground, nor could her companions lift her. Again and again they tried to move her, but to no purpose, she seemed to have become rooted to the ground. Finally, she persuaded them all to return and obtain help from the village.

"Will you not be afraid, sister, if we leave you alone?" they asked.

"Of what shall I be afraid?" Takane replied. "It is yet light, and the home is near. Haste, for I am hungry, and the night is coming."

The girls then left her and ran home. No sooner had they disappeared, than Takane heard a noise amongst the reeds behind her, and, looking round, she saw Masilo standing there.

"Oh, ho! Takane! You are mine at last! Guessed you not that this was my grave, and that it was I who held you firmly to the ground, so that not even all your companions could raise you? Come now, for we must hasten, lest we be caught by your father's people. By the spirits of my fathers, I have sworn that you shall be my wife."

"But you yourself are a spirit. How, then, can you marry me, and what need have you of a wife? Are you going to kill me even as you were killed?"

"True, I *was* a spirit, but I am now a man, and you are my wife. Come, for I tarry no longer."

So saying, he seized her hand and began to run with her away from their old home, while she, filled with superstitious dread, offered only slight resistance. On they ran, ever onward, all through the night and far into the new day. At length, utterly weary, Takane lay down, and refused to go any farther. All around them were strange mountains and valleys, but no sign of human habitation. Here, then, Masilo resolved to remain, and here he built his hut, with the aid of Takane, who, now that she was powerless to escape, became a happy and devoted wife, obeying Masilo as even a wife should.

Soon other wanderers came to dwell near them, and before many years passed Masilo was chief of a happy, prosperous little village, and Takane the mother of sons and daughters whose beauty made her heart glad.

Lion's Defeat

This story has been edited and adapted from James A. Honey's South-African Folk Tales, originally published in 1910 by The Baker and Taylor Company.

The wild animals, it is said, were once assembled at Lion's. When Lion was asleep, Jackal persuaded Little Fox to twist a rope of ostrich sinews, in order to play a trick on Lion. They took ostrich sinews, twisted them, and fastened the rope to Lion's tail, and the other end of the rope they tied to a shrub. When Lion awoke, and saw that he was tied up, he became angry, and called the animals together. When they had assembled, Lion said:

"What child of his mother and father's love,

Whose mother and father's love has tied me?"

Then the animal to whom the question was first put answered:

"I, child of my mother and father's love,

I, mother and father's love, I have not done it."

All of the animals answered the same, but when he asked Little Fox, Little Fox said:

"I, child of my mother and father's love,

I, mother and father's love, have tied you!"

Then Lion tore the rope made of sinews, and ran after Little Fox.

But Jackal said, "My boy, you son of lean Mrs. Fox, you will never be caught."

Truly Lion was thus beaten in running by Little Fox.

Historical Notes

This section contains some brief biographical notes about the original collectors and their books featured in this collection. These notes have been adapted from those primarily on Wikipedia along with other supporting sources and notes.

W.H.I. Bleek

Wilhelm Heinrich Immanuel Bleek was born in Berlin on 8 March 1827. He was the eldest son of Friedrich Bleek, Professor of Theology at Berlin University and Augusta Charlotte Marianne Henriette Sethe. He graduated from the University of Bonn in 1851 with a doctorate in linguistics, after a period in Berlin where he went to study Hebrew and where he first became interested in African languages. Bleek's thesis featured an attempt to link North African and Khoikhoi (or what were then called Hottentot) languages – the thinking at the time being that all African languages were connected. After graduating in Bonn, Bleek returned to Berlin and worked with a zoologist, Dr Wilhelm K H Peters, editing vocabularies of East African languages. His interest in African languages was further developed during 1852 and 1853 by learning Egyptian Arabic from Professor Karl Richard Lepsius, whom he met in Berlin in 1852.

Bleek was appointed official linguist to Dr William Balfour Baikie's Niger Tshadda Expedition in 1854. Ill-health (a tropical fever) forced his return to England where he met George Grey and John William Colenso, the Anglican Bishop of Natal, who invited Bleek to join him in Natal in 1855 to help compile a Zulu grammar.

In 1859 Bleek briefly returned to Europe in an effort to improve his poor health but returned to the Cape and his research soon after. In 1861 Bleek met his future wife, Jemima Lloyd, at the boarding house where he lived in Cape Town (run by a Mrs Roesch), while she was waiting for a passage to England, and they developed a relationship through correspondence. She returned to Cape Town from England the following year.

Bleek married Jemima Lloyd on 22 November 1862. The Bleeks first lived at The Hill in Mowbray but moved in 1875 to Charlton House. Jemima's sister, Lucy Lloyd, joined the household, became his colleague, and carried on his work after his death.

When Grey was appointed Governor of New Zealand, he presented his collection to the National Library of South Africa on condition that Bleek be its curator, a position he occupied from 1862 until his death in 1875. In addition to this work, Bleek supported himself and his family by writing regularly for *Het Volksblad* throughout the 1860s and publishing the first part of his *A Comparative Grammar of South African Languages* in London in 1862. The second part was also published in London in 1869 with the first chapter appearing in manuscript form in Cape Town in 1865. Unfortunately, much of Bleek's working life in the Cape, like that of his sister-in-law after him, was characterised by extreme financial hardship which made his research even more difficult to continue with.

Bleek's first contact with San people (Bushmen) was with prisoners at Robben Island and the Cape Town Gaol and House of Correction, in 1857. He conducted interviews with a few of these prisoners, which he used in later publications. These people all came from the Burgersdorp and Colesberg regions and variations of one similar-sounding "Bushman" language. Bleek was particularly keen to learn more about this "Bushman" language and compare it to examples of "Bushman" vocabulary and language earlier noted by Hinrich Lichtenstein and obtained from missionaries at the turn of the 19th century.

In 1863 resident magistrate Louis Anthing introduced the first |Xam-speakers to Bleek. He brought three men to Cape Town from the Kenhardt district to stand trial for attacks on farmers (the prosecution was eventually waived by the Attorney General). In 1866 two San prisoners from the Achterveldt near Calvinia were transferred from the Breakwater prison to the Cape Town prison, making it easier for Bleek to meet them. With their help, Bleek compiled a list of words and sentences and an alphabetical vocabulary.

In 1870 Bleek and Lloyd, by now working together on the project to learn "Bushman" language and record personal narratives and folklore, became aware of the presence of a group of 28 |Xam prisoners (San from the central interior of southern Africa) at the Breakwater Convict Station and received permission to relocate one prisoner to their home in Mowbray so as to learn his language. The prison chaplain, Revd Fisk, was in charge of the selection of this individual – a young man named |a!kunta. But because of his youth, |a!kunta was unfamiliar with much of his people's folklore and an older man named ||kabbo was then permitted to accompany him. ||kabbo became Bleek and Lloyd's first real teacher, a title by which he later regarded himself. Over time, members of ||kabbo's family and other families lived with Bleek and Lloyd in Mowbray, and were interviewed by them. Amongst the people interviewed by Bleek was !Kweiten-ta-Ken. Many of the ||Xam-speakers interviewed by Bleek and Lloyd were related to one another. Bleek and Lloyd learned and wrote down their language, first as lists of words and phrases and then as stories and narratives about their lives, history, folklore and remembered beliefs and customs.

Bleek, along with Lloyd, made an effort to record as much anthropological and ethnographic information as possible. This included genealogies, places of origin, and the customs and daily life of the informants. Photographs and measurements were also taken of all their informants in accordance with the norms of scientific research of the time in those fields. More intimate and personal painted portraits were also commissioned of some of the |Xam teachers.

Although Bleek and Lloyd interviewed other individuals during 1875 and 1876, most of their time was spent interviewing only six individual ||Xam contributors. Bleek wrote a series of reports on the language and the literature and folklore of the ||Xam-speakers he interviewed, which he sent to the Cape Secretary for Native Affairs. This was first in an attempt to gain funding to continue with his studies and then also to make Her Majesty's Colonial Government aware of the need to preserve San folklore as an important part of the nation's heritage and traditions. In this endeavour Bleek must surely have been influenced by Louis Anthing.

Bleek died in Mowbray on 17 August 1875, aged 48, and was buried in Wynberg Anglican cemetery in Cape Town along with his two infant children, who had died before him. His all-important work recording the ||Xam language and literature was continued and expanded by Lucy Lloyd, fully supported by his wife Jemima. In his obituary in the South African Mail of 25 August 1875, he was lauded in the following terms: 'As a comparative philologist he stood in the foremost rank, and as an investigator and authority on the South African languages, he was without peer'.

L.C. Lloyd

Lucy Catherine Lloyd was born in Norbury in England on 7th November 1834. Her father, William H.C. Lloyd, Archdeacon of Durban, was the rector of Norbury and vicar of Ranton, two villages in western England in Staffordshire. He was also chaplain to the Earl of Lichfield, to whom he was related through his mother. Lucy Lloyd's mother was Lucy Anne Jeffreys, also a minister's daughter, who died in 1842 when Lucy was eight. Lucy Lloyd was the second of four daughters. Her father remarried in 1844 and had 13 additional children with his new wife. After her mother's death, Lucy and her sisters lived with their maternal uncle and his wife, Sir John and Caroline Dundas, from whom they received a private and apparently liberal education.

In 1847 Robert Gray was consecrated Bishop of Cape Town. And William Lloyd was sent to Durban along with his family in April 1849, when Lucy was 14, as colonial and military chaplain to the Colony of Natal's British forces. In 1852 Gray established the Diocese of Natal with John William Colenso as its first bishop. Colenso established his residence at Bishopstowe, near Pietermaritzburg and a party of 45 accompanied him, including the young Wilhelm Bleek who was to assist Colenso as anthropologist and philologist. William Lloyd later became archdeacon of Durban.

The Lloyd family had limited financial means in Durban even though the four older girls had inherited some money from their mother. Lucy and her sisters are said to have had liberal and unorthodox views and Lucy had trained as a teacher. Lucy and Jemima (who was to marry Wilhelm Bleek) were very close, and both were repelled by their father whom they thought to be a hypocrite. After Lucy had refused to allow him to spend her inheritance he threw her out of their home and she went to stay on a farm owned by people called the Middletons.

In 1858 Lucy became engaged to the sweet and widely travelled man George Woolley, the son of a minister. According to Lucy's sister Jemima the Middletons were wretched people who sowed distrust and pain between the couple. Lucy broke off the engagement, but she regretted this all her life, blaming herself for George's early miserable death. In a letter she wrote much later to her niece, Helma, on the occasion of the latter's engagement she said: 'May yours (with your dear Mother beside you), have a very different ending. I missed my dear Mother so sorely then, and the loving counsel and advice, which she could have given me. I had only my own theories and inexperience to go upon.'

Lucy's sister, Jemima, married Wilhelm Bleek on 22 November 1862 and they had seven children, five of whom survived to adulthood. In the same year as his marriage, Bleek was appointed curator of the Grey Collection at the South African Library in Cape Town.

Lucy travelled to Cape Town from Durban aboard the Natal mail steamer, the SS Waldensian, in October 1862, for the wedding of her sister. The ship ran aground on a reef near Cape Agulhas and, although the passengers and crew were rescued, Lucy lost most of her possessions and wedding gifts, managing to retrieve only a pair of vases for her sister (which she carried on her lap in the lifeboat) and a set of Sir Walter Scott's novels that had washed ashore in good condition as they were wrapped in waterproof packaging.

Lucy settled with her sister and Wilhelm after their marriage. After living at first in New Street, the Bleek family moved to The Hill in Mowbray. Lucy started her work with oral histories on the arrival of the first ǀXam (Cape Bushman) speaker at Mowbray in 1870, after which she was responsible for two-thirds of the texts recorded until Bleek's death and the publication of their second report to the Cape Parliament in 1875. After Bleek's death, and true to the desire expressed in a codicil to his will written in 1871, Lucy continued working on their joint Bushman studies with the support of her sister, Bleek's widow, Jemima. While Lucy would undoubtedly have done this anyway, his request must surely have bestowed on her work the credibility that, in those days, was usually reserved for male scholars and researchers.

Lucy was appointed curator of the Grey Collection as successor to Bleek after his death in 1875, at half his salary, a position she accepted reluctantly. During this time she worked with the Grey Collection and at editing various manuscripts collected by Bleek, as well as continuing with her ǁXam research in her own time. She began corresponding with George W. Stow in 1875 about his copies of Bushman art, and in 1876 he proposed a book that would eventually be published (with Lucy's support) in an incomplete form as *The Native Races of Southern Africa*. Lucy also played an important role in the founding of the SA Folklore Society, for which she acted as secretary for a while, and in the founding of the *Folklore Journal* in 1879.

Lucy's services at the South African Library were terminated in 1880 when Dr Theophilus Hahn was appointed, after a long and painful saga, in her place. Her relationship with the library had been fraught, and particularly with the Cape Colony's Secretary-General for Education Langham Dale who made the new appointment. She thought Hahn to be a fool and his appointment a disaster. Lloyd and the trustees of the Grey Collection, who supported her, took the case to the Supreme Court for judgment. The appointment, however, went ahead. Hahn resigned two years later, after which no custodian of the collection was appointed.

After Stow's death in 1882, Lloyd purchased his tracings and copies of Bushman paintings as well as the manuscript of *Native Races* from his wife, Fanny Stow. Lucy then engaged the services of the historian George McCall Theal to work with her on the manuscript and edit it. It was published in London in 1905 along with some photographic images taken from Lucy's own collection.

Lucy Lloyd and her sister Fanny went to England for a time in 1883, for financial and health-related reasons. Lucy's letters show her to have been ill at the time. Indeed, she described herself as having endured 'years of overwork and many of ill-health'. After the loss of her position at the South African Library, the family had found themselves in a precarious financial position with too many mouths to feed – at times, whole families, numbers of adults as well as children, often in poor health, lived in their home – and Lucy's last recorded work with the Bushmen appears to have been in 1884. All in all, at least 17 people had lived in the Mowbray household between 1870 and 1884, some for extended periods. Expenses included food, clothing and tobacco (according to

Bleek's list of expenses for 1871 he also budgeted for the arrival of the informants' wives). After Bleek's death in 1875, followed by the loss of Lloyd's job, Jemima Bleek and Lucy Lloyd were responsible for the upkeep of their various guests and their families, as well as their own sisters and young children.

As a result of these financial constraints, Jemima Bleek moved her family to Germany in 1884 to stay with relatives and receive schooling there, and it appears that the other Lloyd sisters joined them. Lucy Lloyd is believed to have gone to Europe in 1887 – around this time she trained her niece Dorothea in Bushman research – and she moved between Germany, Switzerland, England and Wales, with occasional trips to the Cape around 1905 and 1907. She returned permanently to South Africa in 1912. The Bleek family remained in Germany for the following 21 years.

Lucy Lloyd submitted a third report to the Cape Government concerning 'Bushman Researches', dated London 8 May 1889, in which she added 4,534 half-pages or columns to the collection. In 1911 a selection of texts from Bleek and Lloyd's extraordinary project – and a considerable achievement given Lloyd's personal circumstances at the time – was edited by her and published as *Specimens of Bushman Folklore*.

In 1913 Lloyd received an honorary doctorate from the University of the Cape of Good Hope in recognition of her contribution to research. In the words of the time, the citation read: '…an original production worthy of the highest praise. It is not only a masterly exposition of the folklore of a vanishing race that has remained primitive, but the philological value of the work is greater still, and the work will remain an authority on the language of the Bushman and kindred races.' She was the first woman to receive this degree in South Africa.

Lucy Lloyd died at Charlton House on 31 August 1914 at the age of 79, and is buried in the Wynberg cemetery in Cape Town near her nieces and nephew and Wilhelm Bleek himself.

Levine Henrietta Samuelson

To date I have not been able to uncover any biographical data for this author. The preface to Samuelson's book and publisher details are limited in any personal detail.

James A. Honey

To date I have not been able to uncover any biographical data for this author. The preface to Honey's book and publisher details are limited in any personal detail.

Sanni Metelerkamp

Sanni Metelerkamp was born in 1867 in Knysna, South Africa. She was an author and playwright. She was the great-granddaughter of George Rex, who founded the town of Knysna, for whom she wrote a biography, *George Rex of Knysna: The Authentic Story*.

Her one collection of folklore was *Outa Karel's Stories: South African Folk-Lore Tales*. In the preface, she writes about how these folk tales are commonly known by all children in the region, and she shared them because they weren't told by firelight anymore, and needed to preserved.

Her great-uncle was Frank Rex, whom the family claim wrote the play *Kaatjie Kekkelbek*, and her uncle was Frank Muller Rex, editor of the *Oudshoorn Courant*, who was also involved with the first performance of C.J. Langenhoven's *Die Hoop van Suid-Afrika*.

Sanni Metelerkamp passed away in 1945.

Minnie Martin

Minnie Amy Clara Martin was born in London. She was the daughter of Louis Martin, a Frenchman, and raised by her mother's family. She trained as a journalist.

In 1911 she married John Alcindor, and was disowned by her family. The pair had three children, John (born 1912), Cyril (born 1914) and Roland, known as Bob (born 1917). She also helped her husband in his medical practice on the Harrow Road in West London. Together with her husband, Minnie was also active in the Pan-Africanist movement. She was one of only two white women to serve on the committee of the African Progress Union, which John Alcindor led from 1921 onwards.

After her husband died in 1924, Minnie Alcindor established Remi House, a hostel for African students, in Arundel Gardens. However financial difficulties forced her to close the hostel. She later moved to Canvey Island, where she ran a club, Claremont. The singer Paul Robeson visited the family there. She died in 1961.

Andrew Lang

Andrew Lang FBA was a Scottish poet, novelist, literary critic, and contributor to the field of anthropology. He is best known as a collector of folk and fairy tales. The Andrew Lang lectures at the University of St Andrews are named after him.

Lang was born on 31st March 1844 in Selkirk. He was the eldest of the eight children born to John Lang, the town clerk, and his wife Jane Plenderleath Sellar, who was the daughter of Patrick Sellar, factor to the first duke of Sutherland. On 17th April 1875, he married Leonora Blanche Alleyne, youngest daughter of C. T. Alleyne of Clifton and Barbados. She was (or should have been) variously credited as author, collaborator, or translator of Lang's Colour / Rainbow Fairy Books, which he edited.

He was educated at Selkirk Grammar School, Loretto School, and the Edinburgh Academy, as well as the University of St Andrews and Balliol College, Oxford, where he took a first class in the final classical schools in 1868, becoming a fellow and subsequently honorary fellow of Merton College. He soon made a reputation as one of the most able and versatile writers of the day as a journalist, poet, critic, and historian. In 1906, he was elected FBA.

He died of angina pectoris on 20th July 1912 at the Tor-na-Coille Hotel in Banchory, survived by his wife. He was buried in the cathedral precincts at St Andrews, where a monument can be visited in the south-east corner of the 19th century section.

Lang is now chiefly known for his publications on folklore, mythology, and religion. The earliest of his publications is *Custom and Myth* (1884). In *Myth, Ritual and Religion* (1887) he explained the "irrational" elements of mythology as survivals from more primitive forms. Lang's *Making of Religion* was heavily influenced by the 18th century idea of the "noble savage", in it, he maintained the existence of high spiritual ideas among so-called 'savage" races, drawing parallels with the contemporary interest in occult phenomena in England.

His *Blue Fairy Book* (1889) was a beautifully produced and illustrated edition of fairy tales that has become a classic. This was followed by many other collections of fairy tales, collectively known as *Andrew Lang's Fairy Books*. In the preface of the *Lilac Fairy Book* he credits his wife with translating and transcribing most of the stories in the collections.

Lang was one of the founders of "psychical research" and his other writings on anthropology include *The Book of Dreams and Ghosts* (1897), *Magic and Religion* (1901) and *The Secret of the Totem* (1905). He served as President of the Society for Psychical Research in 1911.

He collaborated with S. H. Butcher in a prose translation (1879) of Homer's *Odyssey*, and with E. Myers and Walter Leaf in a prose version (1883) of the *Iliad*, both still noted for their archaic but attractive style.

Lang's writings on Scottish history are characterised by a scholarly care for detail, a piquant literary style, and a gift for disentangling complicated questions. *The Mystery of Mary Stuart* (1901) was a consideration of the fresh light thrown on Mary, Queen of Scots, by the Lennox manuscripts in the University Library, Cambridge, approving of her and criticising her accusers.

Lang was active as a journalist in various ways, ranging from sparkling "leaders" for the Daily News to miscellaneous articles for the Morning Post, and for many years he was literary editor of Longman's Magazine.

George McCall Theal

George McCall Theal was born in 1837, in Canada, and died in 1919 in South Africa. He was the most prolific and influential South African historian, archivist and genealogist of the late nineteenth and early twentieth century.

The son of Canadian physician, William Young Theal, who wanted him to become an Episcopalian minister, Theal left home early, sailing with his uncle, Captain Francis Peabody Leavitt, and lived briefly in the United States and Sierra Leone before emigrating to South Africa. There he became a teacher but soon moved to journalism, publishing, and an unsuccessful stint as an amateur diamond miner, all in South African frontier communities. His career as a historian began with the publication of his *Compendium of South African History and Geography* in 1873 following his return to teaching.

Theal spent five years at the Lovedale Seminary outside Alice in the Eastern Cape, working amongst missionaries and Africans. Lovedale was an important institution in the early 1870s, being a non-sectarian and non-denominational theological seminary and Christian school, founded by Presbyterian missionaries in 1841. Lovedale's principal, Dr. James Stewart, attached great importance to the teaching of printing and bookbinding. In 1872 Stewart needed someone who could teach and manage the printing works – Theal was the man. He had taught first at an elementary school in Knysna and from 1867 at a public school in King William's Town, later to become Dale College Boys' High School. He had also been editor of three minor British Kaffrarian newspapers between 1862 and 1865, and later worked for the *Kaffrarian Watchman* in King William's Town, where he printed his first contribution *South Africa As It Is* in 1871. From King William's Town he had travelled to Du Toit's Pan, then seen as the richest diamond mine in the world, and was present when Britain raised the Union Jack over the area. Theal wrote some articles for the *Diamond News* and called the takeover "a most disastrous change".

Having failed to make his fortune on the diamond fields, he returned to the Eastern Cape. Theal was a religious man, and thus believed that it was the civilised white man's duty to rescue the black man from ignorance and barbarism (in common with others of that period, he saw it in racial terms as well) This made him ready to accept the Lovedale post.

While living in King William's Town, he had read everything available on the history of South Africa and had started on an outline of his own rendition which was a synthesis of all he had read.

By 1875 at Lovedale he was teaching history, geography, English grammar and history of the Bible, and also being in charge of the printing department. He was responsible for the monthly publication of the *Kaffir Express* (later the *Christian Express*) and for the Xhosa version. The press published mainly religious and educational works. Between 1879 and 1882 Theal wrote a large number of articles for various periodicals on South African history. His knowledge of the Bantu was so extensive that in 1877 he was requested by Sir Bartle Frere to persuade some belligerent Bantu chiefs to moderate their attitude. Theal's success in this role led to his being offered a post in the Treasury. He accepted this position, aware that he would then have access to the State archives which were housed in the Surveyor-General's office.

About The Editor

I was born in 1962 into a predominantly sporting household – Dad being a good footballer, playing senior amateur and lower league professional football in England, as well as running a series of private businesses in partnership with mum, herself an accomplished and medal winning dancer.

I obtained a degree in History from Leeds University before wandering rather haphazardly into the emerging world of business computing in the late nineteen-eighties.

I followed a succession of amateur writing paths alongside my career in technology, including working as a freelance journalist and book reviewer, my one claim to fame being a by-line in a national newspaper in the UK, The Sunday people.

I also spent 10 years treading the boards, appearing all over the south of the UK in pantos and plays, in village halls and occasionally on the stage of a professional theatre or two.

Following the sporting theme I worked on live TV broadcasts for the BBC, ITV, TVNZ, EuroSport and others as a rugby "Stato", covering Heineken Cups, Six Nations, IRB World Sevens and IRB World Cups in the late '90's and early '00's.

You can find out more at www.clivegilson.com